RULE BREAKER

WILD CARD - BOOK ONE

NIKKI HALL

FOREWORD

Thanks for picking up this copy of Rule Breaker! If you'd like to go back to where the series begins, grab your FREE copy of Game Changer, the prequel novella for the Wild Card series.

For a FREE copy of Game Changer, go to www.nikkihallbooks.com/signup.

For everyone who doesn't think they're good enough.
You are worthy.

1

Soren

"**S**oren, I need your help."

I pried my eyes open and stared at the fan sluggishly moving the air in my dark bedroom. Faint music came from the phone pressed against my ear after Eva's dramatic hello. Thankfully, she waited the several seconds it took my brain to engage.

Middle of the night calls were never good news.

I scrubbed my hand down my face. "Why didn't you call D?"

She snorted. "He *just* got back together with Nadia, and you want me to interrupt them when there are other useless football players available?"

"I'm hanging up now."

"No, wait." The tinge of panic in her tone made me sit up in bed. Eva was a pain in the ass most days, but she didn't scare easily—or at all, as far as I knew.

"What's going on, Eva?"

Someone spoke in the background, closer than the music, and she sighed. "I'm at a party with some friends and we need a ride home."

Her answer didn't mesh with her tone. I believed she needed a ride home, but something else was happening here. This was why I avoided getting involved, people were never upfront about their situations when they asked for help.

Unfortunately, Eva was one of the few people I considered a friend, and pain in the ass or not, I'd never leave her hanging if she needed me.

"Where are you?"

"Hold on." Eva said something I couldn't pick up and got a muffled reply.

"Kappa house."

I knew the place, hell, everyone knew the place. Those parties were hardcore, and our crew tended to avoid them. Not worth the trouble, especially during the season. What the fuck was Eva doing there?

Her reasons didn't matter. She knew I'd come, just like she'd come if hell ever froze over and I called her for help.

"I'll be there in fifteen minutes."

She thanked me and hung up. I checked the time to find it was after midnight, meaning I'd only gotten about an hour of rest. Not that it mattered. I hadn't been able to get a full night's sleep since Margot showed up this summer. When I did sleep, I tossed and turned until I woke up with my sheets knotted around me.

My phone showed dozens of notifications from my social media feed, but I swiped them away. They were probably all from people wanting an inside story about Derrick and Nadia's pre-game kiss. I shook my head. Fans thought they deserved to know every detail about players' lives, but I wasn't going to be the one to destroy Derrick and Nadia's privacy.

I untangled myself and stood to search for the clothes I'd

discarded not too long ago. My sore body protested being vertical. Eva was going to owe me for this one. She knew how hard game days were, especially ones where we eked out a win against a physical opponent.

Every once in a while, I wondered if the strain on my body was worth it, then I remembered that my other option was being chained to an office for the rest of my life. My ribs screamed as I got dressed from a brutal hit I'd taken near the end of the game, but I pushed past the ache.

Football was the life I wanted, and I'd take any amount of pain to be able to play. I shook the dark thoughts from my head and grabbed my keys. There'd be plenty of time to stress about my future later.

The party was still going when I got there. I lucked out and got a parking spot one house down from the blasting music. Even during my partying days, I tended to stay away from the frat houses. Too many drunk girls looking to score with a football player. Any football player.

Admittedly, I wasn't looking for a relationship myself, but I liked the girls I was with to actually want *me* and not a trophy fuck.

Not that I'd been with any girls this year. There was a certain amount of freedom in not playing that game anymore, but my dick was pathetically lonely. Maybe Derrick had the right idea with Nadia. Those two were stupidly in love with each other, and I wondered what it would be like to have someone be everything—and have them return the feeling.

I shook my head. That wasn't my life, and it never would be.

The Kappa house looked about as I expected. All the windows and doors open despite the early chill in the air.

Drunk college kids draped over every surface. I blew out a breath and wondered when I'd become a cranky old guy.

A couple of blondes I recognized from somewhere called my name, but they weren't even a temptation. My only focus this year was playing the best football I could and hopefully winning a championship. They pouted when all they got from me was a smile, but they'd get over it.

A keg blocked the main door, so I took the open gate to the backyard. Even with the unseasonably low October temperature, girls in bikinis beckoned at me from the pool. A scene I would have been all over last year, but something had shifted in me this summer.

After this season, I had one more year of eligibility, but if my parents had their way, I'd be firmly ensconced in the family business before then. The heir apparent of the Brehm dynasty, unless I could do something to convince them I wasn't wasting my time playing football in college.

If I didn't buy myself some time, I'd never make it through my last year to the draft.

I shook my head at the shivering co-eds and wound through the crowd to get into the house. Derrick would go first round, no question. Especially after our game today. His antics before kickoff had gotten him on every major sports network, and he'd followed it up with the best playing of his career.

I shoved my hands in the pockets of my hoodie and scanned the room for a familiar blonde head. Eva was usually the center of attention, but none of the groups on the first floor included a tiny cheerleader with more attitude than height.

A guy I vaguely recognized from the swim team jostled me, spilling half his drink as he attempted to apologize. I cursed at the cold feel of beer splashing across my thigh. Why had this ever seemed fun?

He wandered off to assault some other poor shmuck, and I caught sight of a different familiar face along his path. Colton Price. New to the team this year as a junior transfer and gunning for my starting position. I was a little surprised to see him at a party. Derrick, team captain and resident control freak, had told us all to get some rest after the brutal game earlier, but not all the guys had the same definition of 'rest'.

My eyes narrowed as I took in Colt's pinched face and the way he cradled his wrist. I didn't know the three guys surrounding him, but they all looked pissed. Colt especially seemed to be spewing an angry tirade.

I pulled the phone from my pocket and forced my gaze away from his spectacle as I texted Eva for her location. Colt wasn't my favorite person—he was vicious and entitled, a combination I tried to stay far, far away from. I'd bet he deserved whatever happened to him.

Eva answered me right away. *Upstairs. Second door on the right. Don't bring anyone with you.*

I frowned at her last order. It sounded like she was hiding, which would explain why she wasn't down here among her adoring fans. The path to the stairs took me closer to Colt, and I caught some of his angry whining as I passed.

"That stupid bitch broke my wrist." He punctuated his statement by using the arm he'd been cradling to throw his plastic cup of beer into the empty fireplace, as if that would take away the pain.

I rolled my eyes. If his wrist was really broken, he wouldn't be able to gesture so violently.

He snarled as he glanced around the room. "She's going

to regret that as soon as I find her." The three goons standing around him nodded enthusiastically.

I almost stopped walking. Colt was a selfish asshole, and he held a grudge. Whatever girl had pissed him off probably didn't know he was gunning for a second confrontation. He wouldn't play fair either. I tapped my fingers against my thigh but decided not to get involved. If he hadn't found her already, she was probably long gone by now.

Eva's last words flashed across my mind. *Don't bring anyone with you.* A heavy sense of foreboding settled on my shoulders, and I picked up my pace.

No one tried to stop me as I climbed the stairs, and the couple making out in the hallway didn't give a shit. My hand hovered over the lever of the second door on the right. The music downstairs was muted up here, but this was still a party house. I could be walking into a laundry room or a sex dungeon for all I knew.

If Eva called me all the way to Kappa house to prank me with a sex dungeon, I was going to leave her ass here. I gave a cursory knock, then entered the room. Light from the hallway illuminated Eva before I shut us in the near darkness. She sat on a big four poster bed in the middle of the space. Despite my response to her call for help, her face held none of the usual snark.

I crossed my arms and took a step closer. "What did you do now, Eva?"

A prickling sensation lifted the hairs on my neck, warning me we weren't alone in the room before a quiet, angry voice behind me confirmed it.

"Why do you assume Eva did something?"

I turned, and my eyes landed on a girl hunched on the floor behind the door hugging her knees. Her long, curly hair blocked most of her face, and she whimpered miserably as yet another girl rubbed her back.

A jolt hit me as I made eye contact with the third girl, and goosebumps rose on my arms. The defiant tilt to her chin told me she was the one who'd spoken, but I couldn't seem to find the words to answer her.

Short hair fell from her stubby ponytail to frame a face that was more interesting than pretty. Thick lashes highlighted wide eyes in a dark color I couldn't pinpoint. She didn't look like she was wearing make-up, which was odd at a party like this, but that didn't stop me from staring at her full lips as she scowled at me.

She shifted to glare around me, and I belatedly remembered Eva was in the room with us. "This was your big plan?"

The bedding rustled as Eva stood. "No, Soren is *part* of my big plan. He's going to get you out of here without Colt seeing you then drive you home. I'll take Lizzy back to the dorm in my car."

Lizzy must be the unhappy one on the floor. I didn't even spare her a glance as the angry one's lips pressed together before she answered Eva.

"Why can't we all go in your car?"

"Because a bunch of people saw us together earlier, remember? The longer it takes Colt to figure out who you are the better."

My brows rose as I finally caught up. "*You're* the one who injured him?"

Both women ignored my question. Eva passed me to crouch next to the other two. "Vi, I need you to listen for once. You know I love you, and I know you can take care of yourself, but it would make me feel so much better if you'd let Soren escort you home. Please."

I knew that tone. She'd probably gone full puppy eyes, and I could see Vi softening. Lizzy groaned, and Vi looked down at her. "You're going to need help getting Lizzy into the dorm. She couldn't even walk up the stairs on her own."

What I could see of Lizzy's face was pale in the way that meant copious amounts of puking were on the horizon. She was bigger than Eva, most were, but in this case, it posed a problem. There was no way Eva could get this girl downstairs, into her car, and into a dorm without help.

I jerked my chin at Vi. "She's right. Why don't I take Lizzy home, and you sneak Vi out, Eva?" That got their attention. I met Vi's eyes, gratified to see a speculative gleam instead of outright dismissal.

She waved her free hand at me. "See? Even the jock agrees with me."

My hackles rose a bit, but Lizzy groaned again before I could make a comment. She'd turned a distinct shade of green, and I hustled for a container. A trash can caught my eye, so I dumped it on the floor and brought it over just in time.

"Why are you even here, Eva?" I muttered over the sound of her friend vomiting.

She sighed. "Lizzy heard some of the football players might be here, and I was being a good wingwoman."

"What about her?" I jerked my chin at Vi, who was making soothing noises at Lizzy.

"We were supposed to hang out tonight and work on choreography. When Lizzy insisted on the party, she came along."

I nodded and made note of the information. Vi must have some connection to the cheerleaders, though I didn't think I'd ever seen her on the sidelines. Eva adopted people from everywhere, so the options for how they knew each other were nearly limitless.

Once Lizzy stopped heaving, Eva turned her glare on me. "Look, I appreciate the input, but all I need is someone sneaky enough to get Vi out of here and to her place without being noticed. Mac is on his way to help me with Lizzy."

I should've realized she'd call Mac first. They'd been friends since before college, and he was supremely protective of her. He'd be good backup, but Mac was never subtle. If the situation was as dire as it seemed, he'd have to be in charge of Lizzy, and I'd get Vi.

The thought sent a little thrill of anticipation through me, but I told my dick to stand down. Even if I weren't foregoing sex, we'd all promised Eva years ago not to mess with her friends.

I'd already heard Colt's complaints, but I wanted to hear the details from them. "Tell me what happened."

Vi glanced up at me while holding Lizzy's hair. "He thought he'd take advantage of my drunk friend here despite her telling him to back off multiple times."

I swore. Colt was an asshole, but I hadn't realized how big of an asshole. "How did you get involved?"

"I made him listen."

2

Soren

Her tone dared me to argue, but I respected that steely glint in her eyes. There was no excuse for his actions, and I was glad someone had stepped up to protect Lizzy. As a matter of fact, I was tempted to go downstairs and add my own stamp to the message.

Eva must have figured out the direction of my thoughts because she put a hand on my arm to stop me. "Don't. This is a big enough mess as it is. Vi did some kind of ninja move on his arm, and while I enjoyed hearing him yelp in pain, you know he can't afford an injury right now."

Vi scoffed. "Are you actually concerned about him?"

Eva sent Vi a warning look. "I'm concerned about *you*. Colt is a local, and his family owns like half of this crappy little town. They're big contributors to the university too. All I'm saying is he has connections and a reason to hate you if you messed up his season."

"Even if you *didn't* mess up his season." I stood, and they both stared up at me. "Colt won't forget that you got in his way, and he definitely won't forget that you embarrassed him in front of his friends." I didn't add in the rumors I'd heard about his transfer—that his parents had buried some scandal at his previous school and forced him home.

Vi and Eva shared an uneasy look, and I sighed. Eva wasn't wrong. Colt was already hunting for Vi, which meant I couldn't leave her here to find her own way home. For a brief moment, I considered walking her out and letting Colt have his confrontation. I wasn't overly concerned with his ability to play this season, but a fierce rage tightened my jaw at the thought of him putting his hands on Vi.

I wouldn't be able to stand back and let her take on three guys double her size. If Colt was drunk and stupid enough to take a swing at me, we'd both be kissing our seasons goodbye. Stealth really was the best option.

"Fine. I'll take Vi." I conceded to her plan.

"Vi is sitting right here and capable of making her own choices," she said.

Eva ignored her and nodded at me. "Good. Maybe next time just agree first to make things easier. Where's your truck?"

I pointed toward what I thought was the front of the house. "Parked down the street a bit. Whoever's running this party has the door blocked off, so we'll have to go the long way around the back." I eyed Lizzy again. "How far is your car, Eva?"

"A couple of houses away, but I don't think Colt will bother Lizzy again if she's with me and Mac, especially since he'll be looking for someone else." She sent Vi a pointed look.

Vi rolled her eyes. "Alright, I give up too. Soren can smuggle me out of here and escort me home, even though this is all ridiculous."

Lizzy moaned again from the trash can, and Eva edged Vi out of the way to take the support spot. "I can handle this until Mac gets here. You two better go before Colt calls in reinforcements."

I pulled my hoodie off and tossed it at her. "Put this on and keep your head down."

Eva sighed in relief, but Vi's brows came together as she fingered the material. I fully expected her to argue with me. Instead, she shrugged into the sweatshirt, which hung down to her thighs. My gut clenched as she lifted the hood over her stubby ponytail and met my eyes.

Resentment shimmered there, but something else too. Heat. A bolt of electricity passed between us, and for a moment, I forgot all about Eva and Lizzy and Colt. My hands tingled with the urge to reach for her, so I shoved them in my pockets. Not only was she off limits, but this was the worst possible timing to break my new celibate streak.

"You ready?" I asked her.

She nodded and pushed the sleeves up until her hands were free. "I'd like it on record that I'm still not convinced any of this is necessary."

"Noted." I opened the door and led her out of the bedroom, sending a final wave at Eva who was crooning nonsense to Lizzy. "Your friend is going to be really unhappy tomorrow."

Vi snorted behind me. "She should have known better than to start with tequila. It always makes her shoot right past buzzed to spewing in someone's new tote bag full of resistance bands."

I glanced back at her as I took the lead down the stairs. "That's a very specific example."

"It was a very specific memory."

We reached the main floor where a full-contact beer pong game had taken over the living room, and Vi scooted closer to me. The stairs ended in the middle of the room, so

I worked my way to one of the walls where there were less people.

A rowdy group of party-goers started in our direction. They wouldn't be a problem, except I noticed one of Colt's buddies stumbling along with the others. I turned and crowded Vi against the wall, using my body to hide her from the rest of the room.

She sucked in a breath, and her eyes shot to mine before skittering away. "I should have known you'd use this as an excuse to cop a feel."

I braced myself against the wall behind her and leaned closer to speak quietly in her ear. "Am I currently copping a feel?"

I hadn't touched her. Even now, when we were only an inch away from temptation, I'd yet to make contact. She stared over my shoulder and pursed her lips. "Hard to tell. Maybe you're just bad at it."

"Sweetheart, when I touch you, you'll know."

The others moved past, and despite my words, I hesitated. This close to her, I could smell her fresh scent, and I wanted to press my mouth against her neck to see if she'd taste as sweet. Her chest rose and fell with uneven breaths, making me wonder if she was fighting as hard as I was to maintain control. A second longer and I might have given in, but Colt's voice rose above the crowd behind me.

"Anybody seen Vi Malone? Short hair, red shirt, freckles..."

He trailed off to a chorus of *no*'s, and I stared down at Vi's freckles. It pissed me off that Colt had noticed them before I did. He didn't deserve to know anything about this girl. His voice moved farther away, and Vi let out a silent breath.

I glanced around to be sure it was safe to move, then

grabbed her hand and led her out the back door. The blondes had vacated the pool in favor of the guys on the deck, and though several people called out hellos to me, no one stopped us.

Vi did as asked and kept her head down. My hoodie effectively hid her shape while helping her blend into the shadows around the house. The night air nipped at me through my thin tee-shirt, but I didn't hurry. Hurrying would draw attention.

We made it through the gate and down the street with no more close calls. I had to admit that all the spy shit was starting to feel a little silly. Colt didn't scare me, and he deserved a real beating for what he'd pulled with Lizzy.

Then again, Coach would definitely bench me if I started a fight with a teammate, no matter how much he deserved it. And Eva wasn't wrong about Colt's family's influence. One of the science buildings was named after them for fuck's sake.

From what I'd seen in practice, Colt would go to great lengths to get what he wanted, be that retribution or something that he thought belonged to him. Like my starting position. I'd been keeping my eye on him since he tried to convince Derrick of some bullshit rumor about me.

Too bad for him our captain happened to be my best friend. He picked the wrong strategy if he was trying to get me booted.

Vi wouldn't have that kind of protection, especially now that he knew her name.

She stopped walking a few steps from my truck and pulled her hand away. "I appreciate the concern, but you don't actually have to take me home." She started to pull the hoodie over her head, but I stopped her by tugging it back down.

Unlike Derrick, I'd never seen the draw of a girl wearing my clothes, until now. Only I knew what she had on under the sweatshirt, and the baggy material offered up a casual claim. Anyone looking at her would know she was with me. More importantly, anyone looking *for* her wouldn't recognize her.

"Keep it on until we're away from here. As much as I'd relish breaking Colt's nose, I'd like to play next Saturday."

"All the more reason for you to take your sweatshirt and leave me be."

I narrowed my eyes at her. "You wouldn't be planning to try to scare Colt away, would you?"

Her frown gave her away, but the stubborn tilt of her chin arrowed straight into me. I knew that impulse. The absolute need to handle everything without help.

She could be an actual ninja, and she'd still have trouble with several guys built like Colt. No way was I letting her stay at the party to make the situation worse.

I shook my head. "You surprised him the last time, but he's strong and fast, and that doesn't factor in his asshole posse. If that's not enough to convince you, I should warn you that I have no problem calling Eva and explaining why you're still here."

Her nose wrinkled. "You'd tattle on me?"

I shrugged. "You're the one who agreed to follow her plan."

Her shoulders slumped, and I knew I had her. Colt didn't scare her, but Eva did. Even leaving wouldn't really protect her for long. I knew the way Colt's mind worked. He'd hyper focus on her until he passed out, maybe longer. She wouldn't see it coming because she didn't see him as a threat.

"I take it you don't live in the dorms. Do you have room-mates? Anyone to stay with you tonight?"

"No, and I can take care of myself."

Why the hell did her stubborn insistence turn me on so much? She speared me with those dark eyes, full of confidence and fire, and all I could think about was sliding my hoodie up over her curves to see if she had freckles anywhere else.

"Get in the truck, Vi."

She took a shallow breath and raised her chin. "I can find my own way home."

With measured slowness, I backed her against the passenger door, invading her space but being careful not to touch. Part of me wanted to get her to listen, but the other part just wanted to see how she'd react.

"You're not going home tonight."

3

Vi

Fire ignited inside me—a side effect of having Soren mere inches away, but moreso, a reaction to his arrogant tone. I didn't need another overbearing male telling me my business. "And where exactly do you think I'll be staying tonight?"

He chuckled, despite the clear murder in my voice. "You can stay with me. I have a guest room with a zero percent chance that a pissed off, drunk football player will try to exact revenge. I'll drive you home in the morning."

"And everything will magically be safer in the morning? If he's that much of a danger—and I want to make it clear I'm not arguing that point—we should call the police."

"Sure." He pulled his phone from his pocket and held it out to me. "Go ahead. It'll be fun listening to you explain how you assaulted him but *he's* the threat."

I reared back. "If you think he's innocent, why are you so hellbent on helping me?"

"I don't think he's innocent. I think, best case scenario, the police will laugh at you, and worst case scenario, they'll try to arrest you. Probably closer to the second considering

Colt was in there actively looking for retribution." He tucked his phone away when I didn't make a move for it. "Given his family connections in this town, he'd probably love it if you called the cops."

I rolled my lips together as I considered my options. Eva clearly trusted Soren, and he knew Colt a hell of a lot better than I did. Before tonight, I'd only seen these guys from a distance at the training center. Unfortunately, Colt knew my name, and it wouldn't take much to figure out where I lived. I wasn't exactly a hermit. As a matter of fact, I sometimes did personal training in my living room. Half the cheer squad had been to my apartment.

The longer I thought about it, the more I realized Soren seemed like the safer bet.

He still stood close enough for me to feel his body heat, and my reaction to him might pose a problem if I stayed at his place. I wanted to touch him—especially after he'd flashed those abs when he pulled his hoodie off before tossing it to me. I had a weakness for guys who took care of their bodies. Soren did not disappoint.

I met his eyes and lied to his face, determined not to let him know how much he affected me. "I'm not interested in anything you have to offer besides a place to sleep."

He backed up a step and crossed his arms, emphasizing the long tribal tattoo—vaguely Nordic and completely sexy —that trailed down his arm to his wrist. "I don't remember offering anything else."

A pang of disappointment shot through me. "I just wanted to be clear."

"Fair enough, as long as you're sleeping in my guest room." His biceps strained against his shirt as if he were physically holding himself back, and I wondered if his words were a warning or an offer.

I blew my hair out of my face and forced my stiff shoulders away from my ears. I hated being told what to do, but I hated it even more when I reacted by making a bad decision. The jury was still out on which way this one would go.

"Fine. You can take me to your place, but you never explained why you thought I'd be safe going home tomorrow instead of tonight."

"I have an idea about tomorrow, but first I want to sleep for at least eight hours. We can talk about it before I take you home if you don't come up with something else."

"Something else in the middle of the night while I'm supposed to be sleeping under your questionable protection?"

"Yes. Now get in the truck."

I glared at him while I reached for the handle. *Something else,* my ass. He could take me home in the morning, and if Colt tried anything, I'd kick *his* ass for a second time.

"Don't expect me to make breakfast or anything," I muttered.

"I'd never dream of it." His sarcasm came out thick, but amusement glittered in his eyes as he backed away.

———

I HAD an image in my head of what Soren's apartment would look like—a dirty, messy, bachelor pad—but he surprised me. Everyone else I knew resided on campus, but Soren lived in one of the nicer neighborhoods of our little college town.

His building gave off the subtle sheen of money, like a place young business professionals frequented. We didn't see anyone as we climbed the stairs, but I imagined his neighbors got up early for normal office jobs.

I snuck a glance at Soren—tall and muscled, with tattoos etched down his right arm all the way to his fingers. He moved with the grace of an elite athlete, and he belonged here as much as I did, which was to say not at all. The disconnect made me curious.

"Why do you live here?"

He arched a brow at me as he led me to an apartment on the second floor. "What do you mean?"

"Most college students don't have their own smoothie bar in the workout center."

Soren shook his head as he pushed the door open and snapped on a light. "How do you know about that?"

I grimaced and followed him inside. "Occupational hazard. I always check the gym facilities when I go somewhere new. You live across the parking lot, and it looks like you have twenty-four-hour access."

I tried to keep the jealousy out of my tone, but I was pretty sure I failed when he tilted his head to study me. Eva had warned me more than once that Soren would get under my skin if I met him. I hadn't believed her—Eva lived for drama—but the moment the door clicked shut closing me in with him, a delicate shiver ran over my skin.

"You're not what I expected."

He strolled past me, and I took stock of the plain furnishings. It looked like he'd taken a generic picture of an apartment and replicated it. A lot of neutrals. Soren hadn't struck me as the beige type.

"Are you sure you live here?"

He barked out a laugh and headed for the single hallway. "The bedrooms are down here. Guest room on the right. It has an en suite, and I think it's stocked with towels and shit."

I ran my hand along the couch as I passed, then almost collided with him when he turned around.

"I have a shirt you can sleep in." His gaze trailed down my body, still hidden by his giant sweatshirt. Heat pooled in my belly at the immediate image of sleeping in his shirt, in his bed, curled up next to his body.

I snorted, desperately trying to hide my reaction. "I bet you say that to all the girls."

"I don't bring girls here."

I wasn't sure how to take that. Was he saying I was special? Or was he pissed that he'd been forced to break his rules? I had trouble reading Soren, so probably the second.

He hadn't moved away, and neither had I. We stood inches from each other in his dark hallway, and I couldn't tear my eyes from his. I'd never been so aware of my breath, trying to control the airflow through the sudden tightness in my chest.

Soren's jaw ticked and the moment passed. He took a step back and waved at the guest room. "The only other person who's slept here is D. I promise I've changed the sheets since then."

I knew from Eva—and from being a university student with working eyeballs—that D was the hot as fuck quarterback and Soren's best friend. Eva had tried on multiple occasions to get me to come with her to chill at D's apartment, which I'd managed to avoid. No need to get friendly with her group when I barely had time for her.

Unlike other college guys I knew, Soren didn't seem like he belonged with the six people to an apartment crowd, but he didn't belong here in beige purgatory either. His reasons were none of my business, but a deep-seated need to know more wouldn't let me leave it alone.

"Why don't you live closer to D?"

He paused in his retreat and shook his head. "My parents pay for this apartment as a reminder of what they want me to be."

"Boring and colorless?"

His lips tilted up in a smile. "That's a good interpretation. I usually spend my time at D's place, but lately I've been having trouble sleeping, so I stay here where my nocturnal habits won't keep anyone up."

There was a lot to unpack in what he'd just told me, but he didn't give me the chance.

"Good night, Vi." His door closed quietly behind him, and I tried not to imagine him getting naked as I went into my own room.

———

THE SMELL of bacon woke me from a dream that involved Soren and an inventive use of stretch bands. I sat up in his cushy guest bed and blew my hair out of my face. His hoodie was twisted around my torso, attempting to strangle me, which probably explained the dream.

I sniffed the air again, definitely bacon, and snatched my jeans from where I'd left them on the nightstand. My phone was dead because I hadn't thought to ask for a charger, but it didn't matter much. Only Eva would care where I was, and she could call Soren's phone.

The thought made me frown as I came down the hallway. Eva would definitely jump to the wrong conclusion if Soren told her I'd stayed the night.

The man himself stood at the stove, stirring eggs in a skillet. He'd put on clean clothes, but he didn't look any more rested than he had last night. Well, that made two of us. I felt grubby, so I took the seat across from him at the breakfast bar instead of joining him in the kitchen. At least he wouldn't smell my morning breath over the bacon.

"You made breakfast?"

He set a plain white coffee cup in front of me. "And coffee."

I eyed the mug, and he set down a plate covered in eggs, bacon, and toast.

"You're welcome, by the way."

"Are you buttering me up for something?"

That same amused glint from last night lit his eyes, and my senses went on high alert. "I thought you might appreciate some food while we discuss your predicament."

I took a bite of the bacon, crispy and perfect, and ate half my breakfast before I answered him. "There's nothing to discuss. You can take me home, and we'll go our separate ways. If Colt happens to come to practice with a broken wrist, you'll know he didn't learn his lesson the first time."

He crossed his arms and leaned back against the counter. I tried valiantly to keep my eyes on his face, but it was a losing battle when his shirt hugged his chest so well. It should be a crime to cover up such defined biceps.

"He's sneakier than you think. You've already proven you can take him one on one, so he'll come at you from the side next time."

"He's not a raptor."

"Might as well be," he muttered.

A small laugh snorted out of me. "I'm not afraid of dinosaurs *or* football players."

Soren nodded slowly. "I think we can help each other."

I shook my head as I skirted him to raid his fridge for milk. "I don't need help."

"Maybe I do."

When I turned, I expected smug satisfaction, but Soren's

face was a blank slate. Interesting. He must actually want something out of this if he was putting the effort into keeping his emotions hidden.

I took a big sip of my coffee and leaned back on the counter opposite him. "Okay, I'm listening."

"We should date."

I nearly spit coffee at him. "What?"

He didn't react to my near shout, speaking as if this were a completely normal conversation. "Pretend date. We convince Colt and his buddies that you're with me, which should offer you a certain level of protection."

I narrowed my eyes. "Because we live in a feudal society where my worth is tied to who I'm dating?"

"Because Colt fears me more than he wants revenge on you. At least for now. I don't date, so we'd have to sell it, but I don't see how that will be a problem." Fire warmed his blue eyes as he met my gaze, and I felt that same jolt from last night.

The temptation was there, almost a physical need to agree and see what it would feel like to be on the receiving end of Soren's dubious affections. That alone warranted me saying no, but I wanted to know the other side... and how far he'd go to sell it.

"How does this help you?"

"I'd get to parade you in front of my family."

My brows flew up. "To piss them off or make them happy?"

He ran a hand through his hair, the first sign that he had stock in this conversation. "They're threatening to cut my funding if I stay and play another season unless I show some sign that I'm considering a future outside of the NFL."

I whistled low. "Did they give you any indications of what they're looking for?"

"A serious relationship would go a long way toward convincing my parents I'm not partying my college years away while wasting my life with football."

"I've never been much of a trophy girlfriend."

A challenge lit his eyes, and he grinned. "I think we can work around that."

That smile nearly had me changing my mind. Soren was an intriguing combination of bad boy and reluctant hero—and he made great coffee, a necessary trait in any pretend boyfriend. I blew out a breath and firmly locked that temptation away.

"I appreciate the offer, but I'm going to respectfully decline."

Soren nodded, as if my answer hadn't mattered in the least. "You ready to go?"

His easy acceptance melted away the tension building in my shoulders. I'd expected him to argue—a tiny part of me was sad he hadn't—but maybe we could be real friends instead of pretend dates.

"One second." I drained the rest of my coffee and put the cup in the sink. "Okay, Jeeves, let's ride."

4

Vi

"You can't do this." I crinkled the paper in front of my landlord's sweaty face. Dave hadn't met my eyes once since he'd delivered it.

"Sorry, Vi. Word came from the head office. You're being evicted."

I threw my hands in the air and paced the ten steps across my tiny living room. "For what?"

"They didn't say."

"They have to say. It's the law."

He sighed and finally focused on my face. "There's a morality clause in your lease. They claim you broke it. I'm really sorry, but I need this job. You have twenty-four hours to vacate, or I have to call the sheriff's office."

I clenched my jaw shut to keep from spewing the litany of curse words flowing through my head. The lease was bullshit, but it would take time and money to fight it. Neither of which I had. Dave must have sensed the danger level rising because he turned and hightailed it out of my apartment. The cheerful fall sunlight outside made me want to puke. Or punch someone.

Most of the anger drained away with his exit, leaving me tired at nine o'clock in the morning. I had a class in an hour but dealing with this situation seemed more important than analyzing training case studies.

Who gives a tenant *one day* to move? I propped my hands on my hips and blew my short hair out of my face. At least I didn't have much to pack. I'd been so proud when I'd scored the on-campus apartment and could live on my own without annoying roommates. Of course, living on my own meant paying for everything myself, so I'd settled for finding random furniture on the curb.

I could get boxes for my stuff, and I knew Eva would let me store things at her place if I needed to, but what the fuck was I supposed to do with a couch, a dresser, and a bed? I hated feeling impotent, but short of burning the place down, I had no other choice than to start looking for somewhere else to live.

Thanks to Dave and his archaic lease, I skipped my classes to spend the day packing and searching for a new apartment. Luckily, it was one of my few days off from the gym, so I didn't miss any shifts. Not a single apartment complex would rent to me. I didn't make enough money to pass the credit check of anywhere except the on-campus apartments I was currently vacating.

As night fell, the tight spiral of panic inside me grew until I couldn't take a full breath. I'd worked my ass off to be self-sufficient, and everything I'd built in the last three years was crumbling in front of me. The eviction notice gave me until noon tomorrow, and I was out of ideas.

I could rent a storage unit for my meager belongings, but I couldn't live there. Eva didn't have a spare room, and her couch was smaller than me. She was the only person I knew

—the only person I'd ask, anyway—who had her own place outside the dorms.

Soren's face flashed across my mind, and I had to correct myself. I knew *two* people who lived outside the dorms. The beginning of a very bad idea started to form.

It had been two days since he'd strong-armed me into staying at his place, asked me to be his fake girlfriend, then dropped me off as if he didn't give a shit. I leaned back on the couch and stared at the plain white ceiling. Could this mess be connected to that asshole football player, Clayton or Colton or whatever?

I didn't even have Soren's number, though I was sure Eva would be glad to give it to me. When I'd left, I'd thought we could be friends, if I could just get past the annoying urge to run my tongue over the ridges of his abs.

His suggestion that we pretend to date still seemed wildly unlikely to work, but I knew he'd be more likely to take me in if I agreed to help with his parents. Maybe we could work out some ground rules and a schedule of sorts. Pretend dating would still mean real physical contact. A little thrill shot through me at the memory of his words at the party.

Sweetheart, when I touch you, you'll know.

I shivered and shook my head. This was *such* a bad idea.

Soren might not even go for it. I knew from experience he had his own set of boundaries. I also knew from experience that being in close contact with any part of Soren's body short-circuited all my self-preservation instincts.

I sighed. His stupidly attractive face should be the least of my worries at the moment. Dave hadn't left me any other options. I wasn't a quitter, and I wasn't about to ask my family for help—they'd come *rescue* me from my silly independence by carting me home regardless of how close I was to graduating.

Which meant Soren was my last shot if I wanted to stay at school for the remainder of the semester, possibly the year. Assuming he opened the door at—I checked my watch —almost midnight.

I heaved myself off the couch and grabbed my keys. Only one way to find out.

———

SOREN OPENED the door wearing black sweats slung low over his hips and nothing else. My lips parted on a strangled gasp, and I swallowed hard at the sheer expanse of muscle standing in front of me. Did he train *all* the time? I worked in a gym and my body wasn't nearly that defined. My eyes traced the lines of his tattoo and followed the sharp V that bracketed his abs to drop into his sweats.

He moved aside to let me in, and my gaze belatedly shot to his face. His lips tipped up in a tiny smirk, but I refused to be embarrassed by my appreciation of the human form. The guy was beautiful, and he knew it.

I glided into the living room with my head high, determined not to spend any more time ogling him. A single light from the hallway cast the furniture in heavy shadow, but I could see enough to get around. Like the last time, his apartment was hotel-room clean. Soulless and tidy—nothing like the Soren I was starting to know. It made me wonder what his room would say about him.

He closed the door and leaned against it, then tilted his head to study me. "I thought you weren't interested in anything I had to offer."

The faint taunt in his voice almost made me turn around

and go home. I could sleep in my car. I'd done it before. Instead, I made myself comfortable against the back of his couch, determined to see this through. His lips twitched like he could read my mind, and I shrugged.

"I changed my mind."

"Interesting. I usually have to put in a little more effort for a booty call."

He rubbed a hand over his bare stomach, and through Olympic levels of willpower, I kept my eyes on his face. "Your abs are impressive, but that's not why I'm here. The school is kicking me out of my apartment as of tomorrow afternoon. I don't have anywhere else to go."

The smirk left his face, and he pushed away from the wall. "Just to be clear. You're here, in my apartment—alone —late at night, because you need my help."

I stood my ground as he approached. Soren moved through the darkness like he belonged there, and for a split second, I questioned my decision to invade his space. We'd argued more than we'd talked since meeting. How well did I really know him?

He stopped directly in front of me and crossed his arms. "Am I wrong?"

"No. I need your help—and your apartment. I can pay my way."

He chuckled low and looked away for a beat. "I don't want your money, Vi. I want you."

His silky comment ignited me in a way that usually took half a bottle of wine and a really smutty book. My damn body leapt at the chance that he'd take a different kind of payment.

With my heart pounding in my ears, I couldn't tell if my voice shook like the rest of me. "I already told you I'm not here for a booty call."

He leaned closer to whisper in my ear. "My proposition didn't include sharing my bed, but I'm open to amending the terms."

Of course, he still wanted a trophy girlfriend. I took a long, slow breath to calm my racing pulse, but just ended up inhaling the warm, sleepy scent of Soren. Not helpful when I didn't trust myself to actually push him away if I put my hands on him.

"I want to talk about your proposition—your original proposition. We'd need ground rules, and I have to know what specifically you need me to do as your fake girlfriend."

Soren eased back enough that I had to tilt my head up to look at him, but he didn't move away. "I have a couple of specific appearances in mind for my parents, but this is a full-time gig. For the foreseeable future, you'd be my girl-friend as far as anyone else is concerned. For both of our protections."

That wouldn't be a problem for me. Eva was already half-convinced we'd be a good fit, and no one else would care. But was he really going to lie to his best friend?

"Even D?"

He didn't hesitate. "Even D. You're the only person who knows about my family life, and I want to keep it that way."

Warmth curled in my chest at the surprising show of trust. "I won't say anything, and I can fake it with the best of them." He yawned, and I felt myself softening even further. "Still not sleeping well?"

"No, but it shouldn't bother you in the other room."

I narrowed my eyes at the hint of a dare in his tone. He'd said himself that he wasn't opposed to changing the arrangement—tempting, but a supremely bad idea.

Mixing sex with this ruse was a surefire way to screw it all up, which didn't at all stop me from wanting to rise to the challenge. What *did* stop me was the prospect of my family discovering I was homeless because I couldn't keep my raging lady boner to myself.

I shook my head. "Not tonight. I'll be going home to finish my packing for tomorrow. I'm still not convinced this will keep Colt away from me, but I'm willing to pose as your serious, committed girlfriend as long as we're roommates." I held up a finger. "Roommates, Soren. Not fuck buddies."

He grinned at me and inclined his head. "Understood. Just so you know, I would have let you stay either way. The guest room is yours as long as you need it. See you tomorrow." He sidestepped me to head down the hallway, and I let out a silent breath as his door closed.

5

Soren

Contrary to what Derrick's girlfriend believed, I did actually go to classes. The morning after Vi surprised me by agreeing to my crazy idea, I was supposed to be sitting in a 9:00 a.m. business lecture, trying not to fall asleep.

Instead, I parked in front of her apartment and laid on the horn. Her neighbors weren't going to like me very much, but they wouldn't be her neighbors for much longer. Her blinds twitched, and I grabbed my phone to text her.

Get your ass out here. It's moving day.

Three dots appeared, and I didn't have to wait long for her response. *I think I hate you.*

We'll work on that.

Anticipation knotted in my chest as Vi's door cracked open.

She blinked at the bright morning light a couple of times, then her eyebrows hit her hair when she recognized my truck. I'd definitely gotten her out of bed because she wore a tank top and the skimpiest excuse for shorts I'd ever seen. They showed off long, toned legs, and I wanted to run my tongue up the inside of her thigh until she wrapped those legs around me.

Vi clearly didn't give a fuck, propping her hands on her hips and glaring at me. That image of her prickly response and her endless legs would join the other ones haunting my dreams.

The last time she'd stayed at my place, she hadn't brought any pajamas. I knew because I'd checked on her after lying in my bed for two hours staring at the ceiling. She'd left the bathroom light on, along with my hoodie. Her pants, though, were elsewhere.

Vi had curled one long, toned—naked—leg around the outside of the blanket. One glimpse was enough to make it clear I was playing a dangerous game with myself.

I'd given up the partying and the women after Margot fucked me over. Vi hit me differently though, enough that I'd proposed this insane agreement. We could help each other, yes, but that wasn't my only motivation. Despite my need to keep myself aloof, I wasn't ready to say goodbye to her yet.

When I stayed seated in the warmth of my truck, she shook her head and went back into her apartment. I was tempted to follow her, but I needed a minute to calm my raging hard-on. My sweats wouldn't hide a damn thing, and as much as my dick thought he was in charge, I was strictly there to help her move today.

My phone buzzed with a text. *Are you coming or am I supposed to move boxes in my underwear while you watch like a creeper?*

I scrubbed the smile from my face. No wonder I couldn't get enough of this girl. *Was that an option?*

I'm not making you coffee.

I laughed at her threat and repeated football stats in

my head until I could walk with relative safety. By the time I got inside, she'd pulled on yoga pants. The smell of coffee filled the small space. Her place was sparsely furnished, and there were a lot less boxes than I'd expected.

The one closest to the door was labeled 'sex toys' in big letters, and I raised my brow at her. "That's an impressive collection."

Her eyes flicked to the box, and one side of her lips tipped up. "You have no idea."

I laid a hand on my chest. "I feel like, as your boyfriend, I *should* have an idea. We could have explored that toy collection together."

She snorted and took a long pull from a bright red mug. "I didn't realize we'd be starting right away. That box is actually fitness gear."

"I'm devastated."

Vi shook her head. "Why are you here?"

"Why waste any more time? Besides, I thought you might need a hand today." I'd also wanted to see her, but I wouldn't share that little tidbit.

Her stiff shoulders relaxed slightly. "Thanks. Even if you get bored after ten minutes, your truck will be useful."

"Sweetheart, I can last all day."

She tilted her head at me. "I can't tell if you're genuinely hitting on me or if you just can't help the smolder-y attitude."

"Smolder-y isn't a word."

"I beg to differ, since I just used it."

"As my girlfriend, you should be swooning when I smolder."

Vi finally gave in and laughed. "Fine. You win. It's too early in the morning for whatever bizarre flirty battle of wits we've fallen into. Is this something I should expect on a daily basis?"

"Only one way to find out."

The truth was my flirting skills were dangerously rusty. Even before Margot, I didn't let people get close to me. With Eva and the others, I maintained a certain distance. For some reason I didn't understand, that distance disappeared around Vi.

I joined her in the kitchen and took the cup from her hand. Coffee, as expected. She crossed her arms and leaned against the counter while I took a sip. More milk than I liked, but passable. I set the mug on the counter next to her and nodded toward the door.

"We can get to know each other while we get you settled into my place."

"*Our* place."

I inclined my head. "Our place."

She sighed and finished off her coffee, setting the empty cup in the sink. "The first thing you should know is I'm not a morning person. I require some form of caffeine, preferably coffee, to act like a normal human."

"I figured that out already, and I have a working coffee maker at the apartment... as you already know. Maybe we can skip to the fifth or sixth thing on your list."

Vi tsked at me. "You can't skip ahead—you'll miss the fun parts."

Our eyes locked, and the light, playful atmosphere ignited. I *wanted* the fun parts—wanted to be able to reach out and touch her, taste her, hoist her onto the cheap laminate countertop and see how far she'd let me go.

Instead, I broke the connection and reached for the closest box. She wanted a roommate, not a fuck buddy... and

I couldn't afford to let my guard down. "Let's get moving. I still have practice this afternoon."

Vi watched me for a long moment, then grabbed her own box. I started a silly game of twenty questions as we loaded my truck. It took five trips and three hours to empty the apartment.

Her meager furniture and most of the boxes went into the storage space assigned by my complex that had been empty since I moved in. I had a heated underground parking spot too, but it was faster to use the one outside my building. Vi opted for the underground parking, and we made one more trip to the office to get a permit for her car.

Every mundane step we took toward moving her in should have terrified me. I'd never given anyone this much access to my life. But Vi needed this situation to work out as much as I did.

As we made the final trip to the apartment, we lapsed into silence. I wondered if claiming Vi as mine would paint a bigger target on her for Colt instead of offering her protection. He already wanted my spot on the team, and I was giving him something else to covet.

Vi claimed she could take care of herself if the situation called for it, but I didn't like the idea that she'd pay a high price for her defiance if she did. She'd already lost her home. I wouldn't let her lose anything else.

Vi hopped out of the truck as soon as I stopped and waited for me at the foot of the stairs. She could have gone up on her own, I'd already given her a key, but the way she chewed on her lip made me think she had something to say—something she couldn't say in the close confines of my vehicle.

I didn't have much time left before I had to meet Derrick and the others to prep for practice, but I wasn't going to hurry her. She stepped in front of me as I approached, and I tucked my fingers in my pockets to wait.

Vi didn't hesitate long. "We need rules."

I nodded, not in the least surprised. "Okay. Rule one: we can't tell anyone this is fake."

She visibly relaxed at my quick acceptance. "That's a given. Rule two: either of us can call it off at any time."

My fingers flexed in my pockets at the idea that she was already having regrets. "I meant what I said, Vi. The second bedroom is yours for as long as you need it." If she couldn't handle the fake relationship, I'd find some other way to convince my parents I was responsible.

Her eyes narrowed. "I pay my way. I'll be the best fake girlfriend you've ever had."

"Well, the bar is pretty low since you're the first. Rule three: you have to say something if I cross a line."

"That goes for both of us." She tangled her fingers together in front of her. "Rule four: no falling in love."

My first impulse was to veto that rule. I had no intention of falling in love, but the idea of her adding it to the rules— as if falling for me would be the worst possible outcome— made me irrationally pissed. "Not sure I can promise that one, but I'll try."

She gave a distracted laugh. "You're just going to have to resist my many charms. I have one more request. Can we wait to tell Eva and the others that we're together?"

I nodded slowly, letting the slight hurt drain away. "If that's what you want."

Vi sighed. "We don't have any proof that Colt is behind the apartment thing—" I scoffed, but she ignored me. "And I don't like lying to my friends. I appreciate you giving me a place to live, but I just want a couple of days to get used to the idea."

"Don't think of it as lying. The relationship is real. I have every intention of treating you like a girlfriend, and no interest in dating anyone else. The only difference between us and a normal couple is there are zero expectations for a future. It's like a marriage of convenience without all the messy legal paperwork."

That got a real laugh out of her. "What about sex?"

I shrugged. "What about it? Plenty of couples don't have sex. Plenty of strangers do. Our sex life is no one's business but our own." I wanted to add that whether or not we had a sex life was up to her, but I didn't want her to feel pressured.

Her nose scrunched. "I'm pretty sure adding in sex would massively complicate things."

She didn't sound entirely convinced. Hell, *I* wasn't entirely convinced, but I didn't want to fuck around with the plan. This was my last-ditch effort to appease my parents, and as much as I liked Vi, I wasn't willing to sacrifice my future for her.

She shook her head with a tiny smile when I didn't respond. "Nevermind. You're right, of course. I don't owe anyone an explanation of our sex life, fictional as it is."

My cock throbbed painfully at the thought of a real sex life with Vi. At this rate, our fictional sex life might very well kill me. I returned her smile and hooked my arm around her neck, leading her to the stairs.

"If you do decide to give details, make sure you expound on my prowess and how very, *very* happy you are. Maybe quote some Shakespeare. Emphasis on the happy."

She laughed, and the sound wound its way inside me, burrowing deep where my own happiness lived.

EIGHT DAYS. Eight days of Vi the roommate, and I felt like she'd always been there, haunting me.

I'd thought there might be a transition period—I'd never had a roommate, let alone a serious girlfriend—but Vi slid smoothly into my life.

She mostly stayed in her room for the first few days, but signs of her slowly took over. Extra coffee cups in the cabinet, a throw pillow on the couch, and once, a set of weights next to the door that I tripped over. They were gone the next day, but I wouldn't have cared if she filled the apartment with her stuff.

I'd lived there for three years, and I'd resented every second of it, refusing to make it feel like home out of some misplaced need to tell my parents to go fuck themselves. I hated that I took their money and gave them some semblance of control over my life.

My own fault though. TU had offered me a scholarship that would have covered all my living expenses, but I'd refused. I didn't want to take a spot on the team from someone who'd worked to get there when I had other options.

Instead, I'd made a deal with my parents that I'd pursue a business degree as long as I could play football, and they'd cover all my costs. After some back and forth, we'd decided that I'd redshirt my freshman year to give me more time for the degree. Not being out there on the field was hard, but I saw it as another year to build for my dream.

Unfortunately, it sometimes felt like I'd traded my soul for someone else's chance to play.

Vi took the soulless apartment and made it feel like real people lived there. Real people that barely saw each other. After our conversation by the stairs that first day, she'd made herself scarce. Or maybe I was so used to being somewhere else I'd never realized how little time I spent at home.

As the week dragged on, I found myself memorizing her schedule and lingering longer and longer in the living room. She spared me a few minutes each day, but the girl spent a *lot* of time in her room.

For the first time ever, I was glad when my mom sent the requisite summons for their annual Halloween cocktail party. My family didn't do anything so crass as handing out candy in costume, but donning designer dresses and schmoozing potential business associates? Yeah, they were all over that.

As the eldest son and successor, I was required to attend. After Margot showed up unannounced at my parents' house this summer, demanding money for a baby that sure as hell wasn't mine, they were pickier about the guest list. They'd made it clear in the invitation that I wasn't to bring a date, one would be provided for me. I responded to confirm and inform them I'd be bringing a date anyway.

They needed to meet Vi sooner rather than later.

The text came through while I was sitting in the living room, pretending to watch film from our upcoming opponents' last game. In reality, I'd been debating knocking on Vi's door to see if she wore those little shorts again tonight.

The party offered a much better excuse.

I turned the game off—I'd have to watch it from the beginning again anyway—and stretched as I headed down the hallway. Silence greeted me outside Vi's door, but I knew she was in there. She'd come home not too long ago with two gym bags draped over her shoulder and grunted at me on her way through the living room.

At her request, we'd kept our arrangement quiet so far, but it was time to step it up. Vi took so long answering my knock that I wondered if she was asleep. I was on the verge of yelling for her when I heard a muffled *come in*.

Like the last time, only the bathroom light was on. Vi lay on the bed, face down on a pillow, with a closed laptop next to her. She still wore the cropped tank and leggings she'd come home in, and I'd bet she hadn't moved since she flopped down.

"You okay?"

She mumbled something unintelligible, then rolled enough to glare at me.

I crossed my arms and leaned against the jamb. "Don't blame me for whatever pain you've inflicted on yourself."

"I'm not. I'm blaming you for this sinfully soft bed that makes me want to sleep all the time instead of working or doing homework or leaving this room ever."

I chuckled since she wasn't wrong. The beds were one of the few things I'd actually picked out in this place. Football season was hell on my body, and I wanted a bed that would inspire tears of joy when I laid on it. Then I put another one in the guest room for the hell of it.

"I have your first assignment."

Her glare smoothed away, and she groaned as she sat up. I knew that feeling too. I'd found out during our twenty questions game that Vi taught fitness classes and did personal training six days a week. It wasn't football, but she understood the constant exhaustion.

She pulled her hair away from her face and into a short ponytail. "Am I going to steal the family jewels?"

"Not quite. We're going to a Halloween cocktail party in Dallas. Not black tie, but fancy."

Her brows rose. "On Halloween? That's only three days from now."

"I can get you a dress and shoes or whatever if you don't have them, but I need you to keep that night free."

"I know, I know," she grumbled. "And I have my own clothes, thanks."

"Be ready. The grace period is over. Tomorrow, we start practicing."

Her gaze drifted down my body as if she were imagining all kinds of things we could practice right now. Maybe that was wishful thinking on my part, but the sudden heat in her eyes wasn't from the thought of a cocktail party. I smiled, perversely pleased that she was feeling some of the frustration I'd been dealing with the last week.

I waited for her to land on my face again before pushing a little farther than was probably smart. "If you want to start practicing early, you know where to find me."

6

Vi

S oren dropped his bomb, then left to finish some
football thing. I was so drained I didn't even eat
dinner before I passed out for the night. The next
morning, I woke up before Soren as usual. I'd picked up a
few extra sessions doing early morning personal training,
mostly to avoid my tempting roommate, but I still had
almost two hours before my first one started. Instead of
heading to campus with my coffee, I took a seat at the breakfast bar to wait.

I hated the pattern of avoidance we'd fallen into—yes, I
took my fair share of credit for it—but I also didn't want to
make this any harder on him. As much as he wanted to fling
himself between me and Colt as some kind of human
shield, I fought my own battles.

We'd both been lying low the last week, but he was right
that we couldn't keep up like that. Especially considering
the notes I'd been finding stuck in my locker at the gym.

Black ink scrawled in messy handwriting across basic
white printer paper. Since I hadn't pissed anyone else off
lately, I blamed Colt for the threatening messages. They

were more insulting than anything else, full of misogynistic bullshit and vague promises—calling me a stupid bitch, saying he'd make me pay if I talked and I'd be sorry.

I couldn't prove they were from Colt, but they sounded like what I'd expect him to say. He seemed to be stealing phrases from a super villain in a cartoon, so I stashed the notes in my bedside table and tried to forget about them.

The situation was so surreal anyway that it didn't take much effort. I was more concerned about my upcoming debut as Soren's girlfriend. If he wanted me to dress up and stay silent, I could probably manage it, but he'd never given me any indication that he wanted me to be someone other than myself. A bold choice on his part.

I didn't know what he had in mind for *practice*, but part of me hoped it involved him prancing around half-naked again. The few times I'd seen him in the living room, he'd been fully dressed, and I was honestly a little sad. What was the point of living with a guy that looked like Soren if I couldn't ogle him once in a while?

The sound of Soren's bedroom door closing cut off my musing. I finished the last of my coffee and tried to keep my breathing even as my pulse picked up. He stumbled out of the hallway, shirtless, in the same low-slung sweats he'd worn the night I agreed to this mess. It appeared dreams did come true.

He stopped short when he saw me and ran a hand through his shoulder-length hair. "Are you done avoiding me?"

"I'm not avoiding you if I have other places I'm supposed to be."

Soren chuckled, a husky, quiet sound that hit me like a shot of whiskey. "It's avoiding if you leave two hours early every day."

He pulled his hair away from his face, linking his hands behind his head with a smirk when my eyes dropped to his chest. For a blond, his chest hair was kind of dark, not that there was much of it, a shadow above his waistband that arrowed down to the promised land.

"Well, I'm here now," I said to his crotch.

"And I appreciate it, but if you keep looking at me like that, you're going to be late to work."

I sighed and returned my gaze to his face with some reluctance. "Two hours is a big promise."

He quirked an eyebrow. "I'm up for the challenge."

The smile slipped out before I could stop it. "Okay, now that we've got the daily innuendo out of the way, what did you want to practice? I really do have to go to work in a little bit."

Soren lowered his arms and circled the island to start pulling things out of the fridge. "I want you to start coming to lunch with me at the training center."

I pushed my cup closer to his side hoping for a refill. "I take it Eva and the others will be there?"

"Yeah." He glanced over and grabbed my mug, filling it with coffee and milk the way I liked it before setting it back in front of me.

"I'm not a great actress." I took a sip and blamed the warmth spreading through me on the hot liquid.

He sent me a knowing look as he tossed fruit, yogurt, milk, and protein powder into the blender. "Do you really think you need to act?"

I pursed my lips as I thought about our interaction this morning... and last night... and every other time we were in proximity to each other. "I see your point."

"All you're pretending is that you like me for *more* than my chiseled abs." He dumped the smoothie into a big, insulated cup, cleaned the blender, and turned to lean against the counter facing me. "With my parents, you need to pretend you want marriage and kids and the whole thing. Think you can do that?"

I nodded, my voice stuck in my throat. I *did* like him for more than his abs, and I wasn't against the idea of marriage and kids—eventually. The implication that *he* didn't want any of those things made me surprisingly sad.

"Good. We have two days before the cocktail party, and I should probably know more about you than your work ethic and how good you look in my hoodie."

That damn warmth came back, but I pushed it away this time. Soren didn't know me, like he'd just said, so any affection he felt toward me had to be based on my willingness to help him. Not exactly romance material.

"What do you want to know?"

"Why didn't you go to your family for help?"

Shock had me taking an extra-long drink of coffee to buy myself time. He'd gone right for the heart of my issues, and I wasn't sure how much I wanted to share with him. I settled on a simplified version of the truth. "My family lives in a small town in east Texas. They would have taken me in, but I wouldn't be able to finish my degree this year."

He frowned. "How close are you to them?"

"Not close enough that you'd have met them." The statement wasn't entirely accurate. My brothers were overbearing asses, but they loved me unconditionally. I was the one who'd pulled away when I started college.

"Good enough." Soren took his smoothie and headed toward the hallway. "I'm going to take a shower and put on some clothes so that you stop with the sexy eyes."

I huffed. "Fine. I have things to do at work anyway."

He peeked back around the corner and pointed a finger

at me. "Stay right there. I'll be five minutes tops, and I have at least seventeen other questions. Besides, I'm taking you to work today."

I didn't get the chance to respond before he disappeared into his bedroom. Luckily for him, I wanted to finish my coffee anyway. I considered arguing about him escorting me to work, but he was right that we should know each other better than acquaintances with hot as fuck eye contact.

That didn't stop me from setting a timer. If he took more than five minutes, I was leaving his ass behind. I could be generous, but I didn't want to give him the impression I would always let him order me around.

Soren was true to his word and ready to go with twenty-three seconds left. I spared a thought for the absolute unfairness of how quickly men could shower when they didn't have to shave or moisturize or do any of the other crap I did.

The jealousy disappeared when he moved past me to snatch my cup and rinse it out, replaced with that inconvenient heat I couldn't seem to control. Why did he have to smell so good?

I tried to breathe through my mouth as we gathered our stuff and headed for his truck. Soren pelted me with questions all the way to the student fitness center where I worked. I'd expected him to drop me off at the front, but he pulled around to the parking lot instead.

"You don't have to walk me inside."

He flashed me a smile. "Maybe I'm not ready to stop spending time with you yet."

"Maybe you're full of crap because there's no one in this truck but us."

"Humor me." He held up a finger, then hurried around

to my side of the truck with surprising grace. I sighed and grabbed my duffel as he opened the door for me with a bow.

"Thanks, Jeeves." My sarcasm slid off him, and he reached for my hand, linking our fingers together.

The questions tapered off, giving me a chance to collect myself. The path around the building wound through a park-like area, and early frost glistened on the grass. A sure sign that I needed to find my fleece-lined leggings if I was going to do any sessions outside.

Soren strolled along next to me, content to let me set the pace. As much as I hated getting up early, I loved my job, loved helping people realize the amazing things their bodies could do. They were the reason I was majoring in kinesiology and sports science.

The sun barely peeked through the trees, but in the quiet morning, I could almost see this as my life, my future. I shut down the image with a shiver. That kind of daydreaming would only lead to pain and heartache. Soren was very clear about his goals, and walking me to work way before any reasonable human would be awake wasn't part of his extended plan.

He was headed for the NFL, and I was a means to an end.

I looked up at the dark sky and tried to swallow the sudden disappointment that made no sense. We didn't need a real future for me to enjoy the present. My breath fogged in the chilly air, but Soren's hand warmed mine. He glanced over at me with a sly grin, and I admitted that maybe mornings weren't so bad if this was the way I got to spend them.

We reached the main doors, and I scanned us through with my badge. As an athlete, Soren had free access to the building, though most of the athletes used the training center instead—and the football team had their own facility on top of that. The rest of the student population had to pay a monthly fee.

The front desk was empty since we didn't open for another forty-five minutes, but I liked to get in early and prep before a session. Stretching countered the early morning crankiness, but today, I was in a surprisingly good mood.

I could credit the two cups of coffee, but I was pretty sure Soren's easy presence had more to do with it. The low level of heat between us never really left, and the playful side of his personality was just as dangerous. I liked his sarcasm and the way he rolled with whatever answer I gave him. I liked him.

Probably more than I should.

We rounded the corner toward the employee locker room, and I slowed. Thus far, we hadn't seen another person, but I knew he'd meant what he said about practic-ing. His thumb swiped across my inner wrist as we came to a stop.

I ignored the rush of sensation that shot up my arm with that simple touch and pointed to the door. "You can't come in here."

He chuckled. "I doubt anyone would stop me, but if you say so, I'll listen."

I waggled my brows. "What else can I tell you to do?"

His voice lowered as he pulled me closer. "Why don't you try it and find out?" He released my hand to skim his thumb along my jaw. Like with my wrist, that tiny motion rippled through me, causing all kinds of havoc.

Before I could respond, not that I could think of a response besides spontaneous combustion, Anne-Marie, one of the perky morning trainers, came out of the locker room. She stopped suddenly, I assume at the sight of Soren standing so close to me. His hand fell away, and Anne-Marie's smile brightened.

"If it isn't Soren Brehm. I didn't know we were entertaining football royalty today. Are you here for a free session? I have some time now." Her gaze trailed down his body, making it clear she wasn't talking about personal training.

My brows rose at the blatant invitation and her ability to completely ignore the fact he was clearly here with me. I hadn't spent much time with her since I preferred evening sessions, but I expected better professionalism—or at least a modicum of respect.

Soren's hand found mine again, but this time he used it to pull me against his side.

"No, thanks. I'm just dropping Vi off." He turned his attention to me. "I'll pick you up after work. We're still good for lunch, right?"

His slow smile said he enjoyed watching my brain finally catch up.

"Yeah, I can make lunch. Send me a reminder, okay?"

He leaned down and brushed his lips against my cheek. "I will."

Anne-Marie broke in, the predatory gleam in her eyes fading but not quite gone. "That reminds me. Vi, I found this by your locker. You might want to make sure you're not missing anything else." She held out a familiar piece of folded paper with my name scrawled on the outside.

7

Soren

V i froze, staring at the paper, but when I reached for it, she snatched it away. "Thanks, Anne-Marie."

The girl shrugged, gave me another once-over, then sauntered past us toward the cardio area. Vi stepped out of my grasp and gave me a tight smile before disappearing through the locker room door.

Part of me wanted to follow her, to hell with the rules. I linked my fingers behind my head and stared at the door as I debated whether she'd *want* me to get involved. Something was off with Vi. She'd been open and warm, even when her colleague had interrupted us, but the sight of that paper shut her down.

Even if I were to bust in on her, she probably wouldn't tell me what was going on. Not yet, anyway.

I was supposed to meet Derrick in twenty minutes, so I reluctantly turned and headed back to my truck. We used to do our morning workouts in the training center with everyone else, but ever since Coach had fucked around with Derrick and Nadia's relationship, we'd been meeting at my apartment's fitness center. Might as well make use of the fancy equipment my parents didn't realize they paid for.

I'd canceled twice on Derrick to haunt my apartment with Vi, so he told me in no uncertain terms that he was coming over this morning whether I wanted him to or not. Since I'd gotten Vi to agree to lunch, I only had a few more hours before my friends got in the way. Derrick deserved to know first, but I couldn't come right out and tell him. It wasn't my style. I'd have to play hard to get with the information.

As usual, Derrick showed up right on time, meeting me outside the fitness center. I grunted my hello, and we got to work. Drama aside, I still needed to put the time in to stay at the top of my game on the field.

We did our reps in near silence, like usual, but the air felt thick between us. He kept sending me curious glances when he thought I wasn't looking, and I knew my reprieve was just about over. Maybe I should have recruited Nadia to distract him.

He made it all the way to the final section of cardio before cracking. We lined up on the treadmills for a slow run, and I shook my head at his settings. Like always, I reached over to turn down his speed. Three years, and Derrick still didn't know the definition of a cool down.

He nodded his chin at me. "What's the deal, man?"

I locked my eyes on the wall in front of us as I started with a jog. "You're going to need to be more specific."

"You've been quieter than usual, you leave right after practice, and you've been skipping lunch. Plus, Eva has been weirdly evasive since that night Mac had to pick her up from the Kappa party."

Here it was—the real test. Derrick knew me better than any other person in my life, except maybe Vi, now. I planned to stick to the truth with some creative editing since I didn't really want to lie to him, but he might not buy it anyway. He had a surprising capacity to pick up on bullshit. Probably something I should have warned Vi about.

I remembered how easy it was with her this morning— teasing her, touching her, letting her sneak past my defenses. The consequences were steep if we didn't pull this off, but deep inside, the words didn't feel like a lie.

"I've been busy with my girlfriend."

Derrick missed a step and nearly launched himself backwards off the treadmill. "Dammit, Soren." He hopped onto the rails and stabbed at the power button. "You can't just announce shit like that. Someone could get hurt."

I laughed at his disgruntled expression and turned off my machine too. "If we're not cooling down, I'm heading home to take a shower."

He jumped in front of me before I could do more than step toward the door. "Oh, hell no. I deserve more than that pathetic explanation."

"Fine. Buy me a smoothie." I sidestepped him and moved across the room to the smoothie bar.

"You live here," he muttered. "They're free for you."

I snorted. "Everything comes with a price tag." A sentiment I'd do well to remember.

He wisely let that one slide and dug his credit card out of his gym bag. At night, the place became self-service, but during normal hours, the complex paid some poor soul to stand around in the gym in case one of the wealthy patrons wanted extra kale in their drink.

The pretentious attitude wasn't lost on me, but I appreciated the state-of-the-art machines and the solitude. Plus, their smoothies were really good.

We gave our orders to the attendant, then Derrick turned to me. "Okay, talk."

"Vi and I have been seeing each other for a while. Last week, she needed a place to stay, so she sort of moved in."

"She's in your apartment right now?"

I checked my watch and did some quick math. "She's probably making someone cry right about now, but most of the time, yes."

He blew out a breath. "I admit, I was not expecting that. I thought maybe you'd decided to declare for the draft after all."

My jaw tensed. Derrick didn't know why I'd redshirted as a freshman, but he understood the urge to finish college. Too bad that wasn't my reason for staying an extra year. If I had my way, I'd have declared already, but unlike my uber talented best friend, I wasn't guaranteed to go in the first round.

I'd have one shot at the pros, and I couldn't afford to fuck it up.

The smoothie guy put our drinks in front of us, my second of the morning but as far as I was concerned there was no such thing as too many smoothies. Derrick sucked at the cold liquid and winced.

"Tell me about her. Is this the same girl who's friends with Eva? The one that does classes for the cheerleaders?"

I played with my straw wrapper as I considered my answer. It didn't sound like he knew anything about Colt, and I wasn't ready to make that connection yet. "Yeah. That's how Eva met her. She's a personal trainer at the student fitness center."

"Well that explains why you've been somewhere else in your head at practice."

I didn't correct him. Maybe this week I'd been thinking

about Vi, but before that, it *was* the draft on my mind and the very real prospect that next year would be a waste without Derrick.

"You're one to talk. Nay nearly cost you your position because you couldn't get your head out of her ass."

He scowled at me when I used the nickname for his girl-friend that he hated, which was why I'd used it. "She's worth it."

"I know the feeling," I muttered.

Derrick swung around on the stool to face me. "I thought you were loyal to the team and nothing else?"

"Turns out I'm loyal to Vi too."

"Holy shit." Derrick put down his drink to stare at me, but I kept my eyes on my smoothie. "You're serious."

"I'm serious. Our relationship is serious."

"I can't believe you didn't tell me about a girl you've been seeing, *seriously*, after all the shit you gave me about Nadia."

I grinned at him and finally took a pull from my own smoothie. "You seemed busy."

———

AFTER DERRICK LEFT, I spent the rest of the morning watching the clock. I amused myself during my classes by sending Vi increasingly risqué texts along with a reminder about lunch. She only responded to the lunch message, but I knew she was reading them. I hoped she was smiling.

Unlike this morning, the fitness center was busy when I arrived to pick her up. As students streamed past me out the glass doors, I saw the girl from earlier—Anne-Marie?—working the front desk.

For a second, I considered waiting outside, but Vi would never let me live it down if she knew that excuse for a trainer scared me away. Besides, I could use the reminder of what most women wanted from me—a trophy fuck.

Anne-Marie greeted me as I entered, but I didn't spare her a glance. Vi came around the corner before I could get very far past the front desk. Her hair was falling out of her ponytail, and she blew ineffectually at it until she spotted me.

Our eyes locked and a jolt went through me when her lips turned up in a smile. Pink tinged her cheeks, and she raised a brow as she wiggled her phone at me. Clearly, she'd gotten my texts.

I huffed out a laugh at the retribution in her eyes. My girl didn't take a challenge lightly. *My girl...* the thought brought me up short, and I had to fight to keep my steps even. No harm in enjoying the time with her, but I needed to remember that we were using each other. I couldn't let myself get distracted by thoughts of a future she didn't want.

Vi hiked her bag higher on her shoulder and tilted her head to study me. I'd have sworn I maintained my happy expression, but she definitely noticed the change in my demeanor. If she could read me that easily, I was already in trouble.

We hadn't discussed where she stood on kissing in public, so I kept my greeting tame. I circled her waist and pulled her close to brush my lips against her temple. And I ignored the tightness in my chest that released the second I touched her.

"How was work?"

"Fun. One of my clients had to use his big boy words when he half-assed his squats and I made him do them over."

"There's that vindictive streak I love."

She tensed for a split second, then relaxed into my arms again. "Ready for lunch? I'm starving."

I smiled against her hair and ushered her toward the door. "I thought you'd never ask."

Vi let me hold her hand as we walked, keeping up the pretense, but the second we were relatively alone in the truck, she let out a breath and slouched back against the seat.

I sent her a sidelong glance as I pulled out of the parking lot. "You okay?"

"Tired."

"I didn't realize flirting with me would take so much out of you."

"It's not you, it's me." She sent me a weary smile. "For real. Flirting with you is dangerously easy. Anne-Marie wouldn't let up after you left, and the class I had between sessions kicked my ass."

"Tell me about it."

She sat up a little straighter. "Really?"

"Yeah. I want to know."

Out of the corner of my eye, I saw her shift to face me. "You don't have to pretend to care."

"Vi, despite what Eva claims, I'm capable of listening and being a friend."

"Because you need me." She dismissed me to stare out the window.

It was on the tip of my tongue to tell her the truth. That I liked her, and she terrified me. Vi knew more about my fucked-up situation than anyone not actively involved in it, and instead of running or trying to negotiate a better deal, she doubled down to support me. I *should* remember that she was using me too, but I couldn't seem to make myself believe it.

As much as I wanted to deny it, I was already in deep with her. I could fight the pull, try to control the fallout, but Vi had the power to change my future. If we convinced my parents to back off for my last year, I'd be finishing out my time with football as my only focus. Trying anything and everything to make me stand out to the pro teams. She'd graduate and move on.

We were heading in different directions and clinging to her would only slow both of us down. No matter how much I wanted to.

In the end, I didn't say any of that. I couldn't, not without fundamentally altering our agreement.

"I do need you, but that doesn't mean I don't care."

The silence thickened with my admission. She studied me again, like that moment in the fitness center, and I had the feeling I didn't need to tell her any of the thoughts in my head. I couldn't gauge if she believed me or not, but something passed between us as I made the last turn into the athletic center.

I parked and tilted my head to face her. "Show time."

Vi stiffened instead of making any move to get out of the truck. "I know Eva eats with you, but how many others are we talking here?"

"Probably the whole crew. D, Parker, Noah, and Mac along with Eva."

She nodded, chewing on her index fingernail. "I've met Mac, but the others are all new."

"Don't worry. Mac will talk enough for everyone. All you have to do is be yourself and maybe stare adoringly at me from time to time."

"And what will you be doing?"

I sent her a slow grin which earned me an eye roll.

"I actually get to eat, right? Because if not, I might murder you for taking over my lunch time with theatrics."

"There's plenty of food inside."

Her lips twisted for a moment, then she reached for the door handle. "Well, what are we waiting for? Feed me, Jeeves."

8

Vi

We barely made it through the doors before I stopped in my tracks. A giant spread of different foods took up one whole wall of the cafeteria space, and my mouth dropped open a little as I stared in awe.

Soren hadn't warned me that I'd be eating in rich kid paradise. I thought I saw caviar at the far end, but upon closer inspection it was boba. A twinge of guilt soured my joy at the sight.

There shouldn't have been this much of a discrepancy between the abundance available to the athletes and the barely edible dreck they served in the normal food hall. On the other hand, I was going to enjoy every second of my time here in fancy land.

Soren nudged my side, pulling my attention away from the buffet. "Are you okay? I think you might have drooled a little."

I blinked at him and surreptitiously wiped my mouth, in case he wasn't messing with me. "You just moved up several places on the list of people I like."

One side of his lips tilted up in a half-smile. "I wasn't number one?"

"You weren't even in the top ten, but this is one hell of a lunch. You eat here every day? Why aren't you four hundred pounds?"

He laughed and squeezed my hand. "Good metabolism. Our crew eats here most days since it's central to all of us. They always sit at the same table in the corner." He nodded his head toward the far end of the room, around the other side of a decorative wall covered in plants. "It's kind of become a tradition, which they'll expect you to join being my girlfriend and all. Which begs the question... what's my rank?"

"Why do you want to know?"

"I like having concrete goals. How am I supposed to move up if I don't know where I'm starting?"

His words from earlier echoed in my head. *I do need you, but that doesn't mean I don't care.* With Soren, that sentiment was dangerous. I didn't generally let people get close, with Eva as the very determined exception. Even she only knew so much about my family. I didn't like to talk about my life before college. Sometimes it was easier to simply forget—and sometimes it was necessary to move on.

It was these in-between moments that were the most hazardous. I knew he was playing a part, but I *wanted* to believe him. I wanted to think that him caring was enough to let our pretend relationship evolve into reality, even if he didn't need me.

Maybe Soren wanted the same thing, but I wasn't ready to take that chance. Not yet.

I smirked. "Sorry, I'm afraid that information is unavailable at this time, but you're doing great."

"Giving you half an apartment should be enough to get me into the top three at least."

I scoffed. "Housing is nice and all, but food is my love language."

"You sure it's not coffee, specifically?"

"My deep and abiding affection for coffee can never be overstated, but that salad bar has four, count them *four* protein options." I sighed heavily. "I think I'm in heaven."

His gaze turned contemplative. "I'll keep that in mind. What would it take to win the top spot?"

My heart fluttered in my chest at his quiet question, and I found myself answering him with the truth. "It would take every day. Choosing me, every day, as the most important thing in your life, but you're not interested in that."

The air thickened between us for a long moment, then Soren looked away. I forced myself to take a deep breath and push aside the flicker of hurt at his quick dismissal. I knew where we stood. He may care about me, but I'd never be more important than football and his future.

I poked him in the side with my free hand. "You promised me food, and all you've done so far is taunt me with it. Can we get to the eating portion of lunch now?"

Relief passed over his face, then he grinned down at me, back to his usual irreverent self. "Go grab what you want. I'll meet you at the table."

He dropped a kiss against my temple like he'd done it a million times then sauntered off toward the corner. I watched him walk away, greeting people as he passed with that easy confidence. He disappeared around the wall, and I shook my head.

At least he hadn't insisted on escorting me around like a show pony. I scanned the room, looking for any signs of Colt, but as far as I could see, the tables seemed blessedly asshole free. Not that seeing Colt would have stopped me, I just liked to be prepared for confrontation. One of the first rules my brothers had taught me was to always be aware of my surroundings.

I wrinkled my nose as I started loading a plate. That lesson had stuck, but actually avoiding the confrontation brewing was a different thing entirely. They ragged on me constantly for finding trouble, as if I couldn't help but get involved. I guess in this case, they were right.

Which was why they'd never know about my current situation.

I took my time filling two plates and left the buffet with zero regrets. If the athletic department wanted to play favorites, I'd gladly take advantage of a free meal. My nerves flared up when I came around the wall and got my first good look at Soren's friends.

They'd chosen a giant oval table, which made sense considering the size of the guys sitting around it. The five football players took up most of the space, with Eva squeezed between Mac and Soren. An empty chair sat on Soren's left, probably for me, and my steps slowed.

I was used to Eva's tiny perfectness, but the number of stupidly pretty people at that table was a little intimidating. Soren drew my attention, as always, with his hair pulled back into a manbun that didn't make me want to smack him and his arm thrown across the back of the empty chair. He faced away from me, so I couldn't see his smolder-y eyes, but I could enjoy the play of his broad shoulders as he shifted in his seat.

Mac said something that made Soren shake his head, and mischief marked his smile. We'd only met a few times before, but I'd always liked him. He reminded me of a spastic puppy, always happy and intent on making people love him. It would be easy to love him too. Adam Mackenzie oozed charm.

He and Eva had some kind of love/hate thing happening that predated my friendship with her. As far as I knew, they'd been friends since before college, and despite the way she sometimes looked at him, Eva swore there was nothing else between them except annoyance.

The guy on the other side of my seat threw back his head to laugh, and I recognized Derrick Asher, our star quarterback, from games I'd attended. Next to him was a giant with a neatly trimmed reddish-brown beard. He smiled along with Derrick without saying anything.

The other guy I didn't know nearly stopped me in my tracks. Dark hair and eyes with thick lashes and a sharp jaw. He sat back with his arms crossed, listening, but I could see his amusement in the twitch of his lips. This guy could be a model. What was he doing playing football?

Intellectually, I could acknowledge that he was very attractive, but for some reason, he did nothing for my lady parts. I shifted my gaze back to Soren, and even the back of his head made me all squirrely inside.

Mac noticed me first, and a big smile lit up his face. "Vi, you coming over here?"

The others all turned toward me, and Eva's mouth dropped open. "*You're* the girlfriend?"

I put my plates on the table and tried not to feel offended by her clear shock. "Nah, he paid me to pose as his girlfriend. I'm only here for the food."

Soren yanked me down next to him, practically in his lap, and growled in my ear. "Careful."

Goosebumps exploded across my skin, so I jammed my elbow into his rock-hard stomach. "Food first, cuddles later."

Mac snickered as Soren let go so I could sit in my own

chair. "I hope you're ready for the truly monumental amount of shit Soren's going to get for you."

"Worth it," Soren muttered.

I pulled my plates closer and took stock of him through my lashes. He didn't seem upset. In fact, his eyes slid toward me with a slow wicked grin. Under the table, his hand squeezed my knee, then ghosted higher until I clamped my legs shut to stop him. He settled on my upper thigh with his fingers tucked tightly between my legs, inches from where I was suddenly aching.

My leggings offered no protection against the warmth of his touch, and even I wasn't sure if I kept my thighs clenched to stop him or to hold him close. Luckily, Derrick leaned forward and offered me his hand, distracting us both.

"Nice to meet you, Vi. I'm Derrick Asher. Everyone calls me D."

"I know. I've seen you play." I shook his hand and took a chance in relaxing my legs. Soren didn't move his fingers, one way or the other.

Derrick nodded at the big—bigger—guy next to him, then at the walking underwear ad. "This is Noah Olsen, and over there is Parker Shaw."

I gave each of them a finger wave. "I'm glad to finally meet you guys, but you'll have to forgive me while I stuff my face. This is my only chance to eat until late tonight." Mac stole a fry from my second plate, and I slapped at his hand. "That's how you get stabbed. You don't touch a starving woman's food."

Eva waved at the close proximity between me and Soren. "I can't believe you guys pretended like you didn't know each other at the party."

Soren jumped in while I shoved chicken in my mouth. "We didn't pretend. We just didn't explain."

Her eyes narrowed. "So it *was* you making out by your truck when you were supposed to be giving her a ride home. I defended you." She pulled a wrinkled two dollar bill out of the cheer bag by her feet and slapped it against Mac's shoulder.

He chuckled and pocketed the money. "I told you Vi was exactly his type."

Eva pointed a finger at Soren. "You better treat her right. I was willing to accept some rando that caught your attention, but *do not* fuck with Vi."

My heart warmed at her defense of me, and I shared a look with Soren. We hadn't addressed how we'd present our breakup. Ideally, we'd go our separate ways and tell everyone we'd decided we were better as friends. No harm, no foul.

Except Soren's expression shifted subtly. His jaw tightened and some of the playfulness left his eyes, like the thought of going our separate ways made him angry. The separate ways scenario didn't exactly work for me either if I planned to keep living in his swanky apartment for any length of time. I hadn't, at the beginning, but that bed...

Yeah, I scoffed in my head, it was his *bed* I wanted.

Soren squeezed my thigh where his hand still rested, then winked at Eva. "Fucking is exactly what I plan to do with Vi, among other things."

Noah choked on the French fry he was eating, and Derrick had to pound him on the back until he stopped coughing. Eva rolled her eyes and took in my flushed face. I assume she thought I was embarrassed, but I was having a hell of a time not spreading my legs and sliding down in my seat.

I forced a laugh. "We're living together, Eva. He's not wrong."

She turned her finger on me. "I'm going to give you the same warning. Soren acts like an arrogant ass, but he's got a squishy center."

He shifted next to me, and I tried not to laugh at his discomfort that she'd pegged him so accurately—probably more than he realized.

I put my fork down and raised a brow at her. "I'll take the warning because I know you love him, but I'm well aware he's not an ass. Trust me, okay?"

She stared at me for a long moment then nodded. Soren looked back and forth between us with a furrowed brow. He seemed unused to people defending him, but that was going to change as long as we were together. Everyone else got this sleek façade of confidence like he didn't care what they thought, but he softened with me. *I need you, but that doesn't mean I don't care.* Maybe he didn't realize it, but he'd been soft from the beginning when he wouldn't let me go home alone.

I nudged my second plate closer to him. "Eat something. We had a busy morning."

Soren sent me a knowing look and checked to make sure I had enough food on my other plate before grabbing a carrot. He cared a hell of a lot more than he thought he did.

9

Soren

To my great surprise, Eva lasted almost all the way through lunch before dragging Vi to the bathroom with her. In all that time, my hand rested on Vi's thigh, inches from crossing a line. The others didn't notice her heightened color, her shallow breaths, but I did.

The second they were out of earshot, Mac threw a grape at me. "What the fuck is going on? And don't give me any bullshit about suddenly being into Vi. Not that she isn't far, *far* out of your league, but you don't do relationships and suddenly after the Kappa party—"

I interrupted him before he could give the rest of the table ideas. "I *can* do relationships—I just chose not to until now."

He crossed his arms and leaned back. "Uh huh. Are you also going to tell me this has nothing to do with Colt's stupid ass?"

Fuck. Derrick's eyes zeroed in on me. "What happened with Colt?"

I glanced at my friends' curious faces and blew out a

breath. Damn Mac and his big mouth. "He tried to disappear with one of Eva's friends while she was drunk."

Parker's jaw ticked. "*Tried*?"

"The girl was coherent enough to tell him to fuck off, and when Colt wouldn't let go, Vi intervened."

Noah shook his head, and Parker's eyes strayed to the bathrooms where Vi had disappeared. None of them said it, but while Vi was fairly built, Colt still had a solid hundred pounds on her. The girl had balls of steel.

Derrick rubbed the bridge of his nose. "Is that when she moved in?"

All four sets of eyes focused on me again, and I made a snap decision. I trusted these guys on the field and off. They could help me keep an eye on Colt. "Yeah. Vi's campus apartment evicted her two days later—" Mac groaned, but I ignored him. "We're pretty sure Colt, or at least his family, was involved. I wanted to keep Vi close, so she moved in."

They all started talking at once, but I only caught Noah's quiet question. "Is the girl okay?"

I nodded at him, then waited for the others to settle down before addressing all of them. "Mac helped Eva get Lizzy home, but Colt might be a problem moving forward."

Derrick speared Mac with an exasperated look. "You too? Why didn't you call the cops? Or us?"

Mac held up his hands. "Whoa, I didn't find out about any of this until the next morning. Eva conveniently failed to mention the reason Lizzy was upset."

I ran a hand over my hair. "Vi *wanted* to call the police, but I convinced her not to. It would be Colt's word against hers, and he was sporting an injured wrist."

We all stared at each other solemnly. Colt was one of our teammates, asshole or not, but this was a serious accusation. If Vi hadn't been there, what would he have done?

I glanced toward the bathroom. Eva and Vi would be back any minute. "Look, there's nothing we can do about what happened, and you know as well as I do that the police won't be able to do anything. Colt was hyper-focused on Vi at the party, you know how he gets. I don't want him anywhere near her, but I can take care of Vi if you guys can keep an eye on him."

Everyone except Parker nodded, and I raised a brow at him, surprised. "You bowing out?"

He scowled. "Hell, no, but Colt needs to answer for his actions. Maybe we should go to the school."

Derrick snorted. "The school won't do shit. Colt has the protection of being on the football team *and* his family's money. Besides, Eva's friend would need to be the one coming forward with accusations."

Parker shifted to address Mac. "What if it had been Eva?"

Mac stared down at his clenched hands, his smile long gone, but he didn't say anything.

I groaned. "This isn't getting us anywhere. I just wanted you assholes to keep an eye out in case he starts causing trouble for Vi. Obviously, if we see something we'll contact the authorities and let them handle it."

Parker didn't look particularly appeased, but he gave a succinct nod. I understood his frustration. We didn't know for sure what Colt had planned to do with Lizzy, but when she told him to back off, he should have listened.

Mac linked his hands behind his head. "Anybody catch Mercer tossing his socks in the freezer last week?"

The others chimed in, even Noah, about Mercer's disgusting pre-game habits, but my gaze kept returning to the bathrooms. Vi could hold her own against Eva, but that didn't stop me from wondering what story she was telling.

All the talk about Colt prevented the guys from pressing me about my relationship with Vi. I'd expected more shock, but maybe our performance had convinced them. *Performance...* I shook my head slightly. I hadn't been acting—I'd used the ruse as an excuse to put my hands on her.

When she'd looked up at me with fire in her eyes, her breath uneven from my touch, not an inch of me was pretending. All I'd wanted to do was haul her into my lap until she sighed my name.

Then she'd offered to share her food with me, only me, and I was lost. How was I supposed to keep her at a distance when she slipped so easily through my defenses?

Even in the low-key chaos of the dining hall, I heard loud, obnoxious laughter coming from the main doors. People at the tables around us glanced over nervously.

I met Derrick's eyes across the empty seat, then leaned back to try to get a look at the source. The bathroom doors were in view, but the stupid decorative wall blocked me from seeing anything. Prickles on the back of my neck warned me that trouble was coming.

The bathroom door swung open, revealing Eva and Vi just as Colt and his posse rolled around the plant wall. He noticed her immediately and changed direction. A shot of adrenaline that felt suspiciously like fear had me out of my seat in an instant. Behind me, I heard the scraping of multiple chairs being pushed back.

I knew I wouldn't make it to her before he did, but I was ninety-eight percent certain he wouldn't try anything in a room full of witnesses. That last two percent had me practically shoving people out of my way.

Colt positioned himself in front of the girls with a smirk on his face. Eva stopped in her tracks, but Vi hooked their arms together and steered them around Colt, completely ignoring him. She kept her chin high and continued her conversation with Eva as if nothing had happened.

Despite my panic, a rush of pride hit me at her perfect 'don't give a fuck' reaction.

Her gaze found mine, and she smiled. The world slowed as relief replaced the anxiety hidden deep in her eyes.

Then Colt reached out to grab Vi's arm. I lunged forward, uncaring that breaking his face would end my season. Derrick gripped my shoulder to stop me. Some internal sense of danger must have clued Colt in on his imminent demise because he looked up at me with a smirk.

I don't know where the rage came from, but I knew Colt would take his fucking hands off Vi if I had to remove them myself.

Colt proved himself not entirely stupid and released her, holding his palms up and taking a step back. Derrick let me go, but I was done playing Colt's game.

Vi took one look at my face and abandoned Eva to plant a hand on my chest. I finally broke my stare-off with Colt to look down at Vi. Her dark eyes were wide with concern, but I realized it wasn't for her—it was for me.

The fingers on my chest twitched, and I felt that slight movement as if she'd tugged on a string straight to my heart.

My anger drained away. Maybe fifteen seconds had passed since I'd spotted Colt, but something in me shifted. The rest of the room disappeared as I focused on Vi. Her lips curled up into a half-smile, one that said she'd be a lot more fun than my current preoccupation.

"You okay?" I murmured.

"I will be in a second." She twisted her hand in my shirt, giving the smallest tug.

That was all I needed. I slid my hand around her neck, stroking her jaw with my thumb, and lowered my mouth to hers. It took everything in me to keep the touch light, barely a brush against her lips.

She sighed, a tiny sound of surrender, and my muscles tensed with the urge to haul her fully against me. Instead, I pulled away, resting my forehead against hers for a moment.

"You know I could have handled him, right?" she mumbled with her eyes still closed.

"I don't care. If he touches you again, I'll break his fucking arm." I didn't give a shit who heard me—my friends, Colt, the other random people pretending to eat while they watched us—and I meant every word I said.

Vi laughed dryly and patted my chest. "Then you can get in line."

She started to head back in Eva's direction, but I snaked an arm around her waist before she could move very far. Since we'd already announced our relationship to the world at large in a spectacular fashion, I might as well enjoy the moment while cementing the point.

Eva had joined the others behind me, but Colt hadn't moved. Calculation lit his eyes as his gaze flicked to my arm around Vi then back up to my face.

"So she's yours, huh? I should have realized. Are you so afraid of a little competition that you'd send your girl to do your dirty work?"

Vi tensed under my arm, but her tone only reflected boredom. "If you have a problem, I'd be happy to discuss it with the authorities. I'd *love* to explain why I felt justified in my actions."

Colt's confidence never wavered, adding weight to the theory that calling the police wouldn't have achieved anything the night of the party. He ignored her to address me.

"Keep your bitch on a leash or I can't be held accountable for what happens when you're not around to protect her."

I laughed, low and dark. "Vi doesn't need me to protect her, but you already know that."

He scowled at us, but one of his silent buddies called his name. Colt shook his head and turned away without saying anything more. They claimed a table by the door where Colt immediately started flirting with the group of female soccer players next to him.

I still wanted to bury my fist in his face, but with Vi pressed into my side, the urge came from a distance.

"Alright, show's over people. Back to your lunches." Eva made eye contact with several of the closest tables and glared at one guy with thick black glasses that was still filming on his phone.

Derrick slapped me on the back as he sauntered past toward our abandoned lunches followed by the rest of our crew. I hadn't noticed in the moment, but they'd all positioned themselves at our back. A hulking wall of football players and one angry cheerleader.

Vi held herself quiet until they'd all passed, then she blew out a breath. "Secret's out now."

I squeezed her against my side. "That was always the plan, though I'd imagined it a little less dramatically."

She laughed and tucked her arm around my waist. "I have to say, I'm not sure this is going to work out the way you'd hoped. Considering the way he's sneaking glances at us, Colt seems *more* interested now that he thinks we're involved in some conspiracy."

"I wish I could say his attitude stemmed from knowing he'll never win the starting position on his own, but he's actually a good player. If he ever removed his head from his ass, he'd have a real shot. Especially if I'm not here next year."

Vi gave me a strange look. "Why wouldn't you be here next year?"

I glanced down at her as I realized what I'd let slip. No one, not even Derrick, knew I was considering leaving school to declare for the draft. I wasn't really even seriously thinking about it myself, but the option was there in the back of my mind.

I knew I could make up an excuse—distract her or change the subject—but part of me *wanted* to talk about it. Vi already knew about my family. What was one more secret?

"Let's get out of here and I'll tell you."

10

Vi

I spent two days alternating between *holy shit I'll spontaneously combust if he really kisses me* and *holy shit Soren is thinking about joining Derrick in the draft.* I'd heard speculation, anyone who followed college football or walked across campus with working ears had heard speculation, but Soren had yet to comment.

Until he took my hand in his truck on the way back to the student fitness center and surprised me by sharing his thoughts. He didn't swear me to secrecy or anything, but I knew he hadn't told anyone else. I also understood why he kept it quiet. He seemed to think he was just as likely to get drafted as he was to end up working at his family's company, and the risk terrified him.

The whole situation felt surreal to me since I'd love to work at my brothers' gym—as long as they treated me like an adult person instead of a baby sister, which wasn't happening any time soon. Then again, there was a big difference between Soren's family's business and his dream of playing football. At least my passion fell right in line with the rest of my family, even if they didn't see it.

I tried *not* to think about the kiss.

We'd been in front of Colt, and half the student-athletes at Teagan University, so he'd been playing the part as agreed. But it had felt real. His anger, the way he'd traced my face as if I were precious, the badass way he'd supported me without making me look weak. My heart flopped over every time I remembered it.

So I didn't.

I worked and I went to class and I avoided Soren as much as I could considering his insistence on driving me to work every day. Through some miracle, I'd also managed to avoid Eva after that eye-opening lunch, at least until three days later when she guilted me into getting coffee after my shift on Halloween.

The coffee shop on campus was *very* into our school mascot. Wildcats stared back at me wherever I looked as I waited at a table for Eva to show up—framed cat pictures, a cat mural, cat-shaped lights strung along the ceiling. The white walls were covered with scarlet and black cheetah spots, and all the employees wore black cat ears. I'd only been in this place once before, my freshman year, and at the time I'd thought it was the height of cheesiness. That opinion hadn't changed.

Eva came in with a gust of cold wind and blew on her fingers as she searched the small shop for me. I was almost sad to see her in jeans and a sweater for once. If she'd worn her cheer practice gear, she'd have blended in perfectly.

She spotted me and pointed to the counter. I nodded. My next client had canceled, and I was caught up on my reading. For once, I wasn't in a hurry. Eva said something to the guy making her coffee and he laughed, then he looked up and almost dropped the milk he was holding.

I could tell from his reaction she'd put on her flirty face, probably to ask for an extra shot. It never failed. They always fell for the sweet cheerleader persona, completely unaware of how diabolical she could be.

With a subtle hair flip, she collected her extra-caffeinated coffee and added a swing to her hips on the way to my table. I raised my brow as she sat down with a smug smile.

"One day you're going to get a gay coffee guy."

She toasted me with her cup. "And I'll still get my extra shot because he'll see how fabulous I am, then we'll become besties and go on adventures together."

I rolled my eyes. "You already have a gay best friend."

"And how do you think I found him? We met at the coffee shop back home."

Eva loved to talk about Stephen. I'd met him a couple of times during video chats, and I could see why she adored him. If I thought there was a chance I could get through coffee without talking about Soren, I'd call Stephen myself, but he'd just insist on hearing the dirt too.

She'd tried to corner me in the bathroom at lunch, but I'd managed to put her off with the promise of full disclosure. A promise I had no intention of keeping.

As if she could read my mind, Eva cocked her head and eyed me like a predator. "This is where you talk about Soren and your violation of the friend act by withholding important life events."

I sighed. "You have to promise not to freak out."

Her brows shot up to her hairline. "How am I supposed to not freak out when you start by asking me not to freak out?"

"You remember how I asked to store some stuff at your apartment?"

"Yes, then you told me nevermind, disappeared for a week, and never explained?"

"Soren offered to let me move into his place, then I guess I got distracted."

She snorted. "By all the dirty sex. Yes, I understand that part. I need you to go back to how long you and Soren have been dating and follow that up with why you didn't tell me—your closest and most bestest friend—about it."

I picked at the sticker on my paper cup. "I wasn't sure about it, about him, and we haven't been together that long, really."

"Are you sure now?"

I laughed dryly. "No, but it's hard to say no to Soren."

She nodded. "Hard not to care about him too, once you get past the sleek exterior. And I'd say he's sure about you. I thought he was going to dismember Colt right there in front of half the swim team."

I'd thought the same thing. When I looked up and saw Soren coming toward me, violence in his eyes, I'd been relieved. After the notes, I wasn't sure what to expect from Colt. I could fight my own battles, but knowing he'd be there, ready to take over if I needed it, was a heady moment. Soren had genuinely looked like he wanted to kill Colt, but he'd stopped at my touch.

In an instant, he'd shifted from murder to softness. He'd given me that power. Then he'd kissed me, and my insides had become molten goo.

Warmth rose in my cheeks, and Eva laughed. "Okay, tell me everything. What's it like living at Casa Soren? Is his tongue as talented as he claims? Does he sleep naked?" She held up a finger. "Wait, ignore that last one. Of course he sleeps naked."

I propped my chin on my hand. "Living with him is an experience. Soren is intensely personal."

"And possessive. That was a surprise. I've never seen him act that way before. Honestly, I was beginning to worry he wasn't capable of forming a relationship like that with another person."

My brows came together. "Soren has several close relationships... one is with you."

She waved away my contradiction. "He doesn't treat you like he treats us. If that were me, he'd have made a snarky comment at Colt and escorted me back to the table with none of those delicious growly moments."

I couldn't argue with her. I'd seen them together and while it was clear he cared about her, he didn't lose his impervious cool around anyone but me. It should have annoyed me, should have made me push him away with everything in me, but that wasn't the reaction I had to Soren.

Eva reached across the table and put her hand over mine. "I'm betting you haven't told your brothers, but you might want to consider being upfront that you're living with a guy. I'd hate to have you disappear on me because they found out some other way."

"I wouldn't disappear. We're not in the mafia."

She laughed. "Remember that time with Scooter or whatever from the gym? I didn't see you for two weeks because your crazy brothers decided you'd be safer at home. The dance classes weren't nearly as good with you gone."

I sat back, sliding my hand out from under hers. She'd nailed the exact reason I wouldn't be sharing any information with my brothers about my current situation.

"I don't think that's necessary, but your concern is noted."

Eva leaned forward, and her eyes glittered with excitement. "When Jackson shows up, will you call me please? I only got a couple of minutes to ogle him the last time when he dropped you off."

Jackson, my oldest brother, had overreacted to an overly amorous colleague by showing up at my door early one morning during the beginning of my junior year. He'd taken my keys, shoved me in the car before I'd had enough coffee to kick him in the junk, and driven me the four plus hours home. Then he, Corey, Alex, and Ryder had refused to bring me back until I'd been on the verge of failing my classes. Even then, they went with me to "handle the problem", which translated to scaring the shit out of Carter.

They were not subtle—or stable—but they loved me.

In this case, I didn't need them to take over. Thanks to Soren, I'd handled the problem myself.

I pursed my lips as I considered Eva's request. If Jackson showed up, a distraction would be really useful while I escaped out the back way with Soren. Provided I could convince Soren to run. He was surprisingly territorial for someone who'd been so averse to a relationship that he created a fake girlfriend.

Either way, if I had time, I'd probably call Eva.

"Fine. I could use the backup if that situation were ever to happen."

She grinned. "I promise not to corrupt him too much."

"How about you promise not to get him involved in the first place?"

With a dramatic gasp, she stood from her chair. "I would never..."

"Mm hmm." I grabbed my cup and joined her. "I don't need outside help. I have Soren."

The words felt weird coming out of my mouth. Not because they were false, but because they felt so true. We left our dishes in the tub, and Eva paused before opening the door.

"For real, I'm glad you and Soren found each other. I never thought he'd give in, but the way he looks at you... I have to admit I'm a little jealous."

A cold tinge of dread ruined the warm buzz from the coffee. "You never said anything about being interested in him."

She smacked my arm and laughed. "Not jealous because of Soren. Just of the devotion, I guess."

I raised my brows, but somehow refrained from mentioning Mac and his absolute dedication to her despite their bickering. She opened the door and held it for me. I stopped on the sidewalk to wait for Eva, and the cold breeze whipped through my clothes. The door closed behind us with a thud as I pulled my sweater tighter, and I looked up in time to see Colt's smarmy smile from a low-slung car across the parking lot.

His window was open despite the chill in the air, and he lifted a finger from his steering wheel in a douchey wave. Eva poked me in the back, and when I swung around, she looked at me like I was crazy.

Soren had admitted he'd told them about Colt, but I didn't want her to confront him. She would—Eva feared no man—but the last thing I wanted was for him to focus on yet another of my friends. I could handle whatever he dished out at me.

I linked my arm through hers and guided her down the street away from Colt's car. "You never told me how the new stunt worked out. Did Mac finally help you?"

Eva rolled her eyes and launched into a diatribe about how Mac would be such a fantastic stunt partner if he weren't so good at football.

11

Soren

My phone buzzed in my hand, and I flipped it over to read the new message from Eva. *Is this skirt too short?*

She'd included a picture of her in a Bo Peep costume that looked like it was missing three-quarters of the skirt. Mac responded with a mirror pic of himself in full sheep garb giving her two thumbs up.

I barked out a laugh and added another regret to the promises chaining me to my family's party. The group had been sending texts all day prepping for their big night out. Nadia had convinced Derrick to dress up in costume for some volunteer thing at the community center, and he'd encouraged the rest of them to spend their Halloween with a bunch of needy kids.

Honestly, that evening sounded way better than what I'd be doing—dealing with my condescending family and their "helpful" suggestions of how I could improve my life. I tried not to be jealous.

At least Vi would be with me. I filled my lungs with air and let it out slowly. An action I'd repeated over and over since we'd stopped avoiding each other. That kiss at lunch haunted me. I'd forgotten we were performing for an audience, forgotten everything except how much I wanted to taste her, and then I'd let her in on one of my closest kept secrets.

Another deep breath, and I tried to think about anything other than Vi, probably close to naked, as she got ready in her room. My phone vibrated, marking another text from the group. I ignored the notification and glanced down the hallway at Vi's closed door.

I'd been thinking a lot about taking my chances in the draft, but that decision felt a little too close to my parents' accusations. A rash choice made with emotion rather than logic. I'd be burning all my bridges on the chance that a professional football team thought I'd be good enough.

I'd never been good enough.

That's why I worked my ass off to prove myself on the field. My phone buzzed again, and I glanced at the message to distract myself from my grim thoughts. Derrick again, with a message that was probably meant for Nadia alone. My thoughts shot back to Vi moments before I heard the click of heels on the hardwood.

I glanced up from my phone, and the world stilled around me. She wore a halter dress splashed with color, like an abstract painting that hugged her curves. It cinched in at the waist, then flared out into a multi-layered skirt that ended mid-thigh. The short length left her long legs bare all the way to strappy black stilettos.

While I sat there staring at her like a dumbass, she did a little turn, causing the skirt to flare even higher.

"Will this work?" Her voice quivered the tiniest bit, betraying her nerves.

I snapped out of my stupor and stood to tuck my phone

into my pocket. Her chest rose with a deep breath as I approached, then she let it out slowly as I took her hand.

"You look beautiful." Her heels brought her eye level with my chin, and I couldn't stop thinking about how her mouth was at the perfect height.

"Thank you." She pursed her lips and trailed her gaze down my body to take in my charcoal suit. "You'll do."

"High praise coming from you." I held out my arm. "You ready for our first performance?"

She scoffed. "If you don't count lunch and every morning at work."

"Don't forget the afternoons. Those are my favorite." I waggled my eyebrows at her as she slid her arm through mine.

The faint flush on her cheeks told me she knew why it was my favorite. With the biggest audience, I made sure everyone in the vicinity knew she was with me, which meant copious touching.

I'd gone to practice with uncomfortable hard-ons every day this week, but it was worth it to be able to trail my lips over her neck and feel her pulse jump.

Tonight would be twice as bad because we needed to convince my parents I'd settled down into a serious relationship, which did not include running my hands under that flirty little skirt in the first dark corner I could find.

Vi rested her fingers on my forearm as I escorted her down the stairs to my truck, swaying close enough for me to smell her sweet scent. Her steps faltered when I continued past the driver's side. A misstep so slight I almost missed it, but she smiled up at me as I opened the passenger door for her.

"I get the full service tonight, I see." She raised a brow, daring me to make a joke about servicing her.

Heroically, I resisted. "All part of the package." Her eyes darted down, and I grinned. "I thought we weren't including that in the package."

She shrugged and climbed into the truck, baring a dangerous amount of thigh that lit me up like I'd never seen a beautiful woman before. "No one else knows that. Might as well work on the looks while we have the chance."

Her eyes met mine from the shadow of the truck cab, and the smoldering heat there almost convinced me to say *fuck it*—to take her upstairs and finally do something about our very inconvenient attraction.

Instead, I stepped back and closed the door between us. I circled the truck while reciting football stats to ease the ache in my cock. The slacks I wore wouldn't hide my reaction, and my parents expected a certain level of decorum. Vi's dress would fit in perfectly but showing up sporting wood wasn't the first impression I wanted them to have of us.

Even if it was the most accurate representation of our relationship—both of us longing for something we weren't willing to risk.

I paused outside my door to stare at the first stars coming out in the rapidly darkening sky. The sun had already sunk below the trees, but the chilly breeze did nothing to cool me down. I'd put myself in this position by proposing this stupid agreement.

We were supposed to be convincing my parents I'd settled down, that playing football didn't necessarily equal a wild party life. Little did they know that the wildest my life got was the fleeting period each day when Vi the roommate became Vi the girlfriend. I hated the moment we switched back, and I'd been finding ways to extend the time. Tonight,

I'd have hours to touch her the way I wanted because it was part of the show.

Part of me wondered how far she'd let me go in a place where we both knew we couldn't succumb.

That thought was dangerous and tempting, and it wasn't helping me remember our actual goals for the evening. I opened the door and slid into the truck, careful to keep my eyes on the dash instead of Vi's long legs.

"Everything okay?" She sounded worried, so I flashed her a smile.

"Yeah, just getting my head on straight."

Vi left me to my thoughts until we'd turned onto the highway. "Tell me again why we're doing this."

I glanced over at her soft question, but I couldn't read the emotion on her face. "Because my parents think I'm using my football fame as an excuse to drink and fuck my way through college."

She laid a hand on my arm. "I know that part. Anyone who spends five minutes with you knows how hard you work. Why don't they see that?"

The muscles I hadn't felt tense relaxed a little. I hadn't told her about Margot, but there was a good chance my parents would mention her. Not directly, they were classier than that, but in a subtle dig.

Silence stretched between us, broken only by the low hum of the truck wheels on asphalt. Her light touch slid down my arm to cover my hand on the gearshift. Even without knowing any information, Vi offered me steadfast faith. She thought my parents were wrong. I linked my fingers with hers, ignoring the tightness in my chest.

I could choose not to answer, and Vi would let it go. But I didn't want her ambushed like that.

"My schedule doesn't allow a lot of time to go home, not

that I would if I had the chance, but it leaves my parents a lot of room for speculation. A couple of months ago, back at the beginning of the summer, I was hooking up with this girl, a friend of a friend I met at a party. I explained from the start that I wasn't interested in a relationship, and she was still up for some no-strings fun."

Vi squeezed my hand. "I have a feeling I'm going to like your parents a lot less after this story."

I grunted out a laugh. "Maybe you'll like me a lot less too." The words surprised me. I hadn't fully recognized that fear before I spoke it aloud, but Vi scoffed.

"We live together. Your idea of a thrilling night is watching half an episode of Ted Lasso then going to bed like some kind of psychopath." She turned toward me, somehow keeping her legs tucked under herself. "Who watches *half* an episode?"

I smiled despite my sour mood. She'd been paying attention. Maybe I hadn't been alone in all those sleepless nights. "I watched the other half later."

"You clearly don't understand how streaming services work. We'll have to practice your binge watching. Now stop distracting me and finish your story."

"*Me?*" I sent her an incredulous glance. "You started it."

"Only to prove that if your crazy ass television habits haven't scared me off yet, I doubt anything your parents believe would do the trick."

Her reassurance burrowed deep inside me, filling a space I hadn't realized was empty. In that moment, I became one hundred percent thankful that I'd answered Eva's call. I lifted Vi's hand to trail my lips over her knuckles, and she rewarded me with a tiny intake of breath.

"Margot disappeared after a couple of weeks, and I thought that was it. Then about a month later, I got a call from my mom demanding my presence immediately. Margot was in their sitting room when I arrived. She claimed she was pregnant, and I was the father."

I snuck a glance at Vi to gauge her reaction, but I shouldn't have bothered. Her hand tightened on mine as she made a sound of disgust. "That bitch. Women like her make the rest of us look bad. Was she actually pregnant or did she lie about that too?"

I shook my head in amazement. Not a single doubt, and she sounded like she wanted to throw down in my defense. "She was actually pregnant. At least, according to the paperwork she'd brought. She'd fed my parents some story about how I'd thrown her aside, and she only wanted some money to make a new start somewhere else. They didn't question her until she refused a paternity test."

"Why would they believe her over you?"

"They weren't as wrong as you think. Before Margot, I worked hard, but I played hard too. I couldn't tell them definitively the baby wasn't mine. We'd had sex at the right time. I'd used protection, but nothing works one hundred percent."

Vi rubbed her thumb against mine absently as she stared at me. "You didn't bother to defend yourself."

"It would have been a waste of time. It ended up not mattering anyway. Margot disappeared again, and we got a letter from a lawyer claiming someone else was the father and absolving me of all responsibility. We haven't heard from her since, but the damage was done. My parents were convinced of my out-of-control lifestyle."

She shook her head. "This whole situation is ridiculous. You're a grown ass man—a smart, talented, *responsible* grown ass man. I'm sorry they can't see that."

I felt my walls crumble. Literally felt it as if she'd struck me with a sledgehammer and broken something open inside me. Up until now, I'd been able to deal with the minor cracks she'd caused, but I had no protection against her defense of me.

"Me too."

Silence followed my agreement, and Vi must have sensed I desperately wanted to change the subject because she asked me about my morning workouts. The conversation flowed after that, and Vi succeeded in teasing me out of my dour mood.

My parents' house was about an hour and a half drive away from our little college town. By the time we pulled into their gated community, I'd almost forgotten the reason for the trip. Quiet descended as I wound my way through the neighborhood of estates hidden by hedges and walls.

Vi's hand tightened on mine as we passed the open gate to my parents' lane. We moved past the trees and the house came into view. The estate was lit up for the party—a Hamptons mansion plunked down at the end of the road. Cars passed me on the drive up, most likely valets making sure that first impression of the house wasn't ruined.

I parked the car next to the valet stand and tried not to cringe at how pretentious this all seemed. A guy in a red jacket opened the door and helped Vi out of the truck while his counterpart came around to exchange my key fob for a digital stub. Only the best for a simple cocktail party.

The next car pulled up as I joined Vi under the extended portico and urged her to the side. A woman wearing several dozen carats in diamonds breezed past us without a second glance. I didn't recognize her, but then, I'd been out of the circle for a while.

Vi sucked in a deep breath and met my eyes. "Are you sure about this?"

I pulled her close, partly for reassurance, but partly to appease myself after an hour and a half of not being able to touch her the way I wanted. With her scent imprinted on my brain, I'd never be able to smell vanilla again without getting hard.

"Don't worry. At worst, my parents will think we're an awkward couple. Their opinion of me can't get much lower. Of course, if they find out you're here under false pretenses, I'm not sure I can help you. We haven't used the dungeon in at least a year, but I hear it's nice after they redecorated last fall."

She laughed, and the sound burrowed into me, sparking a return warmth that made me want to cancel the whole thing and drag her away for a *real* date. Preferably one where I'd get to peel that dress off of her.

I brushed my lips against her hair, trying to keep a polite few inches between us, when I heard my name. I tensed as we turned toward the house, then breathed a sigh of relief as my Aunt Amelia and Uncle Lukas waved from the front door. Two of the only friendly faces we'd see tonight.

"Soren, it's been too long. Who's your friend?" Amelia rushed down to us for a crushing side hug. Her head came to mid-chest, but that had never stopped her from treating me like the lanky teen I'd been when she'd married my uncle.

I gave her a quick squeeze without releasing my hold on Vi. "Good to see you, Aunt Amelia. This is my girlfriend, Vi. Vi, I want you to meet Amelia and Lukas Brehm."

Lukas approached slower and offered Vi a sly grin as he kissed her hand. "A pleasure." His eyes, the same dark blue I shared, shifted to me. "Your mother will be disappointed as she's also procured you a date for the evening."

12

Vi

S oren's hand settled on my lower back as I smiled at the older couple. He stroked over the fabric with his thumb, and I completely missed what his uncle said. I didn't miss the hand-kissing and Soren's suddenly tense body though.

I extracted my hand and tried not to be obvious as I wiped it on my skirt. "It's nice to meet you both."

Amelia leaned toward me, the gorgeous red necklace she wore sparkling in the evening lights, and lowered her voice. "Don't listen to a thing Soren's mama says. She doesn't like anything that isn't her idea."

Soren cleared his throat as she rejoined her husband. "Leaving already?"

They laughed, and his uncle answered. "Not yet, but we could only handle the stuffiness in there for so long. We're off for a long walk in the garden. You might consider it for future parties."

He waved and escorted Amelia away. They strolled hand in hand across the lawn toward the side of the property. I tilted my head to study Soren, but he was already watching me.

"What?"

He shrugged one shoulder. "Maybe we should start with the dungeon."

I shook my head and started toward the huge double door at the front of the house. "Your aunt and uncle seemed mostly normal. Except for the weird hand-kissing... and the intimidating necklace."

Soren offered me a half-smile. "She wears it to piss off my mom every time she comes here, which isn't that often. My uncle Lukas inherited the rubies from my grandmother despite my dad being the oldest. It was a huge scandal at the time because Amelia wasn't from one of the *right* families. Remind me to tell you the story of their forbidden love sometime."

I was so distracted by Soren opening up about his family that I almost didn't notice the grand foyer, which would have been a tragedy. With some effort, I managed not to stare with my mouth wide open. Luckily, no one else had noticed us.

Two staircases soared to the second floor in lazy curves. Dim lighting highlighted the art on the walls, but my gaze was drawn up to the balcony overlooking the space. Gauzy black material studded with crystals draped dramatically across the railing and trailed down in a shimmery waterfall reflecting a thousand colors across the ceiling. It was like standing inside a kaleidoscope.

Besides the fantastic first impression, tasteful nods to the holiday were tucked unobtrusively into the décor. Soren's parents seemed to have a penchant for skulls and glittering gems under candlelight.

At my urging, we moved closer to the wall so I could get

a better look. The flickering candlelight was fake, but a really good fake. I didn't want to know if the crystals were actually the diamonds they resembled.

I'd known Soren's family had money, but I hadn't realized quite how much until that moment.

"Did you grow up in this house?"

He ran his hand over his hair, pulled back in a short ponytail at his neck instead of his usual bun. "Yeah, until I moved away for college a couple of years ago."

I nudged him in the side as we passed through an archway into another massive room. "How many times did you slide down that banister?"

Soren laughed. "More times than I can count. It's a good core workout."

The background noise gradually grew as we approached what I assumed was the back of the house, but Soren didn't stop until we'd come through yet another archway. Four wide stairs led down into a room bigger than any of the others. The entire back wall was made of glass, and the doors accordioned into each other to open into the lit-up backyard. At the moment, they remained closed against the slight chill.

No one noticed us enter, for which I was profoundly grateful because I'd never seen so many obviously rich people in person. If I hadn't just met his aunt of the enormous rubies, I might have thought these people were wearing costumes. Who put on a diamond-encrusted pendant the size of my fist for a cocktail party?

Unease skittered down my spine. "I'm the only one here not dripping in jewels."

My dress fit in pretty well as long as no one got a look at the tag, and my shoes were designer. A sneaky, expensive gift from Eva when she'd been trying to broaden my clothing horizons beyond the usual fitness hobo look.

Soren gave me a slow onceover, and I had to fight the urge to fan myself. "I like the way you look."

"I'm not sure I fit in with this crowd. Isn't this the part where you whip out a car's worth of sapphires or something to help me play the part?"

"This isn't a *Pretty Woman* situation. I don't want you to be anyone but yourself."

I raised one brow. "You've seen *Pretty Woman*?"

"Blame Eva. She makes us get together once a month for movie night. We take turns picking the movie."

The image of five hulking football players crowded onto Eva's tiny couch as they watched super old chick flicks knocked the nervousness right out of me. I squared my shoulders and scanned the room more carefully a second time.

"Okay, point me toward your parents so I can impress them with my serious girlfriend vibes."

His arm slid around my waist, and he pulled me against him. My breathing became shallow as he leaned down to speak quietly in my ear. "They're standing by the piano in the corner. Black dress, grey suit, huge fake smiles—talking to the woman in the bright pink dress that looks like she mugged a flamingo."

I giggled under my breath and immediately found the pink dress lady. Next to her stood a Viking in a business suit and a beautiful middle-aged woman with striking features. His parents, especially his mom, seemed antsy, but I couldn't pinpoint why. As I watched, she looked up and noticed us standing at the top of the stairs.

Her brows drew together, then she leaned over to say something to her husband before they started our direction.

Soren must have been watching as well because he sighed against my hair, making the short waves tickle my neck. "I'm going to apologize now. The flamingo woman is the daughter of a family friend, and I'm guessing my assigned date for tonight, despite my telling them I'd be bringing you."

I looked away from the oncoming trouble to brush my lips across Soren's cheek. "Don't worry. I can handle myself."

He raised a brow and tightened his grip. "If the last party was any indication, things are about to get really interesting."

His gaze dropped to my mouth, and heat passed between us. In all the time we'd spent together, he'd never really kissed me. Now was definitely not the time, but I wondered how much longer we'd be able to resist the rising tension.

Soren loosened his hold enough for us to descend the stairs, but we didn't make it much farther into the room. Up close, his mom and dad were taller than I expected, which I should have realized considering his size. He'd inherited his mother's features along with his father's blond hair and blue eyes. The flamingo lady trailed along slower than his parents, but she also loomed over me.

We all stopped in an awkward clump surrounded by the din of the party. A quick glance up at Soren confirmed he'd adopted the smug smile that made me want to smack him. I imagined it had a similar effect on his family, though his football crew didn't seem to mind too much.

He met my eyes, and for an instant, his real smile replaced his irritating one. The moment he looked away, the real Soren disappeared. "Vi, I'd like you to meet my parents, Dena and Isak Brehm. Mom, Dad, this is my girlfriend, Vi Malone."

If I hadn't been watching, I would have missed the tightening around his mom's eyes. She hadn't liked his obvious snub of the flamingo lady.

I held out the hand not currently trapped between me and Soren. "It's nice to meet you both."

Dena offered me a sedate smile and a limp shake. "I wish I could say the same, but I'm afraid Soren has caused a bit of an embarrassment by not telling us about you."

My brows shot up without my consent, but I managed to control my tongue. "I'm sorry for any inconvenience."

Isak took my hand with a genuine grin. "A pleasure, sweetheart." He had a faint Texas accent, which surprised me. For some reason, I'd assumed he'd sound... well, less normal. I didn't have a lot of experience rubbing elbows with rich people, so in my head, they all spoke like nineteenth-century dukes.

Soren's smile didn't waver, but I felt his tension along my side. "I told you I'd be bringing a date, as requested."

Dena opened her mouth to reply, but Isak stepped between them to grab two champagne flutes from a passing waiter. "It's no trouble at all. Vi, why don't you tell us a little about yourself?"

He handed us each a drink then stepped back to wind his arm around his wife's waist. I took a sip and nearly snorted bubbles out my nose. I was more of a beer girl, but I was determined not to embarrass Soren.

"I'm a senior at TU, majoring in kinesiology and sports medicine."

His mom snorted quietly. "How do you plan to use your degree in the future?"

My smile became sharper at her frosty tone. "I plan to work as an athletic trainer, most likely with a professional sports team."

Calculation lit her eyes. "I suppose attaching yourself to a well-off football player would be helpful for your goals."

Soren started to speak, but I put a hand on his chest and shook my head. "I'm not interested in your son's money or his affiliation with the team. I'm interested in the smart, kind, generous man that you raised. You do him a great disservice by implying that I'd be here for any other reason."

"We'll see." She took a sip of her own drink.

Isak laughed, awkward and loud. "This is no time for an interview. Please enjoy the party, and we hope to see you for family dinner in the next few weeks."

"We'll be there." Soren had a strange tone in his voice, and when I turned to try to suss it out, our eyes locked. Without breaking the contact, he lifted my hand off his chest to place a gentle kiss across my knuckles like he'd done earlier. Just like before, heat bloomed and raced along my nerve endings.

His parents said something, but the words were drowned out by the pounding of my pulse. What was it about Soren that made me forget about the rest of the world?

I blinked and glanced around, relieved that no one else seemed to have noticed my inattention. Isak turned to address the flamingo lady, who'd stood silently observing the whole exchange, and the three of them wandered back toward the piano.

With any luck, they'd assume I was madly in love with Soren instead of simply losing my mind one kiss at a time.

Soren rubbed his thumb along my wrist, making my breath catch. "You want to take a walk?"

I laughed dryly. "In these heels? Absolutely."

He nodded with a twist of his lips and used my captive hand to lead me back into the bowels of the house. We retraced our steps through the impressive foyer and out under the portico. Soren took a hard right, and we followed the path his aunt and uncle had taken earlier.

"Where are we going?"

"There's a creek just ahead through the trees. It's one of the few areas of the estate that they kept wild. I used to come out here as a kid when I didn't want to be found."

I peered at the trees ahead of us, but I couldn't make out anything other than a chunk of woods. The sun had set a while back, and the moon's light didn't penetrate very deep into the branches. I tried to imagine a little Soren, all on his own, sneaking around to feed his rebellious streak with forest adventures.

The image made my heart hurt.

The burble of running water reached me after less than a minute of walking. A surprising amount of moonlight streamed down through the break in the trees where the creek flowed, reflecting off the water as it raced over small rocks.

Soren pulled me to a stop well before the edges of the little gully. "Don't get too close. I haven't been here in a while, and I'm not confident the ground is stable."

"Noted." The little opening in the trees was pretty, but I'd seen a lot of places like it running wild with my brothers on the other side of Texas. "I can't help but notice we're not currently at the party you required me to attend. Was that single conversation with your parents good enough for tonight?"

"Yeah." He released my hand to approach the creek, rubbing the faint stubble on his chin, and the raspy sound came straight from my wettest dreams. This was the *worst* time to relive any of those fantasies. I may have grown up in the backwoods, but I wasn't big on outdoor sex.

Not that he was offering.

I shook my head, trying desperately to focus. "Why did you bring me here?"

Soren shrugged and stooped to pick up a small rock, as comfortable moving in his suit as he was in his sweats. "I wanted you to see it. My life wasn't all silver spoons and extravagant parties."

I laughed. "I knew that already. If that was all you cared about, you wouldn't be busting your ass playing football at TU."

He tossed the rock in the creek, then stood there staring into the distance. "I'm sorry."

I tilted my head. "For what?"

When he didn't answer, I chanced the uneven ground to approach him. I laid a hand on his back, and the muscles shifted as he took a deep breath before turning to face me.

"This isn't working."

An unexpected flash of fear froze the breath in my lungs. This whole agreement had been his idea. Soren had every right to decide he didn't want to continue it, but I didn't have a backup plan if he kicked me out.

Worse than potentially couch surfing the rest of the semester was the prospect that I'd lose my connection with him. The best parts of my day were the ones where I got to see the real Soren—the one he didn't show to anyone else. He'd said I could stay as long as I needed it, but my chest hurt at the thought of him as a passing roommate and nothing more.

I cleared my throat and tried to sound like I wasn't panicking inside. "What do you mean?"

"This." He waved his hand back and forth between us. "I keep trying to convince myself that this idea isn't completely insane, but it's not working. This relationship isn't fair to you. Colt is a dick, and I'm happy to stand as a shield for you in whatever capacity you need, but you don't deserve the shit my parents are going to lay at your feet."

A relieved breath whooshed out of me. "I thought you were going to end the agreement."

His brows drew together sharply. "No. Why? Do you want to end it?"

"No." I drew the word out because I wasn't sure where he was going with this conversation. "I told you before, I can handle anything your parents dish out. You're the one who has stakes in that part of the game. If you're not worried about me fucking it up for you, I'm not worried about the opinions of people I don't respect."

He stared down at me for a second, and an emotion I couldn't name passed over his face. "Did you mean it?"

"Mean what?"

"What you said to them. About me."

My lips parted as I remembered what I'd told his mom. She'd surprised me, so I'd gone on the offensive with the truth without realizing how it would sound to Soren. I wanted to fall back on a sarcastic response, but the vulnerable note in his voice wouldn't let me. He deserved an honest answer, even if I risked complicating our situation.

"Every word."

He didn't move for a long moment as silence fell between us, broken only by a slight wind rustling the trees. The air thickened, and just when I thought he'd reach for me, he turned away.

"Come on. We can head back."

I shivered as I followed him back along the path, but I wasn't sure if it was from the sudden cold or the sense that something significant had changed between us.

13

Vi

The valets had Soren's truck ready when we got there. I was thankful that whatever voodoo he'd performed included turning on the seat warmers. The temperature had dropped unexpectedly in the last few hours, and I didn't particularly like being cold.

I glanced at the people still milling around talking outside the massive house as Soren helped me into the truck, but no one paid us any attention.

"You're not going to say goodbye?"

Soren shut the door on my question, and I prepared for a return to my grumpy roommate. He waited until we'd reached the main road before answering.

"They only required that I show up. There was no stipulation about how long I'd stay. Goodbyes would imply that they cared I was there beyond the obligation to appear supportive."

I shifted toward him and tucked my cold feet under me. "What about your aunt and uncle? They seemed like they genuinely enjoyed seeing you."

He snuck a glance at me, and his face softened. "You're

right. I wasn't expecting them to be there. My cousin had some big deal happening, but she must have insisted they go. She's more like my parents than Amelia and Lukas, though she's not as self-absorbed. Their 'walk' was an excuse to slip away."

Soren's mind seemed miles away, but I couldn't tell if he was bothered by his thoughts. I debated between asking him directly or trying to distract him. A tiny frown appeared between his brows, and I decided on distraction *then* discussion.

"I have questions. It's only fair you answer them since you rushed me out of there so fast that I missed even a single appetizer."

Soren's lips curled up in that half-smile I'd come to associate with him and trouble. "Okay, but then it's my turn."

I pursed my lips, deciding if revealing my embarrassing past would be worth the answers I'd get in return. There was at least a twenty-five percent chance that he'd just ask about sexual positions or something. I'd be sorely disappointed, but at least it would give me excellent insight into him.

"Agreed. Mine first. If you're from Dallas, why don't you have a Texas accent?"

Soren sent me an incredulous look. "You've met my mom. Do you really think she'd allow something as crass as a blue-collar accent into her hallowed halls?"

I tilted my head. "Your dad has an accent."

"He's the exception to the rule."

"Since when do you follow the rules?"

He grinned at me, and my breath caught. "I've been known to adopt a good 'ol boy accent every once in a while at dinner."

"That sounds horrifying. Why are your parents so against you playing football?"

"They'd always assumed their son would take over the company when Dad retired, except the son they got isn't interested. Even if I don't make it in the pros, I still wouldn't want to be stuck inside behind a desk." He shuddered and spared me a glance. "They don't understand that the life they live sounds like hell to me."

I understood. My brothers had a similar lack of awareness, but I *wanted* the life they had. "Why do they get to decide?"

His fingers tapped on the steering wheel, and he hesitated so long I thought he might not answer my question. Then he blew out a breath.

"My parents are rich—I'm not. All my money is tied in a trust that only reverts to me if I graduate with a business degree. They pay for school and my living expenses, and I get a stipend for spending money. It's almost impossible to work while playing college football, at least at our level, so I can't afford to lose my parents' financial support."

I nodded. "And thanks to Margot they're threatening to pull it, which is why you're considering the draft a year earlier than you planned."

Soren tilted his head toward me in assent. "And why I need you to help me change their minds."

"There have to be other options. What about a scholarship?"

"The school offered me one my first year, but I passed. It didn't feel right to take that away from someone who actually needed it. They haven't offered again because Coach knows I'm not interested. That hasn't changed. I can make my situation work without costing someone else their dream."

I laid my hand on his arm and wished I could help dissolve the tension there. His parents were idiots if they couldn't see what a fantastic son they had already, no matter his job description. "We'll try again. Tonight wasn't a total loss."

He shook his head. "It was certainly the most interesting Halloween party I've been to. Though I'm sorry you didn't get to try the dessert table or dance floor."

At the mention of a dessert table, I narrowed my eyes at him. "I'm going to be honest here. If I'd known about the dessert table, you wouldn't have been able to remove me from that house with an entire team of football players. But I'd pass on the dance floor."

"Why?"

"I don't know how to slow dance."

He raised his brows at me. "You *teach* a dance fitness class."

"Yeah, but that's purposeful, choreographed movement. Slow dancing is awkward. Where do you look? What do you do with your hands? How do you find the right amount of closeness that says you're trying but you're not interested in grinding on the dance floor?"

Soren laughed and changed lanes to pass a slow car. "Let me guess. You didn't go to your prom."

I sent him a smug smile. "I *did* go to my prom, thank you very much. It was a disaster, but I was there with the dress and the hair." I gestured vaguely at my head and shuddered, only partly faking it. "The date sucked, so there's that. Not something I ever want to experience again."

"What did he do?" The danger in his low voice curled in my gut, and all my nerve endings took notice.

Goosebumps rose on my arms as I glanced at him in the dim interior. "Nothing too dramatic. It turned out my date only needed me for the big entrance. He wanted to make his ex jealous, and he succeeded. Didn't make it through even one song. So, no. I'm not a fan of slow dancing."

Soren cursed under his breath and hit his blinker. I frowned as I stared at the dark woods all around us interspersed with deserted turnoffs. Normally, I'd be concerned about being murdered, but I trusted Soren not to pull any shit with me. Despite that, I couldn't make the connection between what I'd said and his sudden ferocious need to stop the truck.

I crossed my arms and waited. Soren pulled into one of the turnouts and parked, leaving the radio crooning a slow song. He almost seemed angry, but he was gentle with his vehicle as he got out and circled to my side.

My door opened, and he stood there in the sparse moonlight with one hand extended. Chilly wind ruffled the skirt of my cute little dress, and I'd already kicked off the stilettos. Had I known I'd be partaking in this many off-road adventures, I might have worn something sturdier.

Cold and barefoot, my eyes caught on his hand before traveling up his arm to lock with his. "What are you doing?"

"Rectifying a mistake."

"I don't want your pity."

"What I feel for you isn't pity. Get out of the truck, Vi."

Despite the logical part of my brain screaming at me to have some willpower, I slid my palm into his and let him tempt me onto the dirt. Soren took two steps back and pulled me against him. His arm came around my waist, holding me so close I could feel the clear indication of how not pitiful he found me.

Soren swayed with me side to side, careful not to step on my toes. I shivered, and his arm tightened then let go for a second to pull the edges of his jacket around me. "Better?"

Surprisingly, it was. Inside the jacket, I slid my free arm around him and tucked myself into his warmth. I tugged on my hand, but he refused to release it, instead holding it against his chest.

"Relax, Vi. Let me give *you* something for once."

I nodded, not trusting myself to speak with the weird fullness in my throat. He lowered his head next to mine, and my hair caught on his stubble. My heart flopped over when he started quietly singing the words to the song into my ear. How was I supposed to keep him at arm's length when he did stuff like this?

My eyes fell closed, and I gave in just this once.

The song ended, but neither of us moved away. My skin felt electrified, like a single touch would burn me—or him. His hand shifted from my back to my side, grazing my breast on the way up to my throat. He tipped my chin up with his thumb, but I didn't open my eyes, even when he rested his forehead against mine.

"I know I shouldn't, but I'm going to kiss you unless you tell me otherwise."

I teetered on the edge of temptation. A small inner part of me screamed that Soren could have his pick of women—he'd only chosen me because I was convenient. He only wanted to kiss me because I was off-limits.

But Soren wasn't like that. I'd seen enough of the *real* Soren to know he didn't take chances without weighing the costs. Off-limits might appeal to him, but not if he had to trade in his future. As for convenience, he'd had plenty of opportunity to take advantage of our situation. This wasn't convenience, this was the same deep-seated hunger I felt.

A tiny smile curled around my lips. "Who says you shouldn't?"

"Open your eyes, Vi." He whispered the words against

my lips, the touch so light I might have imagined it if not for the warmth of his breath. "I want to see you."

I silenced that inner voice and met his heated gaze.

He smiled. "There you are."

The moment etched itself into my mind—frozen toes on hard dirt, his arm strong around me, the press of his fingers against my spine. He lowered his mouth to mine, gentle where I expected roughness.

I filled my lungs with him and melted into the kiss. The world disappeared into a slow dance of breath and lips and tongue that I'd never call awkward again.

A satisfied noise rumbled from Soren's chest, and his hold on me tightened. I'd never had a kiss like this, where I could taste the need as his tongue stroked mine. The heat built, and my movements shifted into a desperate attempt to get closer.

Two steps and he pinned me against the side of his truck. Soren's hand delved into my hair pulling my head to the side so he could slide his mouth down my throat. He sucked the spot below my ear, and my knees trembled while the rest of me went up in flames.

I wanted his hands on me, his mouth, nothing between us but sweat. Soren must have read my mind because his hand left my hair to trail down my aching body. My nipples hardened painfully as he grazed my breast, and a whimper escaped me. I'd never whimpered before in my life.

A trail of fire followed his touch down to pause at my thigh before slipping under my skirt. He skimmed along my bikini line, but when I arched up into him searching for more contact, he pulled away.

Soren's mouth found my ear, and his rough voice eased the sting of denial. "Spread your legs for me, Vi."

Excitement heated my blood at the prospect of whatever

he had planned, but a small part of me remembered the bright moonlight with only a truck between us and the highway.

I gasped as he stroked along the edge of my thong, *so close* to where I wanted him. "We're not exactly on a back road. Anyone could drive by."

He brushed his lips against mine again, and that wicked smile returned. "Then let's give them a show."

14

Vi

I curled my arm around his shoulders to brace myself, but he surprised me by gripping my thighs and lifting me off the ground. Instead of feeling the cool metal on my mostly bare ass, he shifted to the still open door of the truck and set me gently on the passenger seat.

Soren stepped between my legs and took my mouth again. Just as I sank into the kiss, he yanked my ass to the edge of the seat. The hard length of him pressed against me for a hot second as he slowly eased my back down until I was lying across the seat.

His mouth left mine, but our eyes caught and held as he flipped the skirt of my dress up to my waist. Soren's grin widened as he kissed my stomach, my hip—and ran his tongue along the wet line of my slit over the lace of my thong.

I gasped and fisted my hands in his hair. His hair tie gave up the fight, dropping into the darkness somewhere as silky blond locks tickled my skin. Soren nipped my thigh, and I yelped. He laughed, a low, rumbling sound that made my inner muscles clench. Cool air hit my pussy followed by the heat of his mouth.

Soren's fingers dug into the flesh of my ass, holding me still for his talented tongue. Nothing had prepared me for the reality of a man who responded to me. My sighs, my groans, my pleading. He listened and reacted. I should have known Soren would be as generous in bed—or truck—as he was out of it.

Soaking wet, completely lost in the pleasure coursing through me, I couldn't have let go of him if I'd wanted to. When he thrust two fingers into me, I chased that orgasm hard.

"God, Soren, don't stop."

An answering growl came from between my legs and sent me spiraling into the best orgasm of my life. White light exploded behind my lids, and Soren didn't let up until I collapsed back on the seat, trembling.

"Good girl." His stubble brushed my inner thigh, and I nearly had another fucking orgasm.

Light-headed, I propped myself on my elbows and looked down at him. "We should have done that weeks ago."

"I'm not about to argue now." He stood and dropped a hard kiss on my mouth before adjusting my skirt and helping me climb into the passenger seat.

I grabbed his sleeve before he could close the door. "What about you?"

A slow, satisfied smile curved across his lips. "I got what *I* wanted."

Those abused inner muscles clenched again and I nodded, letting him go. I could feel the flush on my cheeks, but that was the least of my worries. My heart hadn't settled down from round one, and I was already gearing up for round two.

What happened to sex making things complicated?

I licked my dry lips. Now that I knew what the heat and tension between us could lead to, the reasons to stay apart seemed trivial. He didn't actually want a serious relationship, hence the agreement with me, but he'd made it clear from the beginning that he wasn't against a casual hook-up.

If my actions over the last hour were any indication, neither was I.

A niggling doubt in the back of my head whispered that nothing with Soren was casual, but I could easily ignore it with my whole body still tingling from pleasure.

With a curious glance at me, Soren started the truck, and we pulled back out onto the highway. I had no idea how much farther we had to drive, but the faint scent of sex lingered in the cab, reminding me that we were going home to the same apartment. With separate rooms and separate beds.

"What does Vi stand for?" His quiet question caught me off guard, and I was too busy debating my decision about keeping things platonic to deflect.

"Violet."

"Why don't you go by that?"

I turned to stare out the window as muscle by muscle my body tightened. "I prefer Vi."

"Violet—"

"Don't call me that. My name is Vi." The words came out sharper than I intended, but I couldn't snatch them back.

He reached over and gathered my hand into his, then brought it up to his lips. "You don't have to tell me anything. You don't owe me, or anyone, a single piece of information about yourself... but I want to know, if you'll let me in."

I looked away, searching for an answer I could give him that would satisfy his curiosity without ripping open wounds that never seemed to heal. A hard ball of anxiety knotted up my stomach, but the thought of telling *Soren* details I hadn't shared with anyone else eased the tightness. He waited with my hand cradled on his thigh—silent—completely willing for me to shut him out after everything we'd shared.

He'd told me about Margot, his parents, the draft. Every time I'd asked, he'd been willing to talk. When I prodded at the box where I kept those memories, I realized the pressure from keeping it to myself might ease if I shared the burden with someone else. Someone who would understand how the loss shaped my life without trying to fix it.

"My mom named me Violet, her long-awaited girl after four boys. I think she hoped to have another feminine presence in the house, but I've been a tomboy since birth, despite her blaming my dad and brothers for treating me like one of them. She was the only one who called me Violet."

"Was?"

"She died at the beginning of my freshman year. Breast cancer." A shallow breath caught in my lungs cutting me off from saying any more.

Soren's brow furrowed as he glanced at me. "Vi—"

I gave my head one quick shake. "I just need a minute."

He squeezed my hand and let the low thrum of the engine fill the silence. My body still hummed with the after-effects of our impromptu stop, making the whole situation feel surreal. Dark trees blurred past outside, but the scenery didn't have any answers for me. No solace or recrimination.

Soren's hand warmed my palm, and I wanted to slide against him until that heat surrounded the rest of me. Anything to banish the chill from my memories.

As if he could read my mind, he tugged me toward him. "Come here."

I scooted as close as I could get. He opened his arm, making space for me next to him, and I hesitated. What were we doing?

We'd created boundaries to keep things simple, but nothing about this felt simple. I'd never talked about my mom with anyone, not even my brothers. I didn't let people see that part of me. Except Soren.

He knew without me needing to say the words.

I closed the distance and curled against his side. His arm circled me, an anchor when my thoughts threatened to drag me down a path I didn't want to take.

"She knew she was sick for a while and didn't tell any of us. That summer after I graduated, she was tired a lot. We didn't have a lot of money, but I'd gotten into TU with enough scholarships to cover most of the costs. She was *so* proud."

Tears gathered, but I clenched my eyes closed until the burning subsided. "I knew something was wrong, but she didn't tell me until the week before classes started, two days before orientation. Too advanced for treatment, so she'd elected to spend her remaining time at home instead of weak and hooked up to machines."

I sniffled, and Soren rubbed his hand up and down my arm. "Did you get to say goodbye?"

"Yeah. She expected me to just pack my stuff and head off to college, as if I'd leave my dying mother behind. I contacted the school and explained my situation. They were very accommodating, so were my professors. Mom didn't make it past that first week. I left the day after the funeral, and I went back as little as possible."

The crushing pain I expected didn't appear. I still felt the sadness and grief, but they were tempered with time—or maybe telling someone else made it easier to bear.

Soren frowned. "What about the rest of your family? Your brothers and dad?"

"They dealt with her death in their own ways. Dad moved to Houston to be closer to his sister. My brothers had a business, so they stuck it out in Harmony. None of us talked about it."

His lips pressed together, and I could feel him restraining himself.

I forced a smile. "You want to make a joke, don't you?"

He nodded. "Yes, very much so. I'm sure Harmony, Texas is delightful, but you didn't stay."

"I had college... and it hurt too much to deal with it on my own when I couldn't escape the memories."

His amusement faded. "You don't have to handle everything yourself. No matter how this situation ends up, I will *always* be here for you. Call me. Show up unannounced. Send me a series of drunk texts culminating in nudes." He waggled his eyebrows, but I knew he meant what he said. "You're not alone."

I levered myself up to press a kiss to his jaw. "Thank you, Soren."

"We still have about an hour of driving to go." His stubble caught my hair as he shifted to look down at me. "Tell me again about the asshat who took you to prom. Maybe include his full name and address this time."

I laughed, surprised that I felt bruised but not broken. "Nope. That memory has been replaced by one a thousand times better."

15

Soren

How had I been so wrong about her? Vi had snuck under my armor somewhere along the way—maybe even that first night—but I'd never really thought she needed protection. I glanced down at her cuddled up against my side and realized she'd wanted me to think that.

The rest of the drive home, I asked her ridiculous questions meant to banish that haunted look from her eyes. Breast cancer. Fuck. There was more to that story too, but I wasn't going to push her to tell me until she was ready.

And after that eye-opening moment by the creek—and the hot as fuck moment on the side of the road—I wasn't going anywhere until I knew everything about her.

Vi believed the best of me, believed in me, and that realization nearly undid me. Watching her come, hearing my name on her lips while she did, finished the job. I may have started this agreement with the intention of holding myself aloof, but screw that. I spent the entire rest of the drive with her taste on my tongue, and I would have given just about anything for another round.

But Vi had given me something else right after—a piece of her past—and I valued her trust higher than getting her naked.

Neither of us moved after I parked the truck at the apartment. We'd made it all the way back without discussing the rather large change in our relationship. Vi's chest rose and fell with a deep breath, then she eased away.

I let my arm fall even though I wanted to tighten my grip, to pull her all the way into my lap and finish what we'd started earlier. She paused with her hand on the door and searched my face in the darkness.

"Are you coming?"

I tried not to laugh, I really did, but her question echoed my thoughts a little too well. "I'll be there right after you."

Her eyes darted down to my lap, and she shook her head. "Thank you again. For listening."

Even properly chastised, my dick refused to settle down. "Go on up. I just need to recite the multiplication tables a couple of hundred times so I can walk."

Vi raised a brow, then exited the truck without another word. I wondered what that brow meant. After our crazy night, the possibilities ranged from 'hurry up, I want to take your pants off with my teeth' to 'put that thing away before someone gets hurt'. Thinking about option number one wasn't helping matters.

I didn't like her thinking sex was all I wanted, but I also couldn't go back to the way we'd been before tonight. The headlights illuminated Vi climbing the stairs in her bare feet, stilettos in her hand, but she didn't look back. Probably not a good sign.

Dammit. Relationships were hard. The lights turned off, and I got out of the truck. No point in keeping Vi waiting. Either she'd change the rules, or I'd spend the night pretending to sleep alone in my bed. I ran a hand through my loose hair as I climbed the stairs. I didn't regret for a second losing that elastic, but I wasn't used to having my hair all over the place.

Vi stood facing the door, staring down at something in her hand. I caught a glimpse of white paper before she heard my footsteps and spun around with a gasp. For a second, she looked like she was braced for a fight—her weight low and her arms coming up to protect her face.

I frowned at her reaction, but she straightened and shook her head.

"Damn, you scared me."

I raised a brow. "I can see how me walking up to our apartment would surprise you."

She shook her head and gestured toward the door. "It's been a long night, and I don't have my key. Can we save the rest of your charm for tomorrow?"

I spotted the crumpled remains of the paper in her hand, but only nodded my head. She moved deeper into the shadows to give me space, and I suddenly needed to remove the distance between us. All this back and forth was bull-shit. Vi was the same woman she'd always been, one who didn't shy away from blunt honesty.

Instead of pulling out my key, I followed her into the darkness and cupped her cheek.

"Before we go inside, I want you to know my expecta-tions haven't changed. I want you more than my next breath, but you get to decide what happens between us. If you need time, it's yours. If you want me to back off, I will. But I'm here when you're ready."

Heat flooded her eyes as she looked up at me, but I could see the denial there before she said a single word. "You have to know how much I want to—" She sighed and started again. "A lot has happened and... it's just not a good idea right now."

She didn't sound happy about her decision, but I wasn't about to try to convince her otherwise after the night we'd had. I nodded and backed away, digging my key fob out of my pocket.

"Soren..."

I flashed her a smile. "Good ideas change all the time, and I'm a hopeful type of guy. That said, we don't have to share a bed for me to like you, Vi." Strangely, I wasn't too sad about her decision. Despite my clear willingness to throw caution into the nearest river, the prospect of adding sex to our relationship was somewhat terrifying. I didn't have many close friends, and Vi hit near the top of the list. How could we go back to simple friendship after tumbling across that line?

She rose up on her toes to kiss my cheek, and I clenched my fists to keep from reaching for her. "I like you too, Soren."

Her scent hit me as she took the fob from my hand and turned away to go into the apartment. I licked my lips, testing to see if I could still taste her, and admitted that it was probably already too late to go back.

This stupid fake dating agreement was going to backfire spectacularly, but I was there for it as long as it gave me Vi. I followed her into the apartment. She disappeared into her room, and my hard-on didn't get the hint. It was a miracle I could function at all after being at least semi-hard for the last few hours.

The gentle click of the door closing sounded loud in the silence of the apartment, but she didn't turn the lock. I scrubbed my face and turned my back on temptation, going into my own room. At least no one expected us to show up for late night partying.

I took a shower, replaying the moments on the side of the road in my mind, and came faster than I had since I was a teenager. With the pressure relieved, I hoped to be able to actually sleep, but an hour of scrolling in bed only confirmed what I already knew. There would be no sleep for me tonight. I wanted to check on Vi one more time.

Something had changed between the truck and the apartment door.

I was almost sure that white paper hadn't been in her hand when she'd gotten out, but I'd been a little distracted. Whatever it was, she'd taken it into her bedroom with her. In general, I tried to respect her privacy. Except for that first night, I hadn't actually gone into her room without knocking. Instead, I haunted the rest of the apartment in case she needed me.

I pulled on a pair of sweats and left my room, shaking my head at the pathetic excuse. It was *way* too late to go back.

From the hallway, I heard Vi whimper behind her closed door. Not like the one earlier when I'd had my mouth on her —I'd never forget *that* sound—this one leaned closer to fear. I frowned and reached for the lever, then stopped myself. If she wanted me there, she'd have said so.

My jaw ticked as I fought off the protective streak that Vi inspired. Before her, I hadn't cared enough to feel protective. Another whimper, louder, came from her room. *Fuck it.* She could yell at me later.

I eased open the door and peeked inside. The space was dark except for a night light casting shadows from the bathroom. We hadn't been back long, but she'd said she was tired. I knew she had an early training session tomorrow because I already had my alarm set to drive her.

Vi was asleep, curled in a ball on one side of the mattress with tears trickling down her face. As I watched, she winced and cried out again. I told myself to close the door and leave her to her dreams, but the sight of her in pain clawed itself into my chest.

I wanted to help, but I had no idea what to do in this situation. Pretty sure the answer wasn't watch her have a nightmare from the doorway like a creeper. I cursed quietly under my breath and stepped into the room, pulling the door closed behind me.

This was probably the stupidest thing I'd ever done, and that included the time my cousin convinced me to jump off the third-floor balcony into the pool. I crouched by the side of the bed where Vi lay, smaller than I'd ever seen her.

Might as well go all the way.

"Vi." She turned toward my voice, and I traced her damp jaw with my fingertips. "Vi, wake up."

Her eyes fluttered open, but instead of relaxing, her face crumpled. Helplessness ate at me as her body quaked with sobs.

"What's wrong?"

She shook her head without answering me, ratcheting up my panic. I sat on the edge of the bed next to her and hauled her into my lap. Her arms snuck around my waist, holding tight as she let loose.

I held her, rubbing her back, until her tears dissolved into quiet hiccups, then the occasional sniffle. "Vi, it's killing me to see you cry. Please tell me what's wrong."

A long sigh shuddered out of her. "Bad dream about my mom."

She spoke so quietly, and with such broken words, that I

almost didn't understand her. I could put the pieces together. Vi had opened up to me about her mom's death, and now her subconscious was punishing her.

I threaded my fingers through her short hair, pulling it away from her wet face. "Have you had this dream before?"

"Yeah."

"Here?"

She nodded.

I cursed silently. I *knew* I'd heard something from her room that first night after the party. If this was how she slept, no wonder she worked herself to exhaustion. It also explained her obsession with coffee.

"What can I do to help?"

"Stay. Please."

I nodded, dropping a kiss against her hair. She could have asked me for a kidney, and I'd have handed it right over. "I'm not going anywhere."

Vi's tense body relaxed as I stretched out on her bed and pulled her down next to me. Like in the truck, she fit me perfectly, one leg tucked between mine as if we'd done this for years. Her head rested on my shoulder, but I kept my grip loose, even when she shifted and brushed her lips across my collarbone.

"Do you want to talk about it?"

"Not right now." Her hand traced the line of my stomach muscles down to the waistband of my sweats before I stopped her.

"This isn't what you want."

She laughed dryly and tugged on her hand. "Oh, *now* you're going to stop me? What happened to it being my choice?"

"It is, but it's mine too. I'm not going to take advantage of you while you're hurting. I'll stay as long as you need me, but all we're doing is sleeping."

Her hair tickled my jaw as she gave a jerky nod. I released my tight grip on her fingers, and she drew my hand up to rest over hers on my chest.

"I'll bet you're going to be so pissed at yourself tomorrow," she muttered.

I grunted out a laugh. "Maybe, but you won't be. Go to sleep, Vi."

She nuzzled my neck, then inhaled a long breath and held it a moment before letting it go. Her body relaxed against mine. "Goodnight, Soren."

I expected to spend the next few hours in an uncomfortable state of arousal, but a sense of contentment filled me. My body felt heavy with the girl of my dreams lying in my arms. I blinked my eyes open, unaware I'd closed them. When had she become the girl of my dreams? I didn't dream about girls—I dreamed about football and being free of my parents' manipulations.

What was I doing? Sleeping with her and saying no to sex when she'd clearly been offering. I cared about her, yes, but I also cared about Derrick and Eva and even Mac. I didn't want to get any of them naked though.

Truthfully, my feelings for her had always been different than those for anyone else. This whole situation was only going to make my damn obsession with her worse. I'd told her I'd stay as long as she needed, but if her slow breathing was any indication, she'd fallen asleep. I was fairly confident I could slip out without her knowing, but deep inside I didn't want to.

I wanted to stay right where I was with her warm and content against me.

My eyes drifted shut again. I felt like I hadn't gotten a full night's sleep since I'd seen Margot sitting on my parents' sofa, but with my arms around Vi, I could push all that drama aside. At least for tonight.

Tomorrow, we'd go back to normal. Separate rooms, separate beds, and a pretend relationship. Except I was beginning to suspect that Vi Malone was everything I didn't know I wanted in one fiercely independent package.

16

Vi

"I don't see why this is necessary."

Soren pulled his head out of the fridge to eye my outfit. The black yoga leggings and long-sleeve training shirt went really well with the dark circles under my eyes. I knew he noticed because his gaze lingered on my face for a beat too long before he crossed his arms and leaned against the counter.

"You saw the social media response to our impromptu announcement at lunch. My feed has been blowing up since then. They gave us a ship name. The people want what they want."

I held up the red jersey he'd given me that morning. "And me parading around like a prize calf with your name branded across my ass is what the public wants?"

"My name won't be across your ass, but yes. They want a show of support."

"Why should I care?"

He crossed the kitchen to take the jersey from me and set it on the counter, probably so I wouldn't toss it in the trash. "If you don't want to wear it, that's fine. Personally, I'd like to see you in it, but it's not worth fighting about. I imagine you're cranky because you're tired. Why don't you take a nap before the game?"

I wanted to lash out at him in the face of his calm logic, but he was right. My eyes felt gritty, and my muscles protested being vertical. I hadn't gotten a good night's sleep in three days—since Halloween when he'd interrupted my nightmare and stayed with me until morning.

No sex—not even a morning make-out session to enjoy. He'd woken me up for my training session then left to get ready himself. The rejection stung, especially after I'd practically thrown myself at him in my half-awake state.

The recurring nightmare was an old one from the bad days right before Mom died. It liked to remind me of my messed-up state in times of high anxiety. I knew how to deal, but it normally took a few days to de-stress my head enough to sleep. The night with Soren was the first time it had gone away immediately.

He believed my belligerent mood was from exhaustion, and I was happy to let him keep thinking that.

"I said I'd go, and I'll go." I tried to keep the grumpiness out of my tone, but I mostly didn't succeed.

One side of Soren's mouth tipped up at my pout. "Think of how pissed Colt will be seeing you cheering for me in the stands while he sits on the bench, unable to do anything about it."

"Which sounds like a great reason *not* to wear your jersey. I thought we were trying to get Colt to forget about that night." Guilt tugged at me as I thought about the stack of notes slowly filling my bedside drawer. If they really were from him—and who else could it be—he hadn't forgotten shit.

Soren pulled me into a hug. "It's not about making Colt

forget you, it's about convincing him you're off-limits. I want him to know, without a doubt, that if he touches you, I will destroy him."

I let my head drop and shivered at the dangerous undertone in his voice. Soren wasn't fucking around. If he found out about the threats, he'd do something stupid that might cost him his future. I wouldn't let Colt take that from him.

With some effort, I pushed past my bad mood in an effort to distract him. "What am I supposed to do with a fan club?"

He dropped a kiss on my temple. "Feed them regular sightings of our love. You can't deny the Voren fans."

"That is the *worst* name," I muttered against his shoulder.

His chest shook as he laughed. "Seriously, get some sleep. You don't have to come to the stadium with me."

I inhaled his clean scent and tried not to think too hard about the last time I'd slept. "I'll be fine. Eva promised me a double espresso if I sat with Nadia and wore your jersey like a good little ball bunny."

"Pretty sure you have to put out to earn that title."

I pinched Soren's side, and he jerked back with a yelp.

"You're violent when you're sleep-deprived." He grabbed the jersey and tossed it at my face. "Suit up, sweetheart. Your coffee awaits."

———

I'd been to plenty of games before—our university boasted a championship team, after all—but sitting practically *on* the field at the fifty-yard line was a whole new experience. Nadia beat me there, but I had no trouble finding the seats. She handed me a giant iced latte as I joined her, and I thanked the weather gods that it was sunny and mild. A rare fall day for north Texas.

The game didn't start for a while, but Soren had insisted on keeping me company until the last possible minute when he had to go get ready. I took a large gulp of my coffee and glanced around at the quickly filling arena. Some of the players were already warming up, which gave me a bad feeling about Soren's timing.

I nudged Nadia. "What time are the players supposed to be here for game days? Is Soren going to get in trouble because of me?"

She sent me a knowing smile. "Usually, they come in the morning and spend all day here, but Derrick covered for him."

Like me, Nadia was swimming in a red jersey. I didn't know her well, but Eva talked about her a lot. Derrick had apparently fallen hard at the beginning of the semester, and after some drama, so had she.

I'd met her once before, when Eva dragged her to one of my classes, but I hadn't realized at the time she was dating the quarterback. I guess these seats were perks of being one of the girlfriends.

Eva waved from the endzone where she was performing stunts with the rest of her cheer squad, and I realized another girlfriend perk—someone to watch the game with who wasn't required to yell the whole time.

We waved back, and I spent the next hour getting dirt on Soren. Nadia did *not* hold back. Some of the stories I'd heard before, some of the habits I'd seen for myself, but one tidbit made me stop her mid-sentence.

I held up a hand. "He warned Derrick to talk to their coach *before* the shit hit the fan with you guys?"

She nodded and pulled out a baggie of carrot sticks.

"According to Derrick, yes. He also swears Soren talked Coach out of benching him right before the game, though Soren hasn't admitted it."

"Weren't you there for that part?"

A pink flush tinged her cheeks. "I was a little distracted."

I chuckled. "If Soren helped, he'd never admit it."

Nadia tilted her head and studied me. "I think he'd admit it to you. Soren gives off this attitude like he has nothing to lose—like he doesn't give a single crap about anything—but there's a lot more to him."

"I know." And I *did* know. If I asked, Soren would tell me what happened that night with his coach. I knew how much he valued his friends, even if he didn't share the inner parts of his life with them.

Like he did with me.

I wasn't a friend, but I wasn't a real girlfriend either. How different would that be from the life I was living now? He'd given me a screaming orgasm and held me while I slept. Even in the confines of the apartment where no one could see, we were completely comfortable touching each other. He took his promise to protect me seriously... maybe too seriously. What was the distinction between fake Soren and real Soren when it came to me? Did *he* even know?

Nadia watched me a second longer, and I got the distinct feeling she picked up on more than I was comfortable with. "Do you want to talk about it?"

I barked out a laugh. "No. Definitely not. Thanks for the offer though."

She shrugged and shifted her attention to the field, then leaned forward. I turned to see the cheerleaders lining up in two rows by the tunnel. A slow thrill built in me. None of the games I'd seen before carried as much weight as this one.

I'd been friends with Eva for a year—and many of the other cheerleaders for longer—but I hadn't particularly cared who won or lost. Now, I knew several members of the team. I knew how hard they worked and how much each game meant to them.

I wanted them to win, if for nothing else than to ease Soren's mind about his future.

The guys rushed out onto the field to the blaring sound of their entrance music, and I immediately spotted Soren at the front of the pack. Derrick elbowed him and nodded in our direction, and I knew that was my cue to make a fool of myself.

Nadia and I both jumped up and waved from our seats. Derrick blew Nadia a kiss, and the crowd around me cheered. Instead of following his captain to huddle with the rest of the players, Soren veered off to jog toward us.

His eyes locked on mine, and my heart took off. The first row of seats was only separated from the field by a wall and a couple of feet in height. I remembered seeing video of Derrick rushing the stands to kiss Nadia before their game on the night of the Kappa party, and I wondered if Soren was planning something similar.

Before he could get very far, his coach snagged him by the arm and pulled him to a halt. The man said something that made Soren scowl, but when he shook himself free, he sent me a smile and a shrug. I pushed the disappointment deep, deep down. The gesture would have been romantic to everyone around us, but I understood the silent message he'd sent me.

Give the fans what they want.

A wolf whistle split the air from right behind me, and I jumped at the sudden loud intrusion. Everyone else had sat down, so I joined them and clapped for the coin toss.

Two orders of nachos and a ridiculously priced beer later, the game was tied with less than a minute left on the clock. Derrick spun out of a tackle and threw a beautiful pass downfield to Soren's waiting hands. I jumped to my feet as he took off across an almost open expanse of turf.

Soren was *fast*. Only one of the defenders had a chance to catch him, and he was right on Soren's ass. They ran together as the entire stadium exploded in sound. I shouted along with everyone else all the way up until the defender dove for Soren's hips.

They went airborne. Soren curled around the ball and landed hard on his back with the other guy on top of him. In the end zone.

The refs called a touchdown, and everyone lost their minds. Screaming, hugging, grown men ripped their shirts off and swung them around their heads. The defender rolled to the side, and his team helped him stand with slaps on the back.

Soren didn't get up.

17

Vi

A tight band across my chest prevented me from pulling in a full breath. The rest of the crowd seemed to notice at the same time because a hush fell over the stadium. Officials and trainers scrambled onto the field, and Derrick pushed his way through to kneel next to Soren.

The crowd blocked my view, and the rush of panic made me light-headed. Nadia rubbed my back as black spots danced in front of my eyes. An old familiar fear from the days with my mom reared up with a vengeance.

I couldn't handle losing anyone else I cared about.

With my attention focused on the men at the end of the field, I didn't notice the distant clapping at first. Derrick stood, then helped Soren up, and the spectators began cheering even louder than before. My strained muscles trembled as they released the tension I'd been holding. I sucked in a breath and might have toppled over if Nadia hadn't steadied me before she sat down again.

The kicking team came onto the field, and Soren walked off on his own legs. Derrick carried both their helmets and said something to him as they reached the bench. Soren's eyes zeroed in on me where I stood against the railing. I hadn't even noticed I'd moved.

His face shifted, and he strode toward me. The wall didn't slow him at all. I barely had time to move out of the way as he reached up and vaulted over the railing to land next to me.

"Are you o—" I didn't get to finish my question.

His hands cupped my face, and he leaned down to kiss me. We both paused for a beat, sinking into the sensation of his lips pressed to mine. All at once, need and relief and several weeks' worth of repressed lust crashed through my system in a confusing tangle of emotions.

I kissed him back with everything in me, plastering myself against him even though his pads got in the way. I couldn't help myself, and I damn sure wasn't performing for an audience. His arms came around me, and he growled out my name against my lips.

He lifted me onto my toes, and I fisted my hands in the silky material at his back. The crowd, the stadium, Nadia, all of it faded into the background.

A whistle echoed from the field, signaling the end of the game, and with a shaky breath, Soren eased back a few inches. He brushed his nose against mine, then lowered me back to my feet.

I didn't want him to let go. The thought came and went with such strength that I was pretty sure it had flashed across my forehead in big neon letters. After all the mental acrobatics I was pulling with myself, that simple truth shined through.

It was a day for uncomfortable realizations, and I hadn't had nearly enough sleep to deal with them.

Someone jostled me from behind, and Soren scowled

over my shoulder at the offender. I'd managed to forget we were blocking the walkway of the stadium after a major college football game. I looked around to see how much of a spectacle we'd made.

Only a small one, it turned out. Fans had rushed the field around us as soon as the game ended, and Nadia had left at some point during the dramatic post-game kissing. I knew the sports reporters would have caught the moment between us, but for the time being, we were lost in the throng of people trying to exit.

He sighed. "I'm sorry."

I tried to lean back to get a better look at his face, but his arms tightened, keeping me in place. "Why are *you* sorry?"

"I didn't mean for it to escalate like this."

I tried to keep my voice light, but my heart sank. "All part of the deal, right?"

"No. It was never part of the deal to make you worry like that."

My brow furrowed. "How did you know?"

"It's how I would have felt. Plus, Nadia texted D."

"Are you okay?"

"Yeah. Daniels knocked the air out of me, and protocol dictates that I stay down until I'm fully functional." He grinned. "I had one hell of a run though."

The last of my unease melted away, and I was suddenly exhausted. The clear joy in his smile reminded me of why we were doing this in the first place. He didn't just want to choose his own future, he specifically wanted to play professional football.

With skills like that, I had no doubt he'd be drafted if he took the chance. He didn't need the extra year of eligibility, which meant he didn't really need my influence—he needed my support to take a risk, even if it cost me a place to live. My blasé reaction to potential homelessness warned me that I was in way deeper than I thought, and I didn't have the energy to deal with the implications.

I offered him the biggest smile I could muster. "Yeah, you scored the game winning touchdown. It doesn't get much better than that. Do you need a ride back?"

He tilted his head at me, probably curious about the disconnect between my happy face and my weary tone. I didn't bother trying to explain. The day had not gone the way I'd expected, and I'd reached the end of my ability to articulate my thoughts.

"No, I have my truck, and I need to finish up here. I'll see you at home?"

I nodded, already planning to be asleep by the time he got back.

He dropped another quick kiss on me, then he was gone from the stands. Jumping the railing again to jog through accolades and congratulations on the way to his gear. I shook my head at the spectacle. Soren played like he loved the attention, but I knew the truth.

He loved the game—and he didn't need *me* to succeed.

———

I HEARD SOREN COME HOME, but coward that I was, I pretended to be asleep when he checked on me like I knew he would. In the intervening hours, I'd listened to him bustle around in the kitchen, watch tv too low for me to hear, and finally go into his room.

The sun set, and though I dozed a little bit, every time I actually fell asleep, the nightmare jerked me awake. It included the added bonus of a motionless Soren after the usual bullshit where my mom blames me for abandoning my family after her death.

After the fourth or fifth awakening, I didn't even try to go back to sleep. Could a person die from lack of rest? The answer seemed like yes, but I couldn't remember if it was a direct death like starvation or if being sleep-deprived led to people making terrible decisions that ended in death.

I flopped over onto my back and threw the covers off. The ceiling didn't offer me any advice, but I thought again about the suspicion that had been floating around in my mind since the morning after Halloween. The nightmare had gone away when Soren slept next to me.

The reasons eluded me, but it was the first time anything had worked except heavy duty sleeping pills. I hated those things. They left me groggy and feeling sick the whole next day. Not a great trade-off.

If Soren's presence worked once, maybe it would work again. Of course, I'd have to deal with the fallout of being up close and personal with the hottest guy I'd ever met, who probably slept naked. The image warmed me, but the real problem wasn't his fantastic body. It was my growing feelings for him. Did I really want to let him in even further when our confusing relationship had an expiration date?

The jumble of conflicting urges made my head hurt—or maybe that was the exhaustion too. It was hard to tell.

I couldn't handle another sleepless night, so I made a decision and hoped it didn't end as poorly as some of the other sleep-deprived things I'd done.

"Soren?" I eased his door open, and the light from the hallway fell across his bed.

He lay with his arms crossed behind his head, staring up at the ceiling. The comforter covered his lower half, but his chest was bare, making it easy to see the tension in his muscles.

His eyes found mine. "Can't sleep?"

The understanding in his gaze quieted the voice in the back of my head warning me this was a bad idea. "No."

The quiet settled between us for a long moment until he exhaled softly. Without looking away, he scooted over and lifted the covers, waiting for me.

Even though I'd been the one to disturb him, I hesitated. The near panic attack, the frenzied kiss after... I'd tried to keep him at a distance, but I sucked at it. If he touched me, I worried I'd toss away what little protection I had left. Judging from my reaction earlier, it was already too late.

Might as well go all in.

"Come here, Vi."

His husky voice helped me let go of my doubts. I moved into the room and pulled the door closed behind me. Soren's breathing matched mine in the darkness—slow and uneven.

I slid in next to him, surprised to find him wearing sweats. He covered us both with the blanket and pulled me back into his chest. I settled against him, truly relaxed for the first time in days. His fingers dipped under my tank to splay across my stomach, anchoring me in place.

"Go to sleep."

Goosebumps raised on my skin even as I closed my eyes. He shifted his hips, nestling his erection against my ass, but I knew without a doubt he'd deny me again if I pushed for sex. Soren, black sheep of his family, would never act if he thought he was taking advantage.

"I'm sorry." I wasn't sure if my quiet apology was for him or for me. Three years of standing strong on my own demolished by a cocky football player with a soft heart.

"I'm not. You can always come to me, Vi."

"I know." The quiet truth hung between us for a long moment, and his thumb stroked a line of fire on my stomach.

He pressed a light kiss to my shoulder. "Go to sleep. You can overthink everything in the morning."

As if he had a direct line to my nervous system, my mind emptied, and my body quieted. I sank into his warmth, letting go of all the reasons this was a bad idea. In the morning, I didn't plan to overthink a damn thing. With his breath in my hair and his body wrapped around mine, I was exactly where I wanted to be.

18

Soren

I'd never been more thankful for a bye week. After the last game, the team had mercilessly teased me about my 'injury'. Some of those assholes didn't know when to quit. D and the others knew better, but Colt thought he was hilarious every time he pretended he couldn't breathe when I walked by.

It's a miracle I didn't punch him in the throat to give him better material to work with. His saving grace was that he seemed to have given up on his obsession with Vi. She'd come by practice a couple of times, and he'd ignored her completely.

I, on the other hand, couldn't keep my attention on the plays I was supposed to be running when I could feel her eyes on me.

We didn't have practice on Saturdays due to games, so the weeks we had off were just off. Instead of sleeping in, Vi woke me up to go food shopping. Stupidly, I wasn't even upset. My parents texted three times while we were at the store, and again as soon as we started putting away the groceries.

Vi arched a brow at me as she shoved spaghetti into the pantry. "You might as well check it."

"I don't need to check it. It's my parents exercising their right to remind me that I have no control over my own life."

She leaned against the counter and crossed her arms. "Don't you think that's a little dramatic? Especially considering you haven't read any of those texts."

To appease her, I pulled my phone out with exaggerated slowness. Vi huffed and snatched it from my hand. I smiled as she scrolled through the messages, her frown deepening as she went.

"Well?"

"We've been summoned." She held the phone out, and I returned it to my pocket.

"They want us to come to family dinner, right?"

Vi pressed her lips together and nodded, then started emptying another shopping bag.

"Should I say I told you so now, or should I wait until we meet with them and they start in on all the ways I'm living my life wrong?"

She glared at me and held up my chocolate peanut butter puff cereal. "I can't believe you eat this stuff. Aren't athletes supposed to treat their bodies like temples?"

I snorted. "You can say that with a straight face after spending time with Mac?"

"Mac works out more than you do." The cereal went into the pantry, and Vi held up a finger before I could get good and offended. "I'm not belittling the amount of work you put into your body."

"Sure sounded like it," I grumbled.

Her eyes lingered on my chest. "I have zero complaints, but I happen to know that Mac does his usual training with you guys and often joins the cheer team for their workouts."

I frowned at the hummus in my hand. "I didn't know that. How did I not know that?"

She shrugged. "There's a lot you don't know."

"I feel like we're dangerously off subject here."

"Your parents have requested that we meet them for a small family lunch today at some French place I can't pronounce."

A feeling of dread settled in my stomach. "La Maison du Chat?"

"Maybe? You rattled that off like you've been there before. Or like you speak French."

"Both, actually." They only insisted on eating there when they planned a hard sell on my familial obligations.

Vi stopped and goggled at me. "You speak French?"

"And Spanish, like any well-bred Texan. And a little bit of Italian, but I'm really bad at that one."

She propped her hands on her hips. "What, not old Norse?"

The gleam of amusement in her eyes woke a hunger that had only been shallowly sleeping. I abandoned the rest of the groceries and advanced on her. "Is that a joke about my heritage?"

Vi raised her chin, refusing to be intimidated as usual. "Your whole family look like they walked off the set of a Viking movie. I stand by my joke."

I caged her in against the island counter. "My Viking ancestors would be very disappointed in me."

Her gaze darted down to my mouth, and she licked her lips. "Hmm?" The distracted murmur was exactly what I'd been hoping for.

"Not a single maiden pillaged today."

She blinked. "I don't think you pillage maidens—"

Vi gasped as I shoved the bags aside, lifting her onto the

counter. I brushed my nose against hers and trailed my lips along her cheek down to her neck. The last few days had wreaked havoc on my best intentions. Things had been heated between us since the beginning, and having her pressed against me all night, every night, had set everything on fire.

I wanted another taste. Just one.

"Soren," she whispered, tilting her head to give me better access.

She reached for me, but I caught her hands in mine and pressed them flat against the granite.

"No touching," I murmured against the rapid pulse in her neck.

"You're touching me."

"Just barely." I swiped my tongue across that pulse point, and her whole body leaned toward me. I wasn't the only one feeling the effects of days of close contact with no release.

Her thighs widened, and she hooked a leg around my hip in an attempt to pull me closer. She was strong, but I was stronger. I moved the other direction, using her leg to slide her ass to the edge of the counter. With her hands trapped in place, the position brought her breasts front and center.

Right where I wanted her.

"I love the way you demand what you want. I know how much you like my mouth on you, my tongue. I know you'll squeeze me tight with your inner thighs when I'm working your clit, two fingers deep in your pussy. I know what you feel like relaxed and sated, but I wonder..." I moved my mouth lower to tease the pebbled nipple visible through the thin material of her top. "What *else* do you want, Vi?"

Goosebumps rose on her arms and a shiver coursed through her. She arched toward me, but my phone went off with a blaring classical ringtone. The one I used exclusively for my parents. Vi took a shuddering breath and unwrapped her leg from around me.

I deeply regretted not leaving my cell phone in the car. With the moment broken, I released her hands and helped her sit up straight.

Vi dropped her head to my shoulder and tangled her fingers in my shirt. "What horrible timing."

I laughed because what else was I going to do. She was right, the timing was spectacularly bad, but they'd keep calling until I gave them confirmation. For a brief moment, I considered tossing my phone out the window. What good was being rich if I couldn't carelessly destroy expensive technology to get into my girlfriend's pants?

The phone rang on as everything quieted inside me. My girlfriend. Not *fake* girlfriend. The thought had come out of nowhere. I could blame poor word choice, but I'd only be lying to myself. All the back and forth this last week came into sharp contrast.

I'd told myself I didn't want to take advantage of Vi— and that was true—but the more complicated reason involved my fear that sex would bring her all the way across my walls. A stupid fear, it turned out. All my possessive feelings toward her reared up and smacked me across the face.

Just like they had at the game. Just like on Halloween. A memory from the Kappa party flashed across my mind— anger that Colt had noticed her freckles before me, had noticed *her* before me.

I was so fucked.

Only a few seconds had passed, but I felt like I'd run a thousand miles then faceplanted in front of her.

Vi's fingers dug into my stomach, then she flattened her hand and pushed me back a step. "Answer the phone." She didn't wait for me to move before returning to the shopping bags.

I answered and listened to my mom drone on about responsibility while I watched Vi pretend like nothing had happened between us. Again.

Well fuck that. I had feelings for this girl that went way beyond getting her naked. She'd probably decide I wasn't worth the trouble, but for once, I was going to put in the effort to make it work.

"Mom." My sharp response cut off the lecture mid-sentence. "We'll be there."

———

THE 'SMALL FAMILY LUNCH' turned out to include my aunt, uncle, and cousin as well as my parents and us. The choice of restaurant had warned me, but the situation was serious if my cousin, Harper, was invited along to witness the lecture.

La Maison du Chat was hidden away in a high-end outdoor mall meant for people who paid other people to shop for them. The front looked like a French cottage in the countryside with clever landscaping to hide the bustle of the pedestrians. Inside, all the waitstaff wore full suits and were well-trained to be neither seen nor heard.

My parents loved the place. I wanted to hate every second of eating there, but the food was fantastic.

Vi and I wound our way to the secluded table frequented by my family, and my tension increased with each step. My dad and Lukas stood as we approached, waiting until Vi had taken her seat to resume theirs. Old school manners that I tried my best to forget most of the time.

I glanced at Vi to see how she was handling the pompous traditions of wealth and found her peeking back at me as she pretended to adjust her napkin in her lap. One side of her lips curled into a tiny half-smile meant just for me.

My mom cleared her throat and reached for her wine glass. "I'm glad you could join us, Soren. Though next time I'd appreciate a warning if you're planning to be late."

Vi reached for my hand under the table and offered my mom a sweet smile. "It's my fault we're late."

I snorted, not quietly. "We weren't late. You told us noon. We arrived at noon."

My mom raised a brow, but Amelia jumped in, always willing to draw attention to herself when I was in the crosshairs. "I'm glad we're all together too. We have some news to share."

Harper's head jerked up, and a quick flash of panic crossed her face. Interesting. I hadn't thought anything could ruffle my ice queen cousin. She smoothed her blond hair back despite it already being contained in a sleek bun and toyed with her napkin as she recovered her mask.

Amelia shared a look with Lukas, and she smiled wide. "We're buying a tiny home. We want to travel the country in quirky style."

Vi laughed in delight, and my mom and dad gave less enthusiastic congratulations. Harper took a large gulp of her wine, then set the glass down slowly when she noticed I was watching. The waiter appeared with bread, and my mom waited until he'd taken our orders back to the kitchen before she focused on Amelia again.

"Why now?"

Amelia's smile became slightly less genuine. "Why not? The business is going well, and we have an excellent team to manage it for us. Why not take advantage of our unique position to enjoy life while we can?"

I caught Lukas shooting a quick glance at Harper, but she ignored him by staring down at her menu. Something was going on with them. Last I'd heard, Harper managed their business, among a few others my parents owned but didn't consider important.

Why would she seem so uncomfortable with this line of questioning? I shook my head once. Why did I care? I just wanted to get through this meal and get Vi home so we could pick up where we'd left off in the kitchen. As long as my parents' poor opinions didn't finally run her off.

In our world—the one around campus—I was a football god, but in my family, I was an embarrassment. I honestly didn't know which one was the truth.

My dad called my name, and I realized I'd missed something while I brooded. "Sorry, what?"

He glanced at Vi with a knowing look, then focused on me again. "Have you decided on a focus for your degree yet? Your mother and I were discussing the finances for next year, and we're concerned you may be spreading yourself too thin to take all the required classes for some of the specialties."

I was saved from answering by the arrival of our food. Politeness dictated that we didn't talk while eating, and for once, I was glad to adhere to the tradition. The impending conversation sat in the pit of my stomach and ruined any appetite I had, though.

Vi must have noticed me pushing my food around instead of eating because she nudged my shoulder and sent a pointed look at my plate. Instead of picking up my fork, I reached for her free hand and kissed her palm. Her face softened, and the air thickened between us. I wasn't the only one thinking of that morning.

"Not hungry?" Harper's pointed voice carried clearly over the subtle background music and other diners, but no one at our table reacted.

I met her dark blue eyes, so much like mine, ready to rip her a new one, and the sarcastic response died on my lips. She looked miserable. Not obviously, Harper would never let that much emotion show, but I knew my cousin.

She gave me a slight shake of her head and mouthed *sorry*. Before I could push, my dad cleared his throat, the usual sign that he planned to switch from eating to talking.

"Soren, you know your mother and I have been generous in supporting you, especially after that debacle last summer. We've noticed your newfound dedication to your responsibilities, so we think it's time to provide you with some real-world experience."

Dread coated my gut, but I had to ask the question. "What does that mean exactly?"

He smiled at me like he was bestowing a great gift. "We want to you work at our main headquarters this summer in a provisional role, mostly shadowing me through the day, but you'll have some duties of your own."

I shook my head. "I can't. I have classes and training over the summer."

My mom frowned. "Of course, we'll work around your classes, but you need to dedicate your time to your future."

"I *am* dedicating my time to my future." Somehow, I kept my voice reasonably low despite the alarm bells blaring in my head.

She scoffed. "Playing a game is no way to earn a living. The chances of you becoming a professional, let alone earning enough to support yourself, are astronomically low."

"You're wrong." The quiet conversation came to a screeching halt, and all heads turned toward Vi.

My mom was the first to recover. "Excuse me?"

She lifted her chin and repeated herself slowly. "You're. Wrong." Her hand found mine under the table, but I didn't think it was because *she* needed the connection. "Soren is an extremely talented football player, and any team would be lucky to have him. He's worked his ass off to get to this tier of play. Have you even come to any of his games?"

My dad looked pensive, but my mom's face closed down. "We don't have time for frivolous hobbies, and neither does he."

Vi laughed. "Playing professional football is a grueling job. When he gets drafted—and he will—you're going to need to find someone else to run your empire. He won't have time for a hobby business."

Shock at her blunt words hit everyone, including me. Her confidence sent a warm spear of hope spreading through my chest. No one had defended me before. Not like this.

Vi was a badass. I'd known it, but seeing it live was a whole new experience.

True to her nature, she didn't give them the chance to respond. Vi stood from the table, all grace and fire, and politely thanked my parents for the meal. I followed suit, offering a real smile to Amelia and Lukas and a nod to Harper.

When Vi turned to walk out, her head high, I was right beside her with my hand at her back.

She didn't have to know how deeply she'd affected me, but I couldn't hide from myself any longer. Vi was a badass when it came to defending me, but who stood for her? Our arrangement offered a half-assed sense of responsibility, but I wanted more. I wanted to be the one she came to when she needed help, the one she let past her walls, deep enough to see the broken parts of her.

But I didn't tell her any of that.

Once we made it outside, she let out a big breath and wouldn't look in my direction. "I'm sorry."

"Don't you dare apologize. That was one of the greatest moments of my life."

She frowned at me then the door. "I really don't think I'm helping your case with them."

I shook my head and pulled her close so I could rest my chin on her hair. "You really are. They may not like what you had to say, but they'll respect that you had the courage to say it. And honestly, they're probably just relieved that you're not claiming to be pregnant with my triplets."

Vi pinched my side. "You have a horrid way of making people feel better."

"Maybe, but it works."

Her hair tickled my neck as she sighed. "What now?"

"After that badass defense? We're doing whatever you want tonight."

She leaned back with a mischievous grin. "Anything I want, huh?"

19

Soren

I f Mac made one more song suggestion, I was going to stuff his head in a toilet. The whole crew sat crammed into a booth at our favorite bar on karaoke night. To Mac's eternal sadness, karaoke night usually fell on the day of our games, and none of us wanted to go out when we could nurse our injuries in private.

This time, fate had smiled down on him in the form of Eva and Vi. I should have known Vi would torture me after the restaurant if given the chance, and she really followed through. Instead of taking her home and spending the rest of the weekend naked, she'd asked to go out with Eva and the others.

I'd told my dick to settle the fuck down and hurried back to TU so Vi would have time to get ready.

The speed had been worth it. We'd arrived at the same time as the first round of drinks to a chorus of cheers. Eva gave me a triumphant smile, and I made a note to work on a revenge plan in the near future. Maybe something involving Mac, who insisted on bouncing song ideas off me, when I'd much rather be focused on Vi sitting in my lap.

She wore jeans, strappy heels, and this sexy little halter top that left most of her back bare. I wanted to run my tongue up the contoured muscles of her arms and kiss my way across the smooth skin of her neck. The girl was *fit*.

And I ached for her.

She leaned forward to say something to Eva across the table, and I bit the inside of my cheek to hold back the groan as her ass rubbed against me. I slid my fingers inside the loose top to rest on her bare stomach, resisting the urge to pull her back and down onto my cock again. If she leaned just a little farther forward...

Mac elbowed my side, and I realized I'd been staring at Vi's back. I scrubbed my free hand down my face and tried to wrestle my mind out of my pants—or hers. The music was loud, and even sitting next to me, I basically had to read his lips to understand him.

"You want some food?"

I tilted my head toward him, careful not to move my lower body too much. "Not really."

Vi suddenly turned, sliding between us. "Food? I'm starving."

Mac and I shared a confused look. How in the hell had she heard us? He recovered first. "How about pizza?"

She smiled. "Pizza sounds great. I'll go put in an order at the bar. Pepperoni okay with you?"

He nodded, and she turned her back on him, swiveling to focus on me. "And you? Do you want anything?"

Her words echoed the ones I'd asked her in the kitchen, right before I damn near lost my mind. My eyes dropped to her mouth, and I shook my head. Distantly, I heard Mac groan. He mumbled something about a room, but I didn't give a fuck if we had an audience.

Vi's lips parted on a tiny inhale. God, that little movement made me so tight. I needed to touch her. Thankfully, despite all her wiggling, my fingers still rested on her stomach, hidden from everyone by her body and her top.

Her abs clenched as I slid my hand lower to the button on her jeans. A little tug, and I had access. Vi braced herself on the vinyl behind me, and oh so slowly slid one leg across my lap. Her weight shifted as she carefully climbed over me to exit the booth, and I found her panties soaking wet.

Her bottom lip trembled as I pressed against the lace, dragging my finger over her clit on my way back out of her jeans. My blood was on fire, but Vi didn't pause as she came to her feet.

I steadied her with a hand at her hip, and the heated look she gave me nearly had me following her. She walked away as if her pants weren't unbuttoned under the drape of her top, but I knew she was fucking hot and wet. For me.

At once, the chaos in the rest of the bar came rushing back. No one seemed to have noticed our little maneuver. Mac and the others were all watching a trio of drunk sorority sisters butcher a Taylor Swift song, but my eyes kept returning to Vi.

I stretched my arm across the back of the booth, tilting my head to follow her progress as she made her way through the crowd. We'd had plenty of practice being together in public, but tonight felt different. Like we'd both rather be at home. Alone.

The trio's song ended, and a curvy redhead got up to sing a ballad. I didn't usually enjoy karaoke night, mostly because Mac insisted he was only playing football because he wasn't interested in a singing career. He wasn't entirely wrong, but every time he got up to croon at the ladies, they followed him back to the table.

I'd been fending off propositions the last few months—

after Margot, I wasn't interested in any more one-night stands—and the scene got old. Before lunch, I hadn't planned to come tonight despite Eva threatening payback if I didn't stop hoarding all Vi's time for myself. Her words.

I noticed Eva watching me from across the table, so I blew her a kiss. It was something I'd done hundreds of times before, but she narrowed her eyes at me instead of playing along like she usually did. Whatever. I didn't have the mental energy at the moment to figure out what went on in Eva's head.

Not while I was replaying the last few minutes over and over again.

Vi looked back at me, the ghost of a smile on her lips, and my heart turned over in my chest. That smile was for me, for what we shared.

A heavy weight landed on my legs, and long, blonde hair obscured my vision for a second. I processed that someone —a woman, judging from the hair and the heavy scent of her perfume—had sat down in my lap.

I immediately shifted to push her at Mac, but the random girl wound her arms around my neck, pressing her breasts against me and bringing her mouth to my ear. She whispered a suggestion that old me would definitely have taken her up on, but all I wanted at the moment was for her to get the fuck off me.

My eyes never left Vi. Her lips parted as she sucked in a breath, and she jerked back as if someone had hit her. I recognized the look on her face, the quick slice of pain. She gave one quick shake of her head and abandoned her spot at the bar to rush toward the bathrooms before I could dislodge the unwanted visitor.

"Mac, take her." I untangled her arms from around me, and Mac pulled her from my lap to his.

Fear quickened my reflexes, and I jumped after Vi. The panic I felt at that flash of pain told me everything I needed to know about the depth of my feelings for her. I was done with the ball bunnies who pretended to care about me—I wanted the real thing.

Groups of people blocked my way as I skirted around the bar, but the crowd thinned out near the propped open door Vi had hurried through. I caught up to her at the end of the dark hallway between the bathrooms and the emergency exit.

"Vi, wait."

Her head dropped for a second, then she turned on me, fire blazing in her eyes. "Rule two, Soren. You can call the agreement off at any point. All you have to do is tell me. I'm sorry the situation with your parents isn't working out the way you wanted, but you should have at least had a conversation with me before picking up someone else two minutes after you had your hand in my pants."

My panic sharpened and mixed with anger. Not with Vi —I understood her fear—but with the whole lifestyle that made finding something real so damn hard. "I wasn't picking up anyone else. I came here for you, and you're the only one I'm leaving with."

She pressed her lips together and ran her hands through her hair. "That's not what it looked like."

I held up my palms in surrender. "I know we haven't gone out in public much, but that happens all the time. People, especially women, want a piece of a football player, assuming we'll take whatever they're offering. They don't care about us personally. To them, we're all interchangeable. I used to enjoy it, but that life has lost its appeal. I didn't know that was her plan. Hell, I didn't even see her until she'd plopped herself on my lap. I was watching *you*."

Her nostrils flared as I slowly approached, like a wild animal scenting danger, but she didn't run again.

"My gaze never left you, even when I shoved her at Mac. I know you're scared by what's happening between us, so am I, but running won't fix anything. Talk to me."

She shook her head and leaned back against the wall next to her, lit only by the garish red light from the exit sign. "I only caught a glimpse, but seeing someone else in my spot hurt. Then I have to remind myself that spot's not really mine—you're not really mine. This whole situation was supposed to protect us from all this emotional bullshit, but we suck so bad at staying detached. You claim you're not into random hookups anymore, and I *want* to believe you. But I watched that woman put her hands all over you, and I couldn't help but wonder if you touched her the way you touched me."

Her voice broke on the last word, and I had to fight not to gather her in my arms. I hated that Vi was hurting, hated even more that I'd caused it, even unintentionally.

"I've never touched anyone the way I touch you." I took a chance and moved into her space, bracketing her legs with mine.

She tilted her head up and met my eyes. Everything I wanted shined up at me. She felt it—just like I did. We'd never been pretending.

The ruse offered an excuse for two closed-off, fucked-up people to let someone in. I was used to giving people the lowest possible expectations for me. That way, when I inevitably screwed up, it wouldn't matter too much. But Vi saw me differently. She believed in me, and damn, it felt good.

"You're right. I want out of the agreement. I don't want a fake relationship that ends at the apartment door." Her brow furrowed, but I didn't give her a chance to respond. "I want everything. Fuck Colt and the school and my parents. They're not a part of this. I want you. All of you. Only you."

I leaned into her, my forearm against the wall above her head. My nose brushed against hers as I pulled myself back from the brink. The connection zinged through me like an electric shock, and I burned from the need to taste her again. We didn't touch anywhere else, despite both of our chests heaving.

"This is your choice, Vi. Don't let anyone, not even me, convince you otherwise."

She let out a ragged breath and closed her eyes. "Soren..."

I didn't think I could feel more torn, but my name quiet on her lips clawed at my hard-won restraint. "Whatever you decide, it won't change what's between us."

She flattened her palms against my stomach—maybe to shove me away, but the push never came. My muscles clenched at her touch, begging for more.

Raucous laughter came from the bar, breaking into the solitude we'd created. Vi looked up at me, all the indecision gone.

"This is such a bad idea."

20

Vi

The hallway smelled like old onion rings, and any second, someone could come rushing out of the bathroom. But staring into Soren's eyes as they heated with understanding made the poor location entirely worth it.

"Why?" he murmured, inches from my mouth.

My mind blanked for a second, then I remembered what I'd just thought—out loud apparently. "We made that agreement because we needed things from each other, and that hasn't changed. Even though I fully plan to take horrible advantage of you later."

"Agreed. We'll still have those things. You'll have a place to live and protection from Colt, and I'll have a girlfriend to parade in front of my parents." He lowered his head enough to brush his lips across mine. "Any other stipulations before I take horrible advantage of you *now*?"

My fingers dug into the hard muscle of his stomach. "I reserve the right for more stipulations when my brain isn't in a fog of lust."

He laughed low, and the rough sound traveled down my

spine straight to my core. "Whatever you need, Vi. Just ask and it's yours."

Soren punctuated his statement by finally, *finally*, touching me. He threaded his hands through my hair and lowered his mouth to mine. His thumb traced my cheekbone as he played at my lips. Searching, pulling kisses that urged me to let him in.

I slid my hands around his waist and pressed myself against all his hard edges. He leaned forward, and my back hit the wall again. His tongue stroked a wicked rhythm, and my body throbbed in response.

The hallway faded—the bar, our friends—everything disappeared except him. Soren trailed his hand down my neck to my breast, pausing to run his thumb over my sensitive nipple. I arched into him, but he moved on, sliding over my hip and into my still unbuttoned pants.

His hum of approval was met with my gasp as he thrust a finger into me. I tilted my hips to give him better access, and he rewarded me with another finger. With slow, torturous movements, he brought me to the edge of orgasm. His thumb drew lazy circles on my clit, and I whimpered his name.

I was so close already, but this time, I didn't want to be alone. It was only fair I returned the favor. I released my clenched hold on his shirt and brought one arm between us to run my hand along the hard length of him.

Soren broke the kiss with a groan. His fist tightened in my hair, holding my head still as he growled in my ear.

"Keep playing and I'll take you right here. But first, you're going to come. Out in the open, where anyone could see us."

His words, his grip on my hair, the rhythmic movement of his hand tossed me over the edge. Trembling that started in my legs crested over my body in a wave of pleasure. Soren kept up the pressure until the last shudders subsided, then slowly pulled his hand free.

"What do you want, Vi. Here or home?"

Had I been wearing a skirt, I might have dropped my panties right there. My body was on fire—even after that mind-numbing orgasm—and I desperately wanted his hands, his mouth, his anything to relieve the persistent ache. But I didn't relish the thought of being interrupted by a drunk patron looking for the bathroom.

I stroked him one more time, and his hips jerked forward. "Home."

Soren immediately pushed away from the wall and tangled his fingers with mine, heading for the front where we'd parked. I was glad I hadn't brought a purse since we didn't even pause as we passed by the table. Eva sent me a smug look and a finger wave.

He didn't slow until we were buckled in for the five-minute drive back to the apartment. Part of me couldn't believe we'd just done that, but my body sure as hell knew. I felt like I'd run a marathon. My heart raced, I couldn't catch my breath, and I was pretty sure my thighs were going to be sore tomorrow.

I glanced at Soren. "How are you so calm? I've *had* an orgasm in the last ten minutes, and I'm fighting the urge to have you pull over."

He caught my eyes briefly, then gathered my hand to bring it to his lips. "I've been waiting for weeks, Vi. A few more minutes is nothing."

The rest of the ride home was mercifully short. Unlike the last time he gave me a fantastic orgasm, I didn't find a note on the door and freak out. We walked into the living room like any other night, but Soren didn't stop or drop my hand. He strode straight through the dark apartment to his bedroom.

I pulled the door closed behind me out of habit, and Soren didn't wait a second longer. He took my mouth with a feral groan, backing me against the wall. The ferocious intensity banished any doubts I had about his hunger. The man had iron-clad willpower, but I was giddy with the evidence that I could tear it all down.

Together, we kicked off shoes and shucked jeans, only separating long enough to toss our shirts into the darkness. Heat pulsed under my skin with the ruthless demand to get closer, to feel the slickness of his skin against mine.

I spread my hands over the planes of his chest and dragged my nails down sculpted muscles that trembled under my touch. He growled against my lips, a supremely masculine warning, and tipped my head back to trail his mouth down my throat.

My eyes drifted closed as his fingers found my breasts. I felt the tiny sting of a bite on my neck followed by the hot swipe of his tongue. The rough pad of his thumb dragged across my nipple, and I shuddered at the pleasure that arrowed through me.

All the other times we'd gone this far, Soren had led the way. He naturally took charge, and I had no problem with that when it made me feel this good. But this time, I wanted a turn to make him lose his mind along with his better judgement, to make him as wild as I felt.

He hissed as my nails dug into his abs. I pushed away from the wall, shoving him in front of me. Soren let me move him—because there was no way I'd budge him if he didn't let me—until his legs hit the bed. His hand fisted in my hair for a beat, keeping me close, but I only smiled against his mouth.

The second I began to lower to my knees, he loosened his hold.

I trailed my tongue along his stomach like I'd imagined doing so many times. His muscles bunched, but he didn't stop me. The salty taste of his skin sent shocks of electricity skittering through my belly.

My fingers wrapped around him, stroking slowly. I looked up and met his eyes, dark with hunger and something else I wasn't ready to name. He brushed his thumb over my lower lip in a surprisingly tender caress. In that moment, I would have given him anything.

I settled for giving him the best damn blow job he'd ever have.

He inhaled sharply when I closed my lips around his cock. With my hands on his thighs, I felt the tension in his body as he fought to hold himself still. Another glance up showed the fierce restraint on his face, and that wouldn't do.

I teased him with my tongue until his hand slid around the back of my head. In the near darkness, I let go of my inhibitions and palmed my own breasts, tweaking my nipples with a moan as I took him deep.

When his grip tightened, I murmured in approval.

His hips tilted forward, and I let him set the pace, using my mouth in a steady rhythm as he groaned out my name. The hoarse rumble urged me on, as did the hand in my hair guiding my movements.

My body felt heavy with need. I needed pressure, needed to feel full, with him inside me, as close as two people could be.

I needed Soren—only Soren. The thought stole my breath, but I refused to let the underpinnings of fear drive me away again.

My hand snaked between my thighs, and I hummed at

the sparks of fire from that first brush against my clit. Soren suddenly pulled himself away, dragging me to my feet. He took my mouth in a violent kiss as he spun me onto the bed. Dropping me onto my back while he quickly dug through his nightstand.

I raised a brow at him, and he shook his head.

"Next time, Vi. Anytime you want to put your mouth on me, you just let me know. But I desperately need to be inside you when you come."

I licked my lips as he rolled on a condom. "I'm going to hold you to that."

He sent me a wicked grin. "God, I hope so."

With agonizing slowness, he lowered himself over me on the bed. I dug my fingers into his hair, loosening the elastic until it fell away as he settled between my legs.

His cock notched at my entrance, and he paused. Soren stared down at me with those soulful eyes, his hair down around his face, with that first thrust. We both drew in a ragged breath, and he began to move. Slow at first, then with increasing force as my thighs gripped tight against his side.

I lifted to meet him, eager for more. He tangled his fingers with mine, stretching my hands above my head as he drove into me. My head dropped back against the mattress, and his breath warmed my ear.

"You are so fucking beautiful. Every part of you. All mine."

I clenched at his words, and he shifted his hips just enough to hit a sensitive spot inside me I didn't know I had.

"Say it, Vi."

My mouth opened, but no words came out. The shocking pleasure gripped me hard, tightening my muscles until I thought I'd die if I didn't find release.

Soren sank deep and held, rolling his hips. "Say it, then you can come on my cock like a good girl."

"All yours," I mumbled.

He gripped my fingers with one hand and slid his other between us to circle my clit, slamming into me with shattered control. White light exploded behind my eyelids, and Soren cursed as I convulsed around him.

With a last thrust, he buried his face in my neck and followed me over.

Once we both stopped trembling, Soren let go of my hands and nuzzled my neck. "Are you okay?"

I giggled, probably because of the sheer amount of stupid-inducing post-orgasm chemicals running through my body. "Yeah. Yes. Fantastic. I'd like to request a lot more of that in the future."

He twitched inside me, and I smothered another laugh.

His tongue swiped across the sensitive spot below my ear, sending a sharp stab of pleasure right to my core. "I think that can be arranged."

His possessive claim came back to me, and I shivered. I'd known getting involved with Soren would shake the foundation of our relationship, but I hadn't expected the intense connection. I'd never given myself to anyone the way I had to him.

And I liked it.

A knot formed in my chest at the thought, and Soren propped himself on his arm to stare down at me. "What?"

I traced the lines of his tattoo and forced myself to relax. It was on the tip of my tongue to tell him it was nothing, but that wasn't fair to him. "Just dealing with the inconvenient realization that I like you a lot more than I thought I did."

He grinned, and the heat returned to his eyes. "You'll get used to it. In the meantime, I'm happy to distract you."

I couldn't help the little wiggle that brushed my still sensitive clit against him, earning us both a quick inhale. We'd just finished, and I already wanted him all over again. Maybe I'd never stop wanting him, but I was strangely okay with that in the moment.

21

Vi

W e spent the next twenty-four hours in bed making up for lost time. Soren skipped his usual morning workout with Derrick, and I didn't have any sessions on Sunday. At some point, he ordered pizza while I was sleeping, which we ate lounging naked in the living room, just because we could.

Sunday night rolled around, and I found myself in my new favorite place—naked, draped over Soren's chest with a pleasant soreness in my muscles that I planned to stretch out the next day.

Part of me still couldn't believe the absolute beauty of Soren's body. My job required me to spend all day thinking about musculature, and none of my athlete clients compared to the way he was built. I wanted to spend all night tracing the ridges and lines of his muscles, the curves of his tattoo, but I had to work at too freaking early in the morning. Several times, I considered calling in sick to make the most of the time before Soren had to leave for practice.

Monday would mark the end of our sojourn, and I wasn't sure I was ready to head back to real life. During this in-between time, I didn't have to think about Colt or my brothers or the murky future. In the darkness, curled up against Soren's warmth, I could pretend none of it mattered.

But pretending wouldn't do me any good in the long run. Not when I was already looking for ways to shape my life around his. Before him, I'd never have considered shirking my responsibilities for a few extra orgasms. Even if they were *really fantastic* orgasms.

Soren brought my fingers to his lips for a sweet kiss. "What are you thinking about so hard?"

I took a deep breath and dove in. "What are we? Fuck buddies? Roommates with benefits? A really annoying new couple that refuses to go anywhere alone... or with pants?"

His chest vibrated under my cheek as he chuckled. "I meant what I said yesterday, Vi. I want you to be mine in every sense of the word. Whatever that ends up entailing for us. No more pretending."

"Then that goes both ways. I get to be all growly and possessive too. Will you be okay with that? As everyone keeps reminding me, you don't do serious relationships."

He trailed a hand lazily up my back and down again before he answered. "I'm rethinking my stance. I can't promise not to fuck things up, but for once, I want to try. *You* make me want to try."

My heart fluttered at his words, but there were so many other complications still in play. I thought of the drawer full of notes in my bedroom that Soren didn't know about—and my brothers, who would definitely become a problem if they found out.

I propped my chin on my hands. "We are *really* bad at following the rules—even the ones we made up. Maybe specifically the ones we made up."

"That shouldn't come as a surprise at all. I think it's time for some new rules."

"Yes, because *these* ones we'll definitely follow."

Soren raised a brow. "Only one way to find out."

I blew out a breath. "Fine. Hit me."

"Rule number one: you sleep in here from now on."

"Technically, I was already sleeping in here."

He swiped his tongue between my fingers, and I shifted restlessly as I vividly remembered him doing the same between my legs. "Rule number two: only naked sleeping allowed."

"Naturally."

"Rule number three: you have to wear my jersey to all my games."

I pursed my lips. "I'll agree to wear it to all the games I attend. I can't promise to be at every game, especially the away games."

"Rule number four..." He gently bit my finger. "Soren is always right."

I sucked in my cheeks to try to maintain a straight face. "Mhmm. Is that all?"

"I'm trying to keep it to a reasonable number."

Need thrummed in lazy beats under my skin, craving more of his touch, as I traced his lips with my fingertips. "I have some rules of my own."

Soren rolled us over, sliding lower to put his mouth right at boob level. "Better list them fast."

He started slow, dropping tiny kisses in a line down the middle of my chest, but it was enough to make me forget what number we were on.

I bent my leg, curling it tight against his side. "Rule number whatever we're on: you have to come to one of my classes."

He glanced up at me in surprise. "Really?"

I brushed hair back from his face and nodded.

Soren's eyes softened. "If you want me there, I'll come."

"Tomorrow?" I knew his practice ended before my class started, but I wasn't sure he'd want to do both in one day.

He grinned and levered himself higher, bringing my leg with him. The position left me open for his cock to glide against me.

I tilted my hips to increase the pressure. "How are you hard again already?"

His eyebrows lifted in disbelief. "I'm seriously starting to question the skills of your previous sexual partners."

I laughed. "My previous sexual partners have nothing on you."

Wild pride filled his gaze. "Damn straight they don't. I plan to ruin you for all other men."

"So humble," I murmured.

Soren leaned in to kiss me, a leisurely exploration of my lips. "I want to be the *only* one you think about." He brushed his nose against mine. "I have one more rule. No hiding things. We trust each other with the truth."

A band of fear squeezed across my chest, and I pulled his mouth back to mine. Soren had the uncanny ability to read my face as if my thoughts were printed there. The notes in my room burned in my mind, but I definitely couldn't tell him now.

He'd rush out and go directly to Colt. It wouldn't matter that the notes were unsigned or that messing with Colt could cost him his place on the team. Soren protected the people he cared about, and somehow, I ended up on that list.

A flutter of warmth—from his kiss, the weight of his body, the certainty of his feelings for me—pushed away the fear. I'd tell him. Eventually. When there wasn't so much at risk.

————

EVEN AFTER THE announcement of the new rules last night, I wasn't sure Soren would actually show for my evening class. I should have known better. He didn't back down when he said he'd do something.

I was standing at the door of the fitness studio before class, chatting with Eva and some of the participants, when I spotted him sauntering down the hallway. His hair was damp, and he wore TU sweats with a ripped-up shirt that revealed a whole lot of sculpted biceps and shoulders, including the full expanse of his tattoo.

Soren sent me a slow grin, and I gripped the doorframe to keep from rushing over to him.

He'd dropped me off at the student fitness center this morning with a lingering kiss that had stayed on my mind all day. My poor morning client had asked me repeatedly if I was okay after he caught me staring off into space when I should have been counting reps. A meeting with one of my professors had taken up my entire break between sessions and classes, so I'd missed having lunch with Soren and his crew.

I'd missed *him*.

Eva followed my gaze to Soren, then ushered the rest of the women into the room to find their spots. He slid his hand along my neck, tilting my chin up for his kiss. I knew the others were watching, but I just didn't have it in me to stop him. Professionalism be damned.

Luckily for me, he pulled back before I did something that could get me fired, like let him bang me against the wall. His thumb traced once more along my jaw, then he stepped back and shoved his hands in his pockets.

"I don't suppose I could interest you in an entirely different workout instead?" The wicked gleam in his eyes made me sigh. I loved my class, but the temptation was strong.

Instead of dragging him into the closest storage closet, I locked my hands behind my back. "I'm afraid you'll have to wait... unless you can't handle it."

Challenge lit his eyes, and damned if I didn't want him to prove me wrong. His eyes bore into me, and he moved closer, careful to keep an inch of space between us. "Are you going to be thinking of me while you teach?" His voice dropped, quiet enough for only the two of us to hear. "Will you imagine me inside you when you roll your hips? When you arch your body?"

I couldn't draw a full breath, and I couldn't look away. The moves in my choreography took on a whole new meaning with Soren painting naughty pictures in my mind. But he wasn't the only one who could.

I raised my chin and leaned forward until my lips almost brushed his. "I'll be thinking about it, but so will you. My class isn't a joke. It's hard work. I wonder how *hard* it'll be for you."

Soren hissed in a breath and pulled his hand from his pocket to spread his fingers along the side of my neck, still not touching me. That barrier of air, hardly a breath between us, held us captive, neither willing to back down.

I licked my lips, and his eyes followed the movement, breaking the moment. No longer trapped on the edge of a supremely bad decision, I straightened away from him. Soren shook his head with a soft growl.

"I can handle it." He trailed his fingers over the racing pulse in my throat, the ghost of a touch. "Can you?"

With that parting shot, Soren entered the studio and found a spot in the front corner. My skin burned where he'd finally stroked me, and I knew I'd never teach another class without Soren in my head. I'd never had foreplay like this, and I was under no illusions that he hadn't intended it this way. Despite our best efforts, we couldn't seem to keep our hands off each other.

Soren looked completely at home among the room full of women. Eva and the other cheerleaders formed a protective circle, but that didn't stop several of the bolder co-eds from inching closer to him.

The last stragglers hurried in as I fought to regain my composure. Thanks to years of practice, I greeted the class without tripping over my words. Hopefully, they'd think the flush on my face was from exertion and not from Soren's evil teasing. Though with him in the corner looking entirely too proud of himself, I didn't think I'd fooled anyone.

Only about half of the participants were listening anyway. The other half were ogling Soren. I maintained the smile on my face, but inside, I was seriously questioning the sanity of having him join my class. Soren was well-known at the school for his athletic talents *and* his prowess with the ladies.

A prowess I could confirm first-hand.

Needing a second to breathe before I started, I turned to adjust the volume on my music and watched in the mirror as a perky blonde ran her hand up Soren's arm. Before he could move, Eva smacked the woman's hand away and positioned herself blatantly between them.

Soren caught my eye in the mirror and shrugged. I didn't want to be petty and jealous, but I definitely imagined making that woman do burpees until she collapsed in a sweaty heap on the floor. Soren was *mine*, and the sooner the rest of the population caught up, the better. Possessive-me didn't play around.

As the fast-paced opening chords of my playlist filled the room, I marched over to Soren and yanked him forward for a hard kiss. He growled low in approval, but I turned on my heel to return to the front of the class before he could truly respond.

A smattering of applause followed me, and Eva let out a whistle that demonstrated why she was such an effective cheerleader. With a giant, shit-eating grin, I held up my hand to count down the beats and cue the first move.

22

Soren

I was so fucking wrong. Vi's dance class kicked my ass, to the utter joy of Eva and her cheer cronies. Not to mention the little problem of watching Vi move her hips in ways that gave me several good ideas for later.

My sweats were not made to contain a perpetual hard-on. I ended up having to recite football plays in my head to keep things appropriate for public consumption. Our little showdown before the class started didn't help.

Vi ended her class with a cooldown that was surprisingly similar to the ones we did during training. I'd never taken a dance class before, especially not dance fitness, but once I was able to move past the room packed with women watching me, I had fun.

That didn't mean I wanted to make it a regular thing, but I was glad Vi had shared this part of herself with me. She shined up there in front of the class. Even the grabby blonde eventually succumbed to Vi's magnetic enthusiasm.

Of course, by the end of class, we were all drenched in sweat, and I felt like I'd endured a two-a-day in the middle of August. No wonder she came home and passed out most nights. After the last song ended, I lay on my mat and hoped no one noticed that it wasn't voluntary.

The other participants recovered faster than I did, and Vi walked around chatting with them while they packed up. I followed her with my eyes until Eva leaned over me, blocking my view. She grinned down at my prone form, and my pride insisted that I at least put in the effort to sit up.

I heaved myself up and draped my arms over my bent knees. "Thanks for running interference."

She propped her hands on her hips. "Anytime. Unless this becomes a regular thing. I'm not sure I can handle a steady diet of all the sexy looks you two were giving each other during the class. I'm here to work out, not get second degree burns."

With some effort, I kept my focus on Eva, even though Vi had returned to the front to collect her things. "Maybe next time I'll bring Mac and you can watch him instead."

She snorted. "You think Mac hasn't come to this class? He tried it once and swore he'd never come back."

I frowned. "I thought Mac helped you with your cheer choreography."

Eva burst out laughing, hard enough to get Vi's attention. She wiped her eyes and shook her head. "No. Mac helps with the muscle-y stuff, like throwing girls in the air. Vi helps with the choreography."

I tilted my head at her. "Then what do *you* do?"

"Mooch and fly, baby."

With a finger wave at Vi, she patted my head and left us alone in the studio. I pushed to my feet and silently cleaned my mat as Vi tossed her things into her bag. She sighed on the way out the door.

"Sometimes I think I'm overdoing it, but then I have a class like tonight, and I'm reminded why I love this job."

"Because you like laughing at football players who are unlucky enough to stumble into your class?"

She laughed. "That did add a fun new dynamic, but no. Those ladies trust me enough to let themselves go in my class. They embrace the joy of movement for an hour every Monday night, and I'm the one they want leading them. There's a certain sense of power that comes with bringing people that joy."

I slung my arm around her waist, stupidly pleased when she leaned her sweaty body against me. "Is that why you wanted me to come? To show me the power of joy?"

Vi shook her head, her stubby ponytail brushing my shoulder. "I want to say no, but maybe?" She glanced up at me, and we slowed. "I think partly I wanted you to see how much work goes into these classes."

My heart turned over at the vulnerable look on her face. "Mission accomplished, though I already knew. I see how hard you work. I just didn't realize how hard *everyone* in your class worked. Coach will probably yell at me tomorrow in practice for running funny."

She searched my face for a second, then the moment passed, and she scoffed. "If Mac can get through afternoon practice after my morning class without any of you knowing, you'll be fine by tomorrow."

"I knew you were listening," I mumbled. We left the cardio area for the main hallway in the building, joining the stream of students coming and going.

Vi laughed again, and our pre-class conversation popped up in my mind, along with the kiss she'd laid on me in front of everyone. A dangerous sentiment heated my blood at the memory. Normally, I was quick to correct any possessive signals from the women I'd been with, but Vi could brand me, and I'd probably ask for more. I'd never wanted to belong to someone quite so hard as I did with her.

Honestly, I wouldn't be surprised if a video of that kiss ended up making the rounds for the Voren fans. I hadn't noticed anyone with their phones out, but I'd admittedly been distracted. Vi in her element showed me a whole new side of her, and like everything else, it fascinated me.

And I couldn't wait to get her back to our place to play out some of the fantasies her class had spawned.

"You ready to head home?"

She grinned. "That depends. Am I going to have to carry you up the stairs to the apartment?"

I lowered my mouth to her ear. "I'd crawl up those stairs if it meant getting you alone."

"Promises, promises," she murmured, quirking her eyebrow.

The need for this girl hit me all at once, a rush of affection and desperate yearning that I couldn't hold back any longer. I hauled her to a stop right there in the main hallway and kissed her the way I'd been dying to since I locked eyes with her before her class.

Vi clutched at my shirt and opened for me immediately, holding nothing back despite being surrounded by her clients and peers. She slid her arms around my waist and pressed all those gorgeous curves against me. I traced her jaw and took my time.

Her quiet sigh sliced right through to my heart. I didn't know why I resisted for so long, but kissing Vi—knowing she was mine to kiss—made all the other shit up to this point worth it.

Someone tapped me on the shoulder, interrupting the moment. I pulled back far enough to note Anne-Marie standing a foot away with her arms crossed. She sent me a frosty smile, then turned her attention to Vi.

"You're blocking the hallway."

Vi pressed a soft kiss to my cheek, then turned to face her co-worker. I kept my arms locked tight around her, and she rested her hands over mine.

"The hallway is plenty big enough for people to go around us." She nodded at a girl I recognized from her class. "As evidenced by all the people currently going around us... and you."

Anne-Marie's eyes flicked up to me and returned to Vi. "You're still on the clock. I'm certain we don't pay you for whatever extra service you're providing."

Vi snorted. "*You* don't pay me at all. We're at the same level of student employment, which is somewhere below the kid that scoops poop out of the pool."

I didn't like Anne-Marie's implication. Even when we'd been pretending—badly—I hadn't wanted Vi to be lumped in with my other supposed conquests. I'd wanted the public at large to believe that I'd fallen hard for her, hard enough to change my ways.

At this point, the story was pretty fucking close to the truth.

Anne-Marie's lips thinned. "Regardless. You need to stop padding your time with a hook-up."

I tensed at the accusation, but Vi squeezed my wrist. "I'm clocking out now, but I'll be sure to keep it in mind the next time you're *busy* in the office."

Her eyes narrowed, then her face smoothed out as she dismissed Vi in favor of me. "You know where to find me for those training sessions when you get bored."

Vi linked our fingers and led me to the front desk where she bent down at one of the computers. I shook my head at the sheer balls it took to proposition me in front of Vi. Anne-Marie was a shark, and even if I weren't completely fucking lost on Vi, I'd steer clear of her.

Out of the corner of my eye, I noticed a husky frame I recognized slinking through the door marked 'Staff Only'. As far as I knew, my head coach had no reason to be at this facility, but his life away from the field was a mystery to me.

After the drama with Derrick and Nadia, anything involved with Coach came with a heavy dose of suspicion. His manipulations could have cost Derrick the rest of the season. Parker was a crazy talented quarterback, but Derrick deserved the chance to finish out his last year. Coach had backed down in the end, but the man's obsession with controlling every aspect of the team wasn't doing us any favors.

Vi cursed under her breath, and when I pulled my attention away from the Staff door, she was fighting with the facility website.

"Everything okay?"

She glared at the computer. "Fine. I've been having problems logging in to enter my class information. It's not a big deal." Vi straightened and sent me a wicked grin. "Let's go home."

23

Soren

"No, you picked the last movie, and it sucked." Vi grabbed a piece of popcorn that had escaped the bowl on the coffee table and tossed it in her mouth.

"It didn't suck. You fell asleep halfway through. It's hard to appreciate a movie when you miss the ending."

She sighed. "That's probably true, but I stand by my statement. The first half sucked." She motioned for me to give her my other hand.

Every night since Vi's dance class, we'd engaged in an epic match of Rock Paper Scissors to see who got to decide on the events for the evening. I'd started the contest in an attempt to get her to relax instead of rushing from work to school to studying. I'd won the first three nights, and I had no regrets about naked sushi or the Ted Lasso marathon.

Vi seemed less stressed, so I assumed the plan was working. To my surprise, it worked on me too. Spending time with her, no matter what we were doing, ended up being fun. She made me happy in a way I'd never experienced before. I could relax around her and know that she *wanted* to be here with me, even if we were arguing about my clearly superior taste in films.

Tonight, I'd lost. Vi chose manicures.

I suggested we do a movie and popcorn too because I was sure as hell going to mess up her nails. Not that she cared. Vi was using this as an excuse to get back at me for the unfortunate cupcake incident. Her tongue peeked out as she concentrated on coating my fingernails with gunk, and it turned out I had no regrets about this night either. If Vi wanted to give me a purple mohawk, I'd hand her the scissors as long as it made her smile.

A sharp band of emotion tightened across my chest, clawing its way up my neck, and I suddenly had a much better understanding of Derrick's choices at the beginning of the semester.

I cleared my throat, but my voice still came out rougher than usual. "You won. Lady's choice for the movie. Now why don't you share some of that popcorn."

She scooted closer to where I had my hands pressed flat on the other side of the table from her and lobbed a piece at my face. I lunged to catch it, but it bounced off my cheek.

Vi tapped my wrist. "Stop wiggling. I don't want to mess this up."

I snorted, then reoriented myself. "If your aim wasn't so terrible, I wouldn't have to wiggle."

She raised a brow. "Isn't it literally your job to catch things?"

"I'm generally not asked to catch a football with my face."

"Semantics."

I nudged her with my foot. "I'm still without snacks in my mouth, and you still haven't picked what you want to watch."

Her eyes flicked to the dark screen and back to my hands. "We could talk instead of putting on a movie."

Something about her entirely too nonchalant suggestion tied knots in my stomach. "What do you want to talk about?"

She finished the finger she was working on and let out a puff of air as she met my eyes. "The draft."

My brows rose all the way to my hair. "What about it?"

"I think you should do it." She leaned forward, invested in making the case she must have been working on for a while. "You *hate* the idea of working in an office job, and while I know you're more than capable of succeeding at it despite that, you haven't really given yourself every chance to succeed at your chosen profession."

My back stiffened, but I tried to keep the anger and hurt out of my tone. "I've worked my ass off to get where I am."

"I know." Her gaze glittered with confidence, and some of my hackles went down. "But you've also been jumping through your parents' hoops to try to make all of you happy."

I wanted to argue that my parents' happiness had nothing to do with it, but the truth burrowed under my skin next to the sliver of guilt I carried with me everywhere.

She nodded as if I'd agreed with her out loud. "I think you always knew you were going to have to make a hard choice at some point. That's why you don't let people close —because you don't want to let anyone else down."

"I let *you* close."

Her face softened. "And I'm telling you that you need to join Derrick in the draft. You can't control the outcome of this, but another year won't give you any more of a guarantee. Make the choice. You won't fail."

Deep down, I'd already made the choice, but having Vi

tell me out loud that I was making the right one released all the tension I'd been carrying, like a shot of caffeine straight into my bloodstream. I shifted, intending to drag her over the table to me, but she slapped a hand down on mine.

"Don't you dare mess up all my hard work. One more thing. You should tell the guys."

I shook my head. "What good would that do? They need to focus on their own futures, not be distracted by the many ways I'm about to fuck up mine."

"You're not fucking up your future by choosing your own timing for it."

An image of that future hit me like a bomb. Vi was right. I'd never let myself visualize that path because the cost of failure seemed so high, especially since my parents had been convinced from day one that I wouldn't succeed.

I swallowed and finally vocalized that fear. "What if I don't make it? What if they're right, and I fail?"

She gripped my wrist, waiting until I met her eyes again before speaking slowly and clearly. "Then we find another way. Not being chosen in the draft isn't failing. It's a temporary setback. You are more than your skill with a football. No matter what, I'm here with you for as long as you want me. You won't be alone."

The last remnants of my walls fell there at her feet, and I knew she belonged in that future with me.

She didn't bother scolding me again as I leaned forward to kiss her.

"I will *always* want you," I murmured against her lips.

Her hand tightened on my wrist, and I realized this conversation was just as emotional for Vi as it was for me. It took a lot of courage for her to confront me. Despite my suddenly ravenous need for her, I ended the kiss without taking it further.

Vi sat back and tilted her head as she stared down at my hands. Her cheeks puffed out as she released a sharp breath, picking up the nail polish again.

"Good. Now that we've settled that..." She added the last bit of color and capped the bottle with a flourish. "What do you think?"

The tension in the room dissipated to a reasonable level, but I got the feeling she was humoring me. Or at least not putting too much stock in my plans for the future. Intellectually, I understood. I'd spent a lot of time convincing her—and me—that I didn't want to be saddled with the responsibility of another person.

I was wrong though. Vi wasn't an obstacle—she was the goal. If she didn't trust my words, I'd need to show her with my actions because I fully intended for her to be by my side at the draft.

She stared at me expectantly, reminding me of the conversation that wasn't happening in my head. I examined my nails, now a dark blue, almost black. Truthfully, I didn't mind it. The look made me feel a little gothy, which isn't seen a lot on the football field. I'd take any chance to distract the other team, but I didn't want to let her win so easily.

"Are you done torturing me?"

She grinned. "Never."

Another tendril of her wrapped around my heart. "Why don't you come over *here* and torture me then."

Her eyes heated, and she set the nail polish down with a definitive snap. "Spread your arms along the back of the couch and rest your hands palms down."

I followed her orders. "I'm not feeling too tortured."

She moved from her position at the coffee table to kneel between my legs. "Keep your arms there. We don't want to smudge your polish."

My pulse took off as if I were doing sprinting drills. "We definitely don't. Nothing more embarrassing in the locker room than smudged polish."

Vi frowned. "If it'll be in the way, we can take it off."

"Nah, I like it. Reminds me of you." I leaned forward to nuzzle her neck, careful to keep my fingers away from everything.

She huffed, a breathless little sound that hit me right in the chest. "Oh good. We can't have you thinking about anything else while you're playing a game where you could get flattened by someone twice your size."

I chuckled. "Not quite twice my size, but it's nice to know you worry about me. At least if I'm not drafted, I won't have to deal with being flattened."

Vi leaned away and framed my face with her hands. My laughter faded at the intensity in her eyes. "You're going to be amazing in the pros. If you want this career, nothing is going to stop you."

The words anchored near my heart. I held her gaze and tilted my head to kiss her palm. For the first time, I wanted more than the career and the freedom that came with it. Vi was still holding part of herself back, but I was determined to change that. I wanted all of her.

And she was right—nothing would stop me.

———

I WALKED into Derrick's apartment, then nearly walked out again. The place was clean to the point of sparkling. He shared the three-bedroom with Noah and Parker, which meant it regularly smelled like ass and burnt toast. It *never* sparkled.

There were throw pillows on the couch.

Parker's speed bag was gone from the living room, and Noah's collection of game systems had been neatly organized in their cheap tv stand. If not for the rainbow llama poster I'd given them as a housewarming joke, I might have thought I was in the wrong place.

I stood just inside the door gaping as Parker walked into the living room and raised a brow.

"What the fuck, man?" I gestured at the living room, and Parker shrugged.

"D made us clean."

"When?"

"He's been on our asses about it all semester, but like this? Since he and Nadia got serious."

I moved into the room and took a deep breath. It wasn't that I missed the smell, but how had I not noticed earlier? "Is he around?"

Parker shook his head. "He left a while ago for the community center. Something about Nadia needing him for a class."

I shared a look with Parker. We both knew what happened to players that ended up in serious relationships —they disappeared. Football required an insane amount of time and dedication, so much that most of us took our classes in the summer during the off season. Girlfriends tended to demand what little time remained, which left nothing for the rest of us.

I'd previously solved that problem by never dating anyone seriously. Parker solved it by never dating.

Nadia made Derrick happy, but I wondered what would happen when he went pro. He swore she was coming with him, but asking her to pack up her life and move to an as yet undisclosed location seemed crazy. I had no doubt he'd get drafted somewhere, but five years down the line, would Nadia still be willing to start over again if he got traded?

Would Vi?

Parker tilted his head at me. "Why do you look like Mac just made cauliflower surprise for dinner again?"

"D's missing out on the glory days of his last year. I hope the pillows are worth it." Even as I said it, the words felt wrong in my mouth. The last few months had been the best of my life. The glory days before that paled in comparison.

He threw one of the pillows at me. "You're one to talk. We haven't seen you much since you hooked up with Vi. I'll bet your apartment is cleaner than this one."

I opened my mouth to argue with him, then looked around again. My apartment had changed a lot more drastically, but Vi lived with me. She deserved the chance to make it hers too.

These throw pillows inexplicably pissed me off.

Yes, I spent all my free time with Vi, but that was my choice. She didn't have any expectations or demands. To be fair, neither did Nadia as far as I knew. I glared at the pillow by my feet and admitted my foul mood wasn't about the changes in décor.

This was about fear.

I sighed in disgust and flipped the pillow back at Parker with my foot. He crossed his arms, but his face remained carefully blank. Parker cleaned up at poker night.

"You can talk to me."

His confident tone made me take a second look at him too. We'd been friends since he joined the team two years ago, but I'd always sort of seen him as a younger brother type. Like Mac and Noah. But this was his last year as a backup. Derrick was graduating and going pro, opening up the quarterback spot for Parker.

Intellectually, I knew the shift was coming, but for the first time, I saw the potential in Parker to lead. Good. The team would need him to step up. Especially since I wouldn't be here to bridge the gap. Dammit. Vi was right. I needed to tell them.

I nodded at the couch. "I can't in good conscience sit there with matching home goods. I'd lose all respect for myself."

He rolled his eyes, then tossed the offending cushions on the floor before sitting down. "Is something actually bothering you or are you just here to harass D?"

"I'm harassing *you* right now."

Parker shifted his weight. "I'm going back to bed."

I sat down next to him before he could make good on his threat. "Since when am I not allowed to stop by randomly and annoy whoever is home? Isn't that why you guys gave me a key?"

His head dropped back to rest on the couch. "Sometimes I hate you."

"I know. It's my superpower."

We sat in silence for a beat, Parker staring at the ceiling while I fought the urge to run back to Vi.

I leaned forward to rest my arms on my knees and just blurted it out. "I'm declaring for the draft."

Parker didn't react, at least not outwardly. I snuck a glance at him, and a tiny smile crossed his face when he noticed me looking.

"Is that all?"

I narrowed my eyes at him. "I expected a little more of a reaction, to be honest."

"That's because you're a closet drama queen. I was almost certain you'd be heading out with D."

"You couldn't possibly know that when I didn't."

He finally faced me with a look that clearly stated I was stupid. "Yes, I could. You've been haunting practice all season like you're in mourning."

I snorted. "Pretty sure the one doing the haunting isn't also the one doing the mourning."

"And you're an expert on ghosts?"

"As much as you are."

He grunted. "That's probably fair, but it doesn't change my point."

"Why didn't you say anything?"

"It wasn't my place. I figured you'd tell us when you were ready... or we'd find out at the Championship."

I heaved out a sigh. The NFL requirements meant I'd need to ask for special permission by the National Championship, and if they approved it, I'd have to give up my final year of eligibility to enter the draft instead. It was a huge risk.

My parents would yank my funding immediately. Tuition and the apartment would be taken care of until school got out in June, but I'd be on my own for other living expenses. I definitely wouldn't get another year at TU, not that I'd need it if I wasn't playing football.

I'd be banking on a team drafting me in April.

Parker clapped me on the back and offered me a smile. "I don't know what was holding you back, but you have my full support. I'd love to have you with us next year to make my throws look good, but any team would be lucky to have you."

His unwavering faith eased the knot in my chest. "Thanks, man."

"Besides, I'll still have Mac."

I shoved him sideways with a laugh. "Yeah, if you can get

him away from the cheerleaders long enough to catch a pass."

Parker laughed, and I hit him in the face with one of the pillows. Then I rubbed the soft material again. Vi would probably like these, actually. They'd be awesome for the next time she lost at Rock Paper Scissors.

I held the pillow up. "Where did Nadia get these?"

24

Vi

"Why are you fidgeting so much?" Soren glanced at me as he navigated the truck into the outrageous garage at his parents' house. I checked my make-up one last time then flipped the visor up. "Because I haven't made the best impression on your parents, and now I'll be eating fancy Thanksgiving breakfast at your freaking mansion."

He turned off the car, and we both got out in a cavernous building that fit perfectly with the rest of their estate. Gorgeous and showy at the same time. Interior lights came on as I walked around the truck to where Soren waited by the open door. The place had to have at least twelve-foot ceilings, trimmed with actual crown molding. I almost expected to hear chamber music playing.

A line of shiny vehicles stretched away from us, and I shook my head. "Why would you possibly need this many cars at once?"

"Don't deflect. Tell me what's going on in that beautiful head of yours."

The compliment hit me sideways, like they always did.

I'd brushed them off until the night I'd painted his nails and he'd spun my vision of the future into something unrecognizable.

I will always want you. Pretty words, but words were easy and 'always' was a lie. No one could guarantee always.

Soren had a way of making me feel like his version of 'always' could happen. At the very least, I was willing to give it a shot until everything crashed and burned. Which meant this family breakfast was a whole hell of a lot scarier than the other events I'd attended with his parents and friends.

I sighed and focused on the expanse of garden that neatly hid the lower-level windows of the house. "Before, it didn't matter what your parents thought of me. I was temporary. If I screwed everything up, you wouldn't be any worse off than you were already. Now..." I groaned and started to exit the garage. "Now, I guess I want them to like me. My mother's insidious influence, taking root at last."

He pulled me to a stop and wrapped his arms around me. "Their opinion matters even less now. I'm declaring for the draft, so their threats about next year are in vain. I don't need you to convince them of anything, and I sure as hell don't give a fuck about their opinion of who I choose to be with."

I dropped my forehead to his chest and my voice came out muffled. "I know, okay. I know I'm acting like an idiot, but I've never dressed up for a holiday before."

"I have fond memories of the dress you wore to Halloween."

His teasing tone coaxed a smile out of me. "That's not what I mean, and you know it."

Soren leaned back a little and tilted his head at me. "What do you normally do for Thanksgiving?"

The question treaded dangerously close to an area of my

life I didn't want to talk about—my family. I'd already cried all over him about my mom, but my relationship with the rest of my family wasn't something I was proud of.

My brothers didn't understand that I needed space after Mom died, and the more they held on, the more I pushed them away. I never voluntarily went home, but my brothers being who they were still dragged my ass back from time to time. I hadn't been there for a holiday since high school though.

Soren waited patiently for me to stop freaking out about answering his question to actually answer his question.

I gave a half-hearted shrug. "I watch the parade in my pajamas, gorge myself on various cheeses during the obligatory football games, then regret eating whatever Eva brings back from her family."

The look of horror on his face would have been funny if it hadn't been genuine. "You spend Thanksgiving by yourself eating?"

"Yes? Isn't that how most of the country celebrates? I'll bet not many of them do a fancy dress-up breakfast." The shame from my family situation was quickly taking second place to my apparently unacceptable holiday traditions.

A cold breeze hit my back and I shivered. Soren shook his head and ushered me toward the house.

"I'm going to show you a real Thanksgiving after this. We can even stop and get some cheese for you to gorge."

I squeezed his hand. "Is that some kind of code for kinky sex? Because if so, I'm in."

He chuckled and sent me a speculative look. "It wasn't, but now I'm curious."

My nerves officially fled at the ridiculous image of Soren seductively holding a wedge of brie. Honestly, Soren could make anything look seductive.

Breakfast wasn't as bad as I'd feared it would be. Soren's aunt and uncle couldn't make it, but Harper was there, looking like a boss in stilettos and a designer suit. The five of us milled around in the parlor, making mostly awkward small talk, until Isak called us to the table. The whole experience felt surreal in that I wasn't sure I was living it or starring in an old sitcom.

For the most part, his family treated me like the set piece I'd been pretending to be. Obligatory girlfriend, check. I caught Harper staring at me a few times like she couldn't figure me out, but never overtly. No one mentioned the scene at Chateau whatever.

I could have done without the stilted conversation, but the food was fantastic. Soren sent me an amused glance when I quietly licked my spoon after finishing off my bread pudding in record time. He nudged his bowl closer to me, and I didn't waste a second switching it with my empty one.

His hand found mine under the table, and the steady warmth made my throat tight for a moment.

Soren leaned closer to brush his lips across my temple, then straightened and faced his parents. I frowned at his stance, like he was preparing for battle. Up until that point, he'd been the relaxed one between us, keeping me comfortable.

"Are you coming to my game this weekend?"

His parents shared a silent exchange, then his mom shook her head. "We promised the Millers we'd have brunch with them. Besides, you know we don't enjoy watching football."

Their answer didn't really surprise me, but I hurt for him.

This weekend marked Soren's last regular game of the season. The team was sitting on one loss with an easily beatable opponent, meaning they were pretty much locked in for the semi-final bowl games. I was unspeakably proud of him for pushing through and playing his best season even with all the crap happening on this side of his life.

Soren carefully set his napkin on the table next to his empty plate. "This might be your last chance to see me play at TU."

His mom's eyes lit up. "Does that mean you're finally going to stop messing around with football and focus on finishing your degree?" Her gaze jumped to me then back.

I saw the moment he gave up the last bit of his hope. Soren shook his head and let out a dry laugh. "No. That's not what it means."

"But then why—"

"I'm declaring for the NFL draft instead of finishing my last year."

When I'd encouraged him to tell his friends about his decision, it never occurred to me he'd tell his parents too. Judging by his grip on my hand, it hadn't occurred to him either. Harper's eyes got big, but she didn't move. His dad's brows winged up, and he sat back in his chair.

Silence reigned for a solid ten seconds, and I could hear the uneven rhythm of my breathing. Soren faced his parents, chin high, shoulders tense as he waited for the inevitable backlash. His mom wiped her mouth with her napkin, folded it neatly next to her, and placed both hands in her lap before she looked his way again.

"Is this *her* doing?"

I jerked back like I'd been slapped. Somehow, despite my trepidation earlier, I hadn't expected to be directly blamed.

Soren's jaw ticked. "No. This is my doing. I'd planned to wait until next year, but I'm ready."

His mom's mouth narrowed to a thin line of displeasure. "I won't let you throw your future away for a capricious dream."

"You don't have a say in the matter. *This* is my future, and nothing is going to stop me."

I smiled at the echo of the words I'd given him and squeezed his hand.

"I'd like you to support this decision, but I recognize that you need time to process everything." He stood and drew me up next to him. "Thank you for the meal, and for all the advantages you've given me. You know where to find us when you're ready."

No one said anything as we left.

Soren led me through two rooms and down a hallway, but I had no idea where we were in relation to the door. I kept pace with him while sneaking glances at his impassive expression.

"Are you okay?"

He slowed, and his face softened. "I'm okay. This was always going to happen, but I'm glad it's out in the open now. I'm tired of hiding things."

A knot formed in my stomach under all the bread pudding I regretted eating. The notes weighed on me, but I didn't want him to overreact, especially now when he was dealing with his parents being complete tools.

Instead, I focused on the bright spot of the meal. "I'm proud of you."

He brought my hand up to his mouth for a kiss. "I'm proud of me too, and I wouldn't have done that without you. I've never had anyone fight for me. Derrick and the others would try if I let them, but by the time we met, I was so used to being on my own that I didn't know how to let them in." He flashed me a quick smile. "You didn't give me a choice."

"I seem to remember *you* were the one who refused to take me home."

"Best decision I've ever made."

The knot dissolved in a warm rush that started in my chest and spread out, filling my whole body. I'd thought broody, sarcastic Soren was hard to resist, but this version of him—the one who looked at me like I was the only thing in the world he wanted—brought all my defenses crashing down.

How was I supposed to protect myself when all I wanted to do was curl up in his lap for the next few forevers?

We made it to the garage before Harper caught up with us. Her heels clicked on the concrete floor, and Soren tensed. I turned and stood between them. He'd been through enough at the hands of his family today.

"What do you want?" I asked.

She stopped at the door, and her eyes flicked past me. Whatever she saw there made her shoulders slump.

Her gaze landed on me again. "I'm sorry for them. They're stubborn and convinced their way is the only way."

I raised an eyebrow in response. "Noted. Now you can run back in there with your guilt assuaged."

Her mouth tilted up in amusement for a second. "I can see why he likes you. Soren, can I talk to you alone?"

Soren tried to move past me, but I sidestepped to block his way. "No, you may not speak to him alone. You can speak to me or you can go on your merry way with your fantastic shoes."

A quiet rumble behind me sounded suspiciously like laughter, but Soren didn't contradict me.

Harper sighed. "Aunt Dena is in there on the phone with the company that owns your apartment complex. She's trying to break the lease immediately, and she'll probably succeed."

I spun around to Soren, who didn't look nearly as surprised as he should. "What the actual hell is wrong with your family?"

He shook his head. "They're trying to control me the best way they know how—with money. I was prepared for this when I made my decision about the draft, but admittedly, I wasn't expecting them to break the lease."

Harper moved closer while I was distracted. "They'll still be required to give you thirty days to move out, but if I were you, I'd move your money immediately. The bank will be her next call."

I narrowed my eyes at her, and Soren slid an arm around my waist before I could take out some of my anger on his perfect cousin.

"Thanks for the warning, Harper," he said.

She nodded, looking significantly more comfortable than she'd been at breakfast. "I'll make some calls of my own, see if I can get you a little longer. I imagine you won't be back here any time soon, so I wanted to tell you this while I could say it in person." She squared her shoulders and raised her chin.

"Your parents are wrong. I've been watching you play football since we were kids, and you belong on that field. I've been... unhappy with the situation here because you had what I wanted—the future of the company—and I thought you'd take it for granted. I was wrong too.

Her eyes shifted to me. "Take care of him."

"I plan to," I said softly.

Soren leaned over to kiss her cheek. "Thank you, Harper. Really. I hope you find your place somewhere that treats you with the respect you deserve."

She smiled, a real, big smile, then walked out of the garage. I shook my head at the absolute craziness of the exchange. Yeah, my version of celebrating Thanksgiving was kind of pathetic, but after this meal, I thought maybe I had the right idea. None of this was normal, and I hoped holidays would never be this eventful again.

25

Vi

Soren multitasked on the way back to TU. He called his accountant to move the money he'd socked away to a new bank, then he did the same with two other accounts I was pretty sure he wasn't supposed to have access to. Harper left a message at one point saying she'd gotten the complex to extend the lease to sixty days, but that was it.

I tried to bring up the impending problem of not having an apartment, but he shook his head.

"We can't do anything about it at the moment, so for the rest of the day, we're going to enjoy Friendsgiving at D's place. Tomorrow will be soon enough."

I wanted to argue that I'd already been through emergency apartment hunting, and it did *not* go well, but the lines around his mouth made me hold my tongue. Instead, I rested my head on his shoulder and challenged him to a bad joke competition, which I promptly forfeited by falling asleep.

Soren woke me up as we pulled into an unfamiliar apartment parking lot. I stretched and wrinkled my nose at the 'classy' dress I'd stressed so much about that morning.

"Do we have time to go home so I can change?"

He glanced my way and laughed. "Are you uncomfortable?"

I pouted because the dress was a very forgiving jersey material and I'd worn leggings underneath it. The strappy shoes I'd chosen to fancy up the outfit were abandoned on the floorboards.

"No, I'm basically wearing secret pajamas, but my shoes aren't made for lounging with friends."

He parked the truck and turned to face me. "I brought those flip-flops you wear everywhere. They're tucked behind your seat."

I would *not* tear up over shoes, at least not ratty old flip flops. When the telltale burn started behind my eyes, I hid my face against the seat as I dug the shoes out. What a pair we were. No one fought for him, and I hadn't let anyone take care of me—not since Mom died.

It was certainly easier to do everything myself, but Soren made me want more. His gaze lingered on my face as I straightened, and I hoped I didn't look like I was about to cry. Stupid holidays were making me emotional.

"Come on, Jeeves. You still have to prove to me why socializing is better than lazing around the apartment naked."

His brows shot up. "This is the first I've heard of the naked part."

I shrugged. "I thought it was implied."

"I've changed my mind."

"Too late," I sang as I got out of the truck.

Despite my years of friendship with Eva, I'd never been in Derrick's apartment. I expected a place one step up from a locker room considering three college football players lived there, but when Soren opened the door for me, I was surprised to find a mostly normal living space.

They had the requisite massive entertainment center with two monster couches, but these guys weren't exactly small. Eva waved at me from the lone recliner that was human-sized. She looked like she belonged there, and I suspected they'd gotten it just for her. None of them would fit in it comfortably.

I wiggled my fingers at her and sniffed the air. "Why does it smell like a Hobby Lobby in here?"

"That would be my doing." Nadia came around the corner from what I assumed was the kitchen, drying her hands on a towel. "It's the twenty-first century—they can be jocks *and* live in a nice apartment at the same time."

Behind her, a candle was burning on the breakfast bar, but I didn't think that little flame would be powerful enough to counteract the stink of three hardcore athletes. I'd know. I'd been around the type all my life.

Eva perked up in her chair, and I realized the parade was rolling along across the gigantic screen. A group of cheer-leaders had taken the makeshift stage to throw each other in the air.

I nodded at the TV. "How did you get them to pick the parade over the football game?"

Nadia laughed. "That was all Eva."

She didn't take her eyes off the screen. "I missed the first half because I slept in. I promised we'd switch it over as soon as we got to the Snoopy balloon."

Soren left my side to snag the remote from the table next to Eva. "I wasn't here for that promise."

Eva glared at him and tried to snatch it back, but Soren held it well out of her reach, taunting her.

He smirked at her growl. "I have a key, so that makes me an honorary roommate—"

"I have a key too, asshat."

Soren ignored her interruption and handed the remote to me. "As a roommate, I vote that Vi gets to decide what we watch since this is her first Friendsgiving with us."

Eva snorted but settled back into the chair.

I took the remote and handed it back to Eva. "I think the current agreement should stand. Parade then football."

He inclined his head. "I'm not going to say no to football. Want something to drink?"

"Sure. What are my choices?" My stomach was feeling a lot better after the drive and the nap, but I didn't want anything heavy after all that bread pudding.

"Let's find out." Soren grabbed my hand and walked backward to lead me into the kitchen. He smiled, looking so pleased with himself that I knew he was up to something.

We rounded the breakfast bar, and I stopped abruptly. "What on earth is that?"

Soren's grin stretched wide. "I called D, and he sent Mac to the store."

The kitchen counter was loaded down with various cheeses, crackers, and weirdly enough, a cantaloupe. Most of the food was still in the packaging, but someone had taken the time to cut the cantaloupe in half.

My hand came to my mouth. Could I fall in love with someone over cheese? My chest got tight again, and I couldn't tell if it was fear of how strongly this surprise had affected me or amazement that he'd put this together in the first place.

Soren wrapped his arms around me from behind, oblivious to my inner scrambling.

I leaned against him. "How did you do all this? Why?"

His lips brushed against my temple. "Before breakfast, when you were discussing the pros and cons of higher reps versus more weight with Harper. I don't know how you got her to talk, let alone about strength training, but I used your distraction to my advantage. And I did it because I wanted to make you smile."

The fear waned, and a much scarier emotion built in my chest until I thought it would burst out with my next breath. Soren had done this for me. The broody, tatted, sarcastic football player had orchestrated a cheese buyout of the local grocery store because it would make me smile.

Tears threatened for the second time in an hour, so I turned and pressed my face into Soren's shoulder until I could get a handle on my jumbled emotions. After a deep breath, I pulled away and dragged him out of the kitchen where I'd be way less likely to say something stupid in front of the others.

They'd switched to the football game, and Eva didn't even glance up when we re-entered the room. Derrick stood by the door with his arms around Nadia, who couldn't stop giggling, but the other guys were notably absent.

"Where's Mac? I want to thank him."

Eva waved toward the other side of the apartment. "He's scheming with Parker and Noah. They'll be out in a minute."

Nadia pushed Derrick's face away and addressed me. "I'm glad you like the surprise. We wanted you to feel comfortable here."

Mac piped up from the hallway. "With that much cheese, no one's going to feel comfortable." Parker and Noah followed him into the living room and took seats on the couch.

Eva rolled her eyes and disappeared into the kitchen.

The whole scene reminded me strongly of my life before, when my family spent time together without regrets. For once, I didn't want to bury myself in guilt and anger. I wanted to be happy and enjoy the day with Soren and his friends—*my* friends.

A cheer went up from the couch, and I felt Soren shift to glance at the screen. I thought the game had taken his attention, but he tilted his head down to put his mouth against my ear.

"Can we still do the naked lounging later?"

I laughed and dragged him down to the empty couch with me. "Depends on how much I eat in the next few hours. I make no promises that I'll be conscious later."

Soren circled my waist and pulled me against his side. "I'll be sure to keep you supplied in coffee."

I leaned over to give him a soft kiss and ran the tip of my nose against his. His hand lifted to my hair, holding me gently in place.

"Thank you," I whispered.

"Anytime, Vi."

A small pillow hit Soren in the back of the head, and he turned to glare at the guys on the other couch. Mac and Noah were engrossed in the action on the screen, but Parker was grinning at us. He raised a brow in a silent message that clearly wasn't for me.

Soren shook his head and tossed the pillow back, narrowly missing Nadia as she and Derrick scooted past to join us on the couch. I briefly wondered about the exchange, but a deluge of pillows being flung at us wiped it from my mind.

26

Vi

I was starting to believe that going to get coffee with Eva caused the weather to magically turn frosty. Granted, it was December in north Texas—we got our fair share of snow—but usually not until after Christmas.

For the second time that semester, I was waiting in Wildcat Coffee for Eva to arrive. Thick grey clouds were spitting freezing rain on all the unsuspecting pedestrians, and I was trying not to panic cry.

After my training session that morning, my boss had pulled me aside and told me that they were cancelling all my dance fitness classes. She gave me some crap story about budget cuts, but I noticed after that Anne-Marie's circuit classes were still on the schedule.

I'd called Soren first, before I remembered that he was at practice. TU had won their last game, catapulting them officially into the playoffs. Soren's parents had declined to come. They'd also declined to answer any messages or offer congratulations.

Every time I thought about how much that must hurt him, I wanted to drive straight over to their damn mansion and set it on fire. Soren assured me arson wasn't necessary, but I remained unconvinced.

Eva was my second call. I didn't tell her the specifics, only that I'd had a hard morning, and she wasted no time in ordering me to meet her at this insane excuse for a coffee shop. As usual, she bounded in with limitless energy and a vicious gleam in her eye. She spotted me right away and pointed at the counter with a raised brow.

I nodded and settled in to watch the show. Eva sauntered up to the front, but her flirty face did nothing for the grumpy guy taking the orders. He frowned down at the tablet as she talked to him, and nothing changed when he glanced up at her to respond.

Nothing changed with *him*. Eva's posture shifted subtly as she straightened and leaned away from the counter. I could practically hear her seething, and I'd bet next semester's tuition that he'd charged her for the extra shot she requested.

The guy seemed new and not at all the type to be working at a coffee shop. Too much lean muscle and not enough school spirit. He'd pushed the long sleeves of his thermal up to reveal tattoos cascading down his forearms. His dark hair fell into his face, and even with the scowl, he had nice features.

A couple of months ago, I might have joined her at the counter to get a better look at the grumpy coffee slinger, but all I could think now was that he wasn't tall enough or broad enough or Soren enough for my taste.

Eva left the counter with two coffees and a grimace. She slid into the booth opposite me and set my coffee down a little more violently than usual.

"What a dick," she muttered as she took a swig.

I clasped my warm cup in both hands and snuck a

glance at the counter again. Coffee guy leaned against the wall next to him with his arms crossed, and he was staring in our direction. Interesting.

"So..." I took a tiny sip. "He's cute."

Eva turned her glare on me. "Are we here to ogle the help or talk about your very out-of-the-ordinary call?"

"Can't we do both? Stephen would be very disappointed in you."

She tipped her cup at me. "Don't you bring Stephen into this. You know he keeps threatening to come up here if I don't send him regular status updates. Now talk."

As grateful as I was for a distraction from my shitty morning, I *did* need to talk about it. Not in the least because I'd have to tell all the cheerleaders before they showed up to a class that didn't exist anymore. Eva could take care of that for me.

"The gym told me today my classes were being cancelled, effective immediately."

Her shoulders slumped. "But why? Everyone loves your classes."

I shrugged one shoulder. "I don't know. It sucks, but at least they didn't straight out fire me. I can still do personal training, but I've had a lot of clients cancel on me lately. I'm starting to think there's something going on behind the scenes."

"Like what?"

Colt came to mind immediately, but I had a lot of trouble believing he had that kind of power. The eviction would have been easy thanks to the draconian lease the school used, but my job was technically a work-study effort governed by several departments. Maybe that's why they didn't fire me outright.

As if thinking his name summoned him, Colt

approached our table, though I hadn't seen him come in. "Well, if it isn't Little Miss Anger Management and her friend, Cheerleader Barbie." He angled himself to block me in on my side of the booth.

I dropped my head back with a deep sigh. Colt didn't scare me—I've been training with guys bigger than him for most of my life—but Soren would lose his shit if I came home with bruises. I didn't want him to miss any chances to play with his team because this asshole didn't recognize a threat when he saw one.

Eva sat up and pulled her drink closer, opting for a bored expression. "Colt. Looking for a new victim to harass?"

Colt ignored her and focused on me, but his usual cocky smirk was absent. "You're lucky I didn't miss any practice because of you."

"Or what? You'd send me threatening notes like a coward?"

His brows drew together. "What the fuck are you talking about? Look, I just wanted to apologize for scaring you at the party. I was wasted, and I didn't know you were fucking Soren."

I blinked at the unexpected words. "What?"

He gritted his teeth, and I got the distinct impression this whole thing wasn't his idea. "Coach said I need to mend fences or some bullshit with Soren. I saw you in here and figured that was my best bet since he won't talk to me. Tell him to cut out the attitude so Coach gets off my ass."

My mouth hung open for a second. "No. Apology not accepted. You deserve every bit of his attitude. Next time, listen when a girl says to let her go."

He shook his head. "Crazy bitch."

I gave him my sweetest smile. "Always a pleasure, Colt."

Coffee guy called his name, so he grabbed his crotch, mumbled something about pleasure, then walked back to the counter for his drink. He left without a backward glance. I frowned after him. The interaction felt off, like we'd been speaking two different languages.

Or talking about two different events.

Eva didn't seem to have the same confusion. "That asshole is going to get arrested someday."

"How's Lizzy?"

"She's fine. The only thing she remembers from that night is puking out the window of Mac's car."

"I'll bet he loved that."

Eva shuddered. "It was a night, that's for sure." She sent me a sly look. "What was that about threatening notes?"

I cursed under my breath. "You can't tell anyone." As we finished our coffees, I told her about the notes, but kept my new suspicions to myself.

Her brows winged up. "Is this related to you losing your classes?"

"I considered it, but it seems really far-fetched."

Eva grabbed my wrist. "You can't just dismiss this."

"I can handle it myself."

"Have you at least told Soren?"

Her face darkened when I didn't answer.

"Let me get this straight. Since the night of the Kappa party, you've been getting stalked through creepy notes and possible harassment. You're convinced it's Colt—as you should be because you're not an idiot—and instead of telling your friends or going to the police, you've hidden it in a drawer and hoped it would go away on its own?"

I pulled my arm away. "The school was within their rights to evict me, and I have no proof Colt was involved in that. The notes are barely creepy. They've never escalated—"

"Moving from your workplace to your living place is escalation," Eva interrupted.

"Fine. They've never escalated beyond notes, and it didn't start at the Kappa party. It started after I moved in with Soren."

Eva dug her hands through her hair. "I retract my previous statement about you not being an idiot."

"Today was the first time Colt has approached me since that day at lunch. He's had plenty of opportunity to do something stupid, and he's hidden behind vaguely threatening anonymous messages warning me not to talk. Besides, Soren and I have some other stuff to deal with that's a much higher priority."

Her eyes widened. "Are you pregnant?"

Shock hit me fast and hard. "What? No. Not that." I must have looked horrified because Eva let out a relieved breath.

"Thank god. I'm too young to be an auntie."

I snorted. "Could you imagine Jackson's face if I told him he was going to be an uncle?"

She laughed, but calculation lit her eyes. "Yeah, Jackson would break every speed limit on his way here to beat Soren into a sad husk of a man."

"No. Absolutely not."

Eva tried to look innocent, but she sucked at it. "What? I'm not doing anything."

I pointed a finger in her face. "You *will not* call my brothers here on false pretenses because you're hoping to do unspeakable things to Jackson."

She took a sip of her drink, then mumbled, "They're only unspeakable to you. Every other female in the vicinity is on my side here."

"No. Are you ready to go? I have a couple of assignments to finish up before Soren picks me up at the gym."

"Yeah. Hypothetically speaking, what would it take to convince you to video call your brother while we walk back?"

I smiled at her relentless push to get a glimpse of Jackson. Eva threw her paper cup away on the way out, and I noticed coffee guy's gaze follow her into the cold. She didn't add any extra sway to her hips, so I doubted she noticed—or she did and chose blatant disregard. With Eva, it could go either way.

At least the topic of my brother distracted her from Colt's unfortunate appearance. Unlike the last time, he wasn't waiting outside. Had he been waiting for us last time, or had I seen a pattern where there wasn't one? For the first time, I wondered if my assumption the last few months had been based on a skewed version of events.

But it didn't make sense for anyone else to send the notes. Who would go to that much trouble to silence *me* when a room full of partygoers had seen the altercation?

27

Soren

The reality of preparing for playoffs meant Vi and I spent very little time together. Saturday was my only real day off, besides the workout that D insisted on. I'd been tempted to stay in our warm bed, snuggled next to Vi, but the rest of the team was depending on us to be leaders. I needed to show up for them.

By the time I got home, Vi was up and nursing a coffee on the couch. She had a class at noon, but she wasn't dressed for work like usual. I dropped my gym bag inside the door and sank down next to her.

"You feeling okay?" I laid my hand against her forehead, but I wasn't sure what I was expecting. I'd never been the nursemaid type, so I had no idea what a fever would feel like.

She didn't look sick, but Vi didn't stray from her routine either. Instead of answering, she dropped her head onto my shoulder and closed her eyes. I'd never seen her look so small. Vi was a force, and she unapologetically took up space.

I pulled her into my lap, coffee and all. She tucked herself against me, and no matter how badly I wanted to ask again, I kept my mouth shut.

Instead, I stroked her hair, her back, whatever I could reach without jostling her. Slowly, Vi relaxed. We sat that way for a while, our arms around each other while she worked through whatever was bothering her. Eventually, she sighed and rubbed her face against my shirt.

"You're stinky," she muttered into my chest.

I chuckled. "That's a championship football team you smell."

A tiny smile crossed her face. "Better get used to it then, I guess."

My cock stirred as she wiggled on my lap. "You want to join me in the shower?"

She leaned forward to set her coffee on the table, then swung her leg around to straddle my hips. "Yes. Yes, I do."

I'd intended to go slow and let her set the pace, but Vi didn't want slow. She reached for me as soon as we were naked and pulled me into the shower. I hissed at the blast of lukewarm water, but Vi's hand on my cock offered an excellent distraction.

The water quickly began to steam, so I spun us to put Vi under the warm spray as our hands roamed. This wasn't our first shower together, but today felt different than the rest. There was a frantic undertone to her movements, like she wanted everything all at once. I was happy to oblige.

Her head tilted, and I licked droplets off her neck. "Spread your legs for me, beautiful."

I followed the water flowing down her curves in gleaming rivers with my tongue until I was kneeling in front of her. Vi moaned my name and widened her stance. I loved the taste of her, the sighs, the way her fingers tangled in my hair as she held my mouth exactly where she wanted it.

She shifted, and I got doused, but I didn't stop. If I drowned, I drowned.

In no time, I had her clenching around my fingers as she whimpered her release. I kissed her stomach on the way up, and Vi opened her eyes to give me a big grin.

"If football doesn't work out, you could probably get by on your oral skills alone."

I pushed my wet hair out of my face and backed her against the tile. "Those skills are only for you."

She curled her hand around my neck and pulled me down to her mouth. "Good."

I boosted her up and pinned her to the wall as I kissed the hell out of her. Vi wrapped her legs around my hips, and our bodies slid against each other. I swept my tongue in her mouth, a preview of what I planned to do with the rest of her.

She gripped my shoulders and eased herself up and down my shaft, shuddering every time I hit her clit. I tore myself from her mouth and thrust forward just a little, making her gasp.

My breath came in pants as we fell into a familiar rhythm. "We need to move this to the bedroom. If I'm not inside you in the next thirty seconds, I might actually die."

Her legs tightened around me. "We're both clean, and I have an IUD."

I dropped my forehead to hers, acutely aware of what she was suggesting. "Are you sure, Vi?"

"I want you with nothing between us."

Vi lifted herself again, this time lowering herself onto my cock. I cursed at the slick glide as she rolled her hips. Her back arched, and I sucked a tight, little nipple into my mouth. My fingers dug into her ass cheeks as she moaned and rode me slow and steady.

"Fuck yes, baby," I whispered against the skin of her neck.

Our movements became more and more desperate until she squeezed me tight with her second orgasm. Her heels dug into my ass, and I took over, pounding into her as I chased my own release.

After, she kissed me, soft and sweet. "You make everything worth it."

Her words etched themselves onto my heart, shifting and growing until I was full to bursting with the need to prove how much she meant to me—how much I loved her. I held her, my lips against hers, as the feeling crashed over me.

I knew Vi. She was willing to commit to me, to live with me, fuck me, but love was scary for her. I didn't want to give her another reason to push me away, so I held tight until the urge subsided enough that I wouldn't blurt my feelings out right there in the shower.

The water stayed hot long enough for us to get clean, and after a wrestling match for the loofah, Vi went back to teasing me like she usually did.

"You should come home without showering more often."

I raised a brow. "Oh yeah?"

She gestured at herself, wet and naked as she stepped onto the bathmat, and I couldn't help the appreciative hum.

"You're right. No more showering unless you're involved."

Vi laughed and tossed a towel at me. "That's going to be awkward after you're drafted."

I watched her as I dried off. She'd meant the comment

as a joke, but I planned for her to be there after the draft. Maybe not in the locker room, but in my life, in our home, wherever that ended up being.

Playing in the NFL was notoriously transitory, since we didn't have control over what the team decided to do with our contracts. Assuming I made it past all the camps and tests onto the roster.

Would Vi be willing to follow me from place to place for my dream? I sure as hell hoped so, since I couldn't see myself doing it without her. We'd need to have that conversation sooner rather than later, but nerves held me back. The draft wasn't for four months, and she wouldn't graduate for six.

Plenty of time to convince her we were worth the risk.

For today, I focused on a more immediate problem. "Are you going to tell me what this morning was all about?"

She hung her towel on the rod and went into the bedroom to start pulling on clothes. "The gym cancelled all my classes."

I stopped rubbing my hair to stare at her from the bathroom doorway. "They fired you?"

"Not technically. I'm still doing personal training, but the classes were half my income." Her indifferent tone didn't mesh with the way I'd found her on the couch.

"Is that what was bothering you?"

She started to nod, then grimaced and shook her head. "It was partly that, partly the apartment, and partly Colt."

Blood pounded in my head with the immediate urge to punch that asshole. "Are you okay? Did he do something?"

Vi glanced pointedly at my fisted hands. "First, you have to calm down."

"I am calm," I said through a clenched jaw.

She raised a brow, and I took a deep breath attempting

to let go of the violent mood. My anger had no place around Vi. I grabbed a random set of clothes out of the closet and pulled them on while I focused on happy thoughts that didn't involve flattening him with my truck. When I rejoined her in the bedroom, I'd purged most of the fury.

Vi sighed and cupped my face with her hands. "He didn't touch me. Eva and I were having coffee yesterday, and he stopped by to apologize."

Shock nearly knocked me back a step. "What?"

"That's what I said, but I don't think he meant it. He was acting on orders of your coach for some team-building purpose. Nothing else happened. He got his coffee and left. I wanted to clear that up first, so you didn't find out some other way. I handled it, and I'm fine. Moving on. My bigger concern is where we're going to live come January."

I covered her hands with mine and kissed her palm. "I don't care if we end up crammed onto Eva's couch as long as you're with me."

A bit of the shadow left her eyes, and she smiled. "Why Eva's and not Derrick's?"

I pulled her close to kiss her nose. "Because Parker would make my life a living hell if I moved in there. Like I told you before, Harper is looking for places that aren't susceptible to my parents' manipulations. She said she'd have some options by next week."

She leaned back to meet my eyes. "And you trust her?"

A knock interrupted me before I could tell her about my suspicion that Harper was keeping her own secrets, which put her at odds with my parents. I wasn't expecting anyone, but Vi didn't look surprised.

The knock came again, louder, and a flash of dread crossed Vi's face. She wriggled out of my hold to bolt for the living room. She beat me to the peephole and visibly paled at whatever she saw on the other side.

"Oh shit," she muttered.

I glanced at her, but she didn't elaborate. Instead, she stood back and winced as I opened the door.

28

Soren

Three lean, muscled guys stood outside with their tattooed arms crossed and scowls on their faces. Even if I hadn't seen Vi's reaction, the resemblance to her would have clued me in to their identities. All four of them shared the same dark eyes.

They zeroed in on me, and for the first time, I wondered if I was about to get my ass kicked. Vi leaned against my back and peered around my shoulder from the doorway. I shifted my weight to keep her behind me. If need be, I'd take on all three of them before I'd let them near her.

"Where's Ryder?" she asked.

The front guy turned his attention on Vi, and his fierce demeanor softened. "Someone had to watch the gym. He lost."

She snorted. "You mean you guys teamed up on him because he'd have stopped whatever stupid plan you have going here."

"That too." He nodded at me. "Is your bodyguard going to let us in?"

Vi sighed and tugged on my arm. "Might as well get this over with."

I narrowed my eyes at him as I let her pull me backward. "You look familiar."

"I get that a lot," he replied.

Vi snorted. "Yeah, because you were an MMA champion. They splashed your face all over the place until you retired. Soren Brehm, meet Jackson Malone, my oldest brother. Lurking behind him are Corey and Alex, the middle brothers."

They gave me a nod, and I returned the gesture. "How can we help you?"

Jackson gave me an inspection I wasn't sure I passed. "Why is my sister living here instead of in her own apartment?"

I raised a brow. "You can ask *her* that since she's perfectly capable of speaking for herself."

His mouth twitched like my answer amused him. "I'm asking you."

Vi pushed between us and smacked him in the chest. "Stop it. I got evicted, okay? Soren let me move in with him. Before you get any ideas, I'm not leaving. This apartment is leagues better than my last one, and Soren has a game this weekend. If I have to kick all your asses, I'll be there wearing his jersey."

Warmth spread through me at her belligerent statement. She was using me to mess with her brothers, but I didn't care as long as she told the world she was mine while she did it.

He sighed heavily. "Ryder was right. There'll be no living with him after this."

Her nose wrinkled. "Right about what?"

"That you'd refuse to leave this swanky place."

"How does Ryder know this place is swanky?"

"We updated him through the family text before we came up here."

Her mouth dropped open. "You have a family text, and I'm not on it?"

Jackson shrugged. "Neither is dad." Her other two brothers stayed wisely silent.

Vi's eyes narrowed, and I wrapped an arm around her waist, just in case she got violent. "See, this is why I never tell you anything. You don't treat me like part of the family."

The other man snorted. "Me? You're the one who ran halfway across Texas to go to school. You don't answer my calls. You don't come visit. Hell, I didn't even know you'd moved in with a guy until Eva sent me some bullshit message about getting more involved."

The animated woman in my arms suddenly became deathly still. "Eva did what?"

I understood her anger. Eva had a knack for finding trouble, but straight-up causing it wasn't usually her style.

Jackson missed the undertones and continued on without answering his sister's question. "The last time I got involved, you blocked my number."

Vi growled under her breath. "You fucking kidnapped me, you asshat. I almost failed two of my classes. My life is *better* without you in it."

I winced, debating if I should intervene, but her brother shrugged off Vi's comment.

"So you've told me. Doesn't mean I'm not going to show up when you need me."

"I *don't* need you. The situation is handled. Eva only got involved because she wanted a chance to stare at you."

I was on the verge of asking her about 'the situation' when Jackson jerked his head at the door.

"What about the guy we saw outside staring hard at your window? As soon as he realized we were heading here, he suddenly got very busy on his phone and walked off."

I frowned, imagining Colt lurking in my parking lot after his run-in with Vi last night. "What guy?"

Jackson looked me up and down. "Are you going to do something about it?"

Vi sidled up to the window so she could peek out the shades. "Okay, that's enough of the pissing contest. Can you describe the guy?"

"I can sketch him for you." He scanned the room, then scowled. "Where the hell do you keep your paper around here?"

She rolled her eyes. "You are such a luddite. At least you're finally using your art for something besides brooding."

A smile tried to break out, but I kept it contained. "I think we have a notebook in your bedside table." Jackson's disapproving gaze followed me into the bedroom, but he could stare all he wanted. As far as I was concerned, my relationship with Vi was none of his business.

I yanked the drawer open, then stared down at the contents.

"Soren, wait." I heard Vi rush to the doorway behind me, but she was too late. I'd already found her stash of notes.

I held up the crumpled one that had conveniently been sitting face up on top of the stack. "What the hell is this, Vi?" Her eyes shifted from the white paper to me, and I could see her reaching for an excuse. A ripping pain clawed through my chest that even now she couldn't just talk to me. "Tell me the truth."

Jackson appeared behind her, but he took one look at

my face and turned on his heel. "Corey, Alex, we're waiting outside."

The other two muttered about food, but I didn't take my eyes off their sister. The black handwriting had been easy to read considering the message was only a few words long.

Talk and you'll regret it.

Vi jumped as the door slammed. "I was going to tell you."

Fear for her competed with the hurt that she hadn't trusted me enough to share this with me. "When? After this moved from notes to something more dangerous?"

She winced and reached for me. "It's not a big deal."

I stepped back, and her hand fell to her side. "This is a *huge* fucking deal, Vi. This was why we made the rules in the first place."

"We changed the rules."

"Yeah, and you don't think I want you safe now that you're so much more to me? How am I supposed to protect you if you keep things like this from me?"

Her nostrils flared as frustration lit her features. "I wanted your apartment, not your protection."

I shook my head, shoving the offending paper in my jeans. She wanted to ignore the problem, but that wasn't my style. "Too bad. You're about to get both. Stay here."

She called my name as I stormed through the living room, but I didn't slow. I'd deal with Colt, then come back after I'd had a chance to calm down.

Her brothers leaned against the railing outside, but I brushed past them without a word. I didn't give a shit about their opinion at the moment. Vi had promised not to hide things—to trust me—and she'd broken that promise. The betrayal burned, and I needed to decide how I was going to move forward from there.

I slammed into my truck and backed out of the parking spot in a spray of gravel. Anger squeezed my throat closed, but the searing pain in my chest was so much worse. For a second, I hated her damn stubborn need to take care of everything herself. She tried to lock away any chance that she might get hurt by controlling the world around her, but it was too late.

We'd come too far to escape unscathed.

———

I KNEW EXACTLY where to find Colt on our day off. Our college town didn't have a country club, but his parents owned the next closest thing—an exclusive tennis club where Colt liked to lord about in his free time.

Something niggled in the back of my mind about the note, but the dangerous mix of fury and painful disappointment forced me to focus on my driving. I wasn't stupid enough to let my emotions get me killed. Especially not before I'd had the chance to shove this paper down Colt's throat.

My family's name got me into the club easily, and finding Colt was a simple matter of asking the closest employee. A teen in a polo shirt gave me a tight smile and pointed me toward a private lounge.

Colt sat in a leather chair facing a view of the tennis courts, where he watched a woman in a short skirt practice her backswing. No one else was in the room. The whole set-up felt pervy, but I wasn't there to enjoy myself.

"Colt."

He looked over his shoulder, then spun the chair to face me. "Soren. I didn't think you slummed it with us non-Dallas folks."

So he did know who my parents were. I hadn't been sure up to that point because I purposefully kept it under wraps, but his family ran in some of the same circles.

"Sometimes slumming is necessary." My insult flew over his head as he waved at the chair next to him.

"Have a seat and enjoy the show."

He started to spin back around, but I grabbed the arm rest. "We need to have a talk."

Colt lifted both hands. "Whatever, man."

I let go and backed away because the rage was still bubbling under the surface, and I wasn't sure I'd be able to stop myself from taking a shot at him if he was in arm's reach.

"Tell me about your wrist injury after the OU game."

His eyes shifted past me to stare at the door. "It was nothing. I just had to ice it a couple of days, and I was fine."

"Vi told me what happened at the Kappa party."

He scoffed, back to his usual arrogant self. "Your girl got it all wrong. That cheerleader was tripping all over herself to get at my balls, but she wasn't my type. I like them less whiny and in multiples of two. I thought I'd get her the hell out of the party because she was depressing people."

I hated that I believed at least part of his story. Colt wasn't overly concerned with protecting his own ass as long as his parents were around to bail him out of trouble. I'd bet my truck that he had no intention of just leaving Lizzy on the curb though.

"And what was your plan once she was outside?"

He smirked, smarmy and annoying. "You know how it goes, man. Chicks change their minds all the time. I thought I'd wait for her cheerleader friend to come looking for her and see if they'd be interested in a private party."

I narrowed my eyes at him and felt my muscles

twitching from the effort of holding myself back. "And when they turned your ass down?"

He shrugged. "No problem for me. Plenty of pussy inside still. It didn't get that far though. Your ball bunny got in the way. Hot as fuck, I'll give you that, but she looks like the type to bite your dick off as soon as suck it. Though I'll try anything once."

"That why you started harassing her?"

Colt held up his hands. "Whoa, man. Not my fault she keeps showing up where I'm hanging."

"What about the notes?"

He stared at me like I was stupid. "Like I told her, I don't know anything about any notes. If that cheerleader had said no once I got her outside, I would've found someone else. I was wasted at the party, but I'm not about to go to jail for some bitch. Pussy is pussy."

I shook my head and turned to leave. Colt hadn't left the notes. He was an asshole, but he didn't care enough to put that much effort in.

He leaned back in his chair to yell at me on my way out. "We're cool, right, man? Coach said to fix things so his effort wasn't wasted."

I stopped in my tracks and closed my eyes for a second as the truth hit me. My world shifted then settled into a new reality—one I hadn't wanted to see.

Outside, I pulled the crumpled note from my pocket and stared at the blocky handwriting. No wonder it had seemed familiar. I'd been staring at it on the whiteboard in the locker room for the last three years.

Coach had pulled that bullshit with Derrick earlier in the semester, but I'd thought it was an isolated incident. Threatening Vi and influencing the school to take away her apartment and her job went so far beyond the bounds of acceptable that I almost had trouble believing it.

Talk and you'll regret it. We'd all assumed Colt was focused on Vi because of the minor injury to his wrist and the major blow to his ego, but he hadn't complained about his arm until I asked about it. He only remembered the way she'd cock blocked him.

Coach, though, seemed to believe that Colt had done something that would negatively impact the team.

I could have done without the reality check to my relationship with Vi, but no matter how much she hurt me, I wasn't going to let him keep targeting her. Our team may be on the brink of a championship win, but I didn't want to work with someone who would protect a player he thought was preying on other people.

Coach had to go.

The university would never believe me without evidence, and even then, they might just try to bury it. I'd need help, and I knew exactly who to call. First, Harper. I needed a back-up plan in case the administration refused to listen, and she got shit done. Second, someone who I knew would feel the same way I did.

Parker picked up on the first ring. "Yeah?"

"You ready to do something about the situation with Colt and Lizzy?"

"About fucking time."

29

Vi

"I am such an idiot." I dropped my head back against the couch and closed my eyes. "I should have burned those stupid notes."

"Why didn't you?"

I opened my eyes to see Jackson sitting on the coffee table in front of me. The three of them hadn't made a sound as they'd snuck back in. Freaking ninjas.

He raised a brow. "Why are you sitting here considering arson instead of kicking his ass like we taught you? Is he not worth the effort?"

I scraped my hair back into a tight ponytail, then realized I didn't have a hair tie with me. "Shut up, Jackson. You don't know what you're talking about."

"So tell me."

My hair fell into my face as I peered at him. He slouched forward with his elbows on his knees, watching me with a steady gaze. He'd inherited Mom's artistic talent along with the gray eyes that we'd all gotten, but the temperament was all Jackson.

The last time I'd seen them, I'd spent the entire time pissed off and literally closed myself in my room at my dad's house until they'd driven me back to school. Except it hadn't been Dad's house anymore. He'd moved to Houston to be closer to my aunt, and Jackson had taken over.

The house wasn't home without Mom there. Everything had been the same and yet so devastatingly different. Just like now. Corey crouched in front of Soren's video games, and Alex was raiding the fridge, but they looked noticeably older, broader... adultier.

And they'd come all the way out here because Eva had said I needed help. After experiencing the way Soren's family dismissed him, I missed my brothers.

The metallic taste of tears coated my mouth, but I wasn't going to cry. Tears wouldn't solve anything. Jackson waited patiently for me to talk, but I wasn't sure where to start.

Corey took care of that for me by holding up one of Soren's games. "Mind if I play this?"

Jackson rolled his eyes. "We're not here to mess around, jackass."

"Speak for yourself. I told you Vi could handle whatever trouble she got herself into." He winked at me. "You remember that move I taught you?"

I smiled at his question—the same one he always asked me. Corey had shown me a wrist lock that I'd promptly used to make Jackson cry during a sparring match. The only time I'd ever beaten him.

Alex popped his head over the fridge door with a piece of string cheese sticking out of his mouth. "If her problem is that Soren guy, then she's fine. Did you see the way he stood between her and us? I think I like him." He waggled his eyebrows then dove back into the cold interior.

Corey shook his head. "I'm reserving judgement considering he's been living with Vi for who knows how long."

I rubbed my temples where a headache was already pounding away. "I'm sitting right here."

Jackson stood, snatched the game out of Corey's hand, and walked over to shut the fridge door in Alex's face. "Go wait in the car."

Corey grumbled about conflicting orders, but he slung an arm around Alex and left us blessedly alone. Silence descended, and Jackson grabbed his own cheese stick before sitting next to me on the couch.

He methodically ate my snack while I took deep breaths trying to relieve the crushing pressure in my chest. Soren had walked out. To my dismay, I wasn't surprised. Some part of me had been preparing for him to leave this whole time. I'd just thought it would happen around the draft when pro football became a reality for him.

"Start with the notes."

Jackson's voice startled me, lost so deep in my own thoughts. He sounded calm, but the whole reason I'd moved in with Soren was so I wouldn't have to tell my brothers about Colt. Some of the pressure diminished as I tried to find a way to explain without giving him any details.

He sent me a knowing look. "Stop. Just tell me."

I grimaced, recognizing that Soren had picked up on the same habit. Maybe I should stop hiding things from the people I cared about.

Once I cleared up one last thing.

"Promise not to kidnap me again."

Jackson shook his head. "I'm sorry for the way we treated you last time." He stared down at his hands. "I didn't react well to a threat to you after Mom."

I swallowed hard and nodded, unable to speak.

"We raised you to be able to take care of yourself, then we didn't give you the chance to ask for help. So I'm sorry, though I fully intend to murder anyone who makes it past your football player bodyguard."

I cleared my throat. "Apology accepted. I had an altercation with one of Soren's teammates."

"And?"

I grinned, despite my horrible suspicion that I'd permanently ruined everything. "And I used Corey's wrist hold on him."

Jackson winced.

"A while after, I started getting notes warning me not to talk, I assumed about that night."

His eyes sharpened. "Were you wrong?"

"Not about the warning, but probably about the sender. I didn't think the notes were important because the author wasn't a threat."

"And now?"

"Now I'm not so sure," I said softly, staring down at my lap. "I found out yesterday that the school cancelled my fitness classes. In the back of my mind, I'd sort of planned to just wait out the year until I graduated. The notes were annoying, but I didn't feel unsafe. I knew I could handle a physical threat, and until my classes were cancelled, nothing had changed. Those classes were important to me, and I had no recourse after they were taken away. I felt powerless, just like when Mom died."

Jackson wrapped his arm around my shoulders. "Did your boyfriend go running off to beat the shit out of his teammate?"

"Probably, which could get him benched during the playoffs right before he declares for the draft."

He nodded. "Good."

I glared at him. "*Not* good. Playing professional football has been his dream his whole life, and he's worked hard to achieve that goal. I could cost him his future."

"I'm sure he's very talented, but Vi, you have to trust him to make his own choices. Personally, I support this one and feel a lot better leaving you with him knowing he'd put you ahead of his goals."

I squinted at him. "You're not going to question our relationship and lecture me about shacking up with strangers?"

He shrugged. "I figured you had to love him if you were pushing him away this hard. Why else would you act like this much of a dumbass?"

"Fuck," I muttered. "I told myself I was protecting him by not telling him about the notes."

A dry laugh came from him. "Yeah. Our family has a shitty track record with that particular skill, but keeping secrets is more about protecting yourself rather than protecting someone else."

"Yeah, I figured that out." I sucked in air past the fear and dismay. "I want to be with him. All the time. He's got this dangerous job that could change his life any second, and I still want a life with him. I love him."

He sent me a sly look. "More than me?"

"Yes."

Jackson nodded. "Did you tell him that?"

I closed my eyes with a groan. "No. I told him I was using him for his apartment because I'm an idiot. We covered that part."

"Are you worried about him getting injured?"

I pulled my knees up to my chest and dropped my head onto them. "I don't even care anymore. I just want the chance to be with him, however long that ends up being."

Pain stretched me open at the thought that I'd fulfilled my own prophecy of him leaving me. He'd walked away because he thought I hadn't trusted him, but he'd also told me to stay here. If he were done with me, wouldn't he have kicked me out?

If I left to go after him, would I make everything worse?

I searched Jackson's face. "What do you think I should do?"

He tilted his head. "You're asking my opinion?"

"Yes. Bestow your wisdom, oh older brother."

Jackson grinned. "Stop sitting on your ass moping and go do something to convince him you realize you fucked up."

I blew hair out of my face. "Yeah, that's where I landed too. Can you do me a favor?"

"Depends. If there's makeup involved, I'm out. That was a one-time thing."

A laugh burst out as I remembered teenage me insisting the whole family go to the Renaissance Faire dressed as pirates, complete with eyeliner. Mom had spent the whole time referring to my dad as her booty. The expected slash of pain from thinking of Mom never came. Actually, it hadn't happened since the night I'd cried all over Soren.

I shook my head. Another reason I was an idiot. It was nice to let myself just enjoy the memory for once instead of punishing myself.

"No. I need you to stop by Eva's place and take her to dinner."

His brows winged up. "I'm not going to lead along your friend with the crush to make you feel better."

I patted his arm. "You can tell her it was my idea. She just wants to stare at you for a while. Besides, if she spends more than ten seconds in your company, her crush will be long gone."

He grunted. "I hope you realize how much I love you."

I kissed his cheek and stood. "You can leave Corey and Alex here. Might as well really test Soren's forgiveness."

30

Soren

Parker met me outside the film room, which happened to be down the same hallway as Coach's office. Normally, this place would be buzzing, but everyone was taking advantage of the rest time before we made our big push in the playoffs.

Probably for the best that no one saw us since Parker showed up in black sweats, a long sleeve shirt, and a black beanie instead of his usual jeans and graphic tee.

I gestured at his outfit. "Are we planning to steal some diamonds after?"

He raised a brow. "Weren't you the one who wore an inflatable t-rex costume to practice once?"

"Yeah, and I was still faster than Mac."

Parker snickered. "You know he's going to destroy your record next year."

I sighed. "Provided there's a team next year. What we're about to do could tank everything, cost us a championship."

"Worth it." Parker looked up, and I saw the same anger and resolve on his face that I felt. "And not just to me. I talked to the others."

My brow furrowed. "What others? D and Mac?"

He nodded. "And Noah, the rest of the team. We're all on board."

I shook my head. Parker was going to be one hell of a leader, and any team with him in charge would be able to come back from this shitstorm. "Thanks."

"Are you sure he'll be in there?"

"He spends all his free time in here. This team is an obsession for him." I knew because at one point I'd admired his dedication.

The first year when I'd redshirted, I'd spent every spare moment in his office learning whatever I could. Strategies, routes, workout regimens, anything that would make me even a little bit better, a little bit more worthy of my spot here.

Coach Lancaster was an institution at this university, and I planned to make use of every advantage I was given.

After the Margot incident this summer though, things began to unravel. Margot simply gave up her claims when I'd expected her to make my life a living hell, as promised. Initially, I'd credited my parents with paying her off, but they denied giving her any money. They had no reason to lie about that since they had no trouble expressing their disapproval for all the other aspects of my life.

It wasn't necessarily Coach's doing, but some of his comments made me think he knew about Margot and had played a part in getting rid of her. He didn't seem to care that I was aware of it, and I had no reason to say anything.

Not until he tried to force D to split with Nadia, going so far as to orchestrate a breakup scenario. I confronted him before the game the same day as the Kappa party. He admitted to nothing, but he agreed to leave D and Nadia alone if I kept my theory to myself. The whole situation was sleazy as hell, and now I planned to use his own play against him.

Voices from down the hallway warned us Coach was on the way, so we ducked into the film room and pulled the door almost all the way closed. His assistant was talking about the depth chart for next year, but Coach sounded distracted. I wondered if Colt had called him to brag about fixing things.

It wouldn't change my plan, but it made me regret not punching him when I had the chance.

I watched through the crack until Coach went into his office and his assistant's footsteps faded. Parker cracked his neck and rotated his shoulders as if he were preparing for an actual fight.

"You remember what to do?" I asked.

He nodded. "Stay out of sight and try to keep both of you in the frame at all times."

"I'll be broadcasting live too, but it'll only be audio since I need to keep my phone in my pocket."

He shook his head. "I want to say I can't believe you're using the internet fame from your relationship for this, but this is exactly something I'd expect from you."

"The Voren fans are rabid and dying for some drama. I say we give the people what they want."

"Did you warn Vi?"

I shook my head, firmly pushing the knot of unease in my chest farther down. She'd find out about the plan soon enough since I intended to tag her on the live. If she was anywhere near her phone, she'd be alerted as soon as we started.

The anger from earlier had faded to a calm acceptance. Yes, she'd kept important information from me, but I could see why. When she'd told me about Colt approaching her at the coffee shop, her first concern was that I would react without thinking and confront him. A valid concern, it turned out, but she was also afraid. Caring about someone and losing them was her biggest fear.

In the end, her choice of how to deal with that fear sucked, but everyone made bad choices sometimes. Maybe I was about to make one, but I wanted to help her see that what we had together was worth the risk.

Hopefully, she'd understand why we had to do this. The situation had started with her—and there was no way in hell I'd let someone fuck with her like that again—but it was a matter of honor now. Who knew what other sketchy shit Coach had pulled from his position of power?

I breathed in deep like I did before a game. The next half hour would change a lot of people's lives—I hoped for the better in the long run. My phone was already cued up to the live, so all I had to do was start the broadcast.

There were already several hundred viewers leaving comments since I'd teased an exclusive earlier. I turned on my camera and gave it a wide smile.

"Hey there Voren fans. I'm coming at you from inside the TU facilities with a show you don't want to miss. Unfortunately, it's all going to be audio because you good people will be in my pocket, but if you want to see the action, check out my buddy Parker Shaw's channel. He's tagged below, along with the lovely Vi Malone. You'll see why."

I added a wink then stuck the whole thing in the pocket of my jeans. Fear caught in my throat as I stared down the hallway. Pictures of previous championship teams hung along the way, and I'd be potentially costing my team that spot. Even with their support, I needed a second to fully accept what I was about to do.

An image of Vi flashed across my mind and the fear

dissolved. I was doing the right thing--*we* were doing the right thing. Parker nodded that he was filming from behind his phone, so I strode down the hall to Coach's office like I'd done a million times before.

Coach's door was open, usually a sign that he was in a good mood. I knocked on the wood, and he smiled when he saw me.

"Soren. Come on in. What can I do for you?"

I made sure to leave the door ajar so Parker could get a good shot and took my usual chair. "I'm worried about the team."

Coach's genial attitude dropped immediately, replaced with a concerned expression that struck me as fake. "What's the problem?"

"Colt." I saw the knowledge flicker in his eyes before he masked it, but I doubted Parker could, let alone his viewers.

"I know you two have butted heads a bit this season, but I thought you'd both done a good job putting it aside when needed."

I shook my head and mimicked Colt's smarmy smile from earlier. "It's not really him so much as Vi. She told me Colt got pushy with a cheerleader during a party earlier in the semester."

Coach's eyes sharpened. "And you believed her?"

"Let's say it's not out of the realm of possibility, but I only wanted to make sure you'd taken care of the situation. We can't have his extracurriculars ruining things with us this close to the championship."

He leaned back, seeming relieved. "Don't you worry about that. I took care of any fallout. Your Vi is confused. Colt is a little hot-headed, but he's never crossed that line. Women are just too sensitive these days. Maybe you could help with keeping her quiet."

I nodded along. "Sure. Honestly, I'm not sure why she waited this long to tell me. I'm guessing I have you to thank for that?"

He laughed like I'd just complimented him, which in his mind I probably had. "You're welcome. She's a tough one to control. You should consider trading her in for someone more malleable."

"I'll keep that in mind. She just lost a big chunk of her job, so she's been pretty malleable lately." I eyed him with forced respect. "Was that you too?"

He tucked his hands behind his head, clearly not worried after all the time I'd spent convincing him I was team first, team only. "Guilty. I wanted her focused on her own life instead of on Colt's activities. If it benefited you, even better. I'm glad you've been as laser-focused as ever while dealing with her. Remember, women are temporary, but championships last forever."

Something started vibrating under a stack of papers—his phone probably. I guessed my time was about to be done, so I slapped his desk and chuckled.

"Man, I just realized this wasn't the first time you helped me out with the ladies. You got rid of Margot this summer, didn't you?"

He sniffed. "She was easy. Once I had her expelled, she ran back to her mommy and daddy on the east coast. If she bothers you again, you come to me. I'll make sure she regrets ever thinking she can interfere with someone on my team."

The shuffle of running footsteps came from the hallway followed by a shout. It sounded like Parker had been busted, so I stood.

"Thanks for everything, Coach Lancaster. I hope you get the ending you deserve."

He tilted his head, confused, but I simply turned and walked out. I shoved my hands in my pockets and gripped my phone, fully expecting security to stop me in the hallway, but the space was empty.

Parker must have led whoever it was away. I hoped between the two of us we'd gotten enough of an admission to nail Coach. I ducked into the first empty room I found—a storage closet—to pull my phone out and finish up.

The comments were exploding, but I didn't have time to read them now.

"Hey folks, so there you have it from Coach Lancaster himself. All the dirty nitty gritty of how not to run a championship football program. You wanted Voren drama, and I provided. Vi, if you're watching this, I love you."

I blew a kiss to the phone, then shut off the whole thing. It was only a matter of time before people came looking for me, but I slumped against the wall to catch my breath.

My heart was racing, and I felt like I'd just run hill sprints for an hour straight, though I couldn't have been in there for more than ten minutes. When I'd shared my plan with Harper earlier in the day, she'd advised me to get out as fast as possible afterward because there were all kinds of tricky legal issues I might have just flung myself into.

She'd also agreed to record the live and send it out to as many sports journalists as her media liaison could contact. If nothing else, finding out Harper wasn't a bitter shrew was a bright spot in potentially torpedoing my career.

And Vi was the aurora borealis. Beautiful, unexpected, and something I'd cherish for the rest of my life, if she'd let me.

31

Vi

I blew on my cold fingers as I stood outside the TU football training facility. I'd eaten lunch in the connected athletic center, but I hadn't spent any time over here. From this side, you couldn't even see the rest of campus thanks to the trees surrounding the buildings.

Sometimes I forgot how much our university spent on the football team alone, then I remembered how much trouble I'd had convincing them to buy us stretch bands for the student athletic center.

I shook my head and tucked my hands into my pockets as I worked up the nerve to go inside.

After I'd left Jackson in Eva's questionable hands, I hadn't been able to find Soren. Derrick's place had only contained three stone-faced football players who hadn't seen him, and Eva hadn't heard from him.

He wouldn't answer my calls or messages, which made me realize that other than during practice, he *always* responded to me. Even if it was just a funny meme or emoji. Soren put in so much effort to make me feel important, and I'd told him I was just using him for his apartment.

Hopefully once I found him, I'd be able to convince him that I was done pushing him away.

As a last-ditch effort, I'd called Harper. She suggested I check the training facility and keep my phone close, which was strange, but I didn't have a chance to ask questions because she hung up on me.

I'd almost made it to the door when my phone started vibrating almost non-stop. A quick glance showed me more notifications than it could list. I stopped at the edge of the parking lot and scrolled until I saw a message from Parker.

Check your feed.

What the hell had they done?

I ducked around the side of the building and opened my feed. Amidst all the mentions was a tag from Soren. Finally.

When I clicked on the live, I groaned. Soren didn't look like he'd just beaten someone to a bloody pulp, but he was about to pull some spy shit that was guaranteed to be a bad idea. Maybe Colt was inside, and he hadn't gotten to the beating part yet.

The screen went dark as Soren shoved us in his pocket, and I switched to Parker's account. I nearly dropped my phone when I saw Soren enter his Coach's office. Icy fear chilled my blood and stole my breath.

A couple of loose ends snapped into place at lightning speed as I watched Soren sit as if it were any other Saturday. I'd wondered how Colt had enough influence to affect my campus apartment and my job. Not just that, but the savvy to understand how best to hurt me. After a few sentences, the truth became clear. Colt hadn't been the one threatening me, his Coach had.

Thousands of people were watching this live with me, and Soren was about to destroy everything he'd worked for.

I took off running through the hallways, only slowing when I approached another person.

Just like in my gym, if I moved with confidence, no one questioned whether I was supposed to be in an area off-limits to the public. Everything was conveniently labeled, so I could just follow the signs to the head coach's office.

I passed a security guard frowning down at his phone, and a shiver of foreboding skittered down my back. How much trouble would they get in for this stunt?

I came around the next corner and found Parker near the end of the hallway crouched outside an open door. That security guard had been slowly heading this direction. I shouted a warning and took off again with my sneakers squeaking against the tile floor.

Parker looked up and nodded at my violent hand motions for him to get away from the door. He checked his phone one more time, then stood and reached my side in a few strides.

"We have to get Soren out of there," I panted, trying not to curl around the stitch in my side. "Security is right around that corner."

"Soren can take care of himself, come on." He grabbed my arm and pulled me into a door marked stairs.

I groaned. "I don't think I can climb stairs right now."

He eyed me with disbelief and started up. "I thought you taught cardio classes."

"There's a huge difference between dancing and running."

"Well, dance your ass up these steps. They won't look for us on the second floor. It's all study rooms. I'll text Soren once we're there."

Thank all that was holy the flight of stairs was short. As soon as we burst into the main study area, I pulled my phone out again to see what was happening with Soren. The visual jostled and there he was on screen again, grinning. I couldn't make out where he was, which was probably a good thing, but he had to still be in the building.

Parker started tugging me down yet another hallway, and I followed along as I turned up my volume. I caught the last part of his monologue before he signed off and stopped in my tracks.

If you're watching this Vi, I love you.

Luckily, Parker had stopped too, but only to groan, "That idiot."

Tears blurred my vision, and I pressed my fingers to my lips. He'd just told *everyone* that he loved me. Even after I'd broken his trust and said stupid shit instead of trying to work through the problem.

Parker propped his free hand on his hip and stared at the ceiling for a second. "Okay, I'm trying to give you time for the moment, but I'd feel a lot better if we were somewhere out of the way."

I glanced at the stairwell door, still well within sight, and started moving again. "Right. I'm coming."

"That's what she said," he mumbled under his breath.

I elbowed him in the side as I caught up.

"Hey! No need for violence. Eva is a bad influence on you." He opened a door and ushered me into a small room with no windows. With anyone else, the setup would trigger a whole lot of warnings in my head, but Parker took one of the two chairs on either side of the desk and pulled out his phone.

My own was still exploding with notifications of people tagging me, most wanted a response to Soren's declaration. I was still floating along with my heart making flapping noises above me, but I chewed on my lip as I considered the audience.

Soren had given the Voren fans exactly the kind of thing that would stir them into a frenzy, thus guaranteeing his little show would get the most attention. What if it was all for show? What if he just left to deal with the aftermath from the safety of somewhere far away? I could find out by calling him, but I was too afraid it would go straight to voicemail again.

I glanced at Parker, kicked back in the chair with his long legs resting on the desk. "Did you get ahold of Soren?"

He nodded but didn't take his eyes off his phone. So much for that avenue of information. My phone continued to beg for attention, so I shut off notifications. With Soren's live likely going viral, there was another possibility if he didn't show up soon.

Campus security could have found him before he made it up here to us. Honestly, we probably should have gotten off the premises immediately, but it was a little late now to change course. Unfortunately, I didn't have a defensive plan for fighting off campus security in a tiny room with only one exit.

My heart jumped into my throat when the study room door banged open. Instead of campus police, Soren stood there breathing hard and grinning.

I launched myself at him, so relieved that he wasn't angry or sad or hog-tied on the floor with zip ties. His arms closed around me, and I buried my face against his chest. From somewhere behind me, Parker mumbled about going home.

The door closed behind him, leaving us alone in the quiet space. Soren sighed, ruffling my hair, and I tipped my head up to see his face.

"I'm sorry."

He traced his thumb along my jaw. "What are you sorry for?"

"Not telling you about the notes... and making you feel like I only wanted you for your apartment. Even at the beginning that wasn't true."

A soft smile crossed his lips. "I know."

"I still shouldn't have said it. I've never really felt at home here because I didn't want to be too comfortable in case it got taken away, but you changed that for me."

I kissed him, and we both sighed into the moment like we'd been apart for a lot longer than a day. The light above us flickered, and we pulled apart to stare at it. Soren peered at the rest of the room as if noticing it for the first time.

He cocked his head at me. "I just realized you were the one I heard outside. That's why Parker was gone when I left the office. He was hiding you up here."

"Didn't he tell you I was up here?"

"No, he said he'd changed the plan and to meet him in the janky study room upstairs."

I laughed. "I guess I wasn't the only one worried about your reaction."

Next to my hip, Soren's pants vibrated. "That'll be Parker letting me know he made it out okay."

"Or asking for bail money."

He let me go to pull his phone out and check. "Nope. We have the all-clear. Coach seems too busy trying to save his own ass to chase after us. At least according to social media and Harper's mysterious sources."

"What happens if Coach Lancaster manages to slide past this? I wasn't even a threat, and he didn't hesitate to try to ruin my life."

"I already have Harper working on the narrative for me.

Apparently, she's well known in the business world for her PR skills, which is one of the pieces of information I took into account before I decided to go full Scooby-Doo."

"What about right now? I can't imagine the campus police are very happy with you at the moment."

"Parker says we should worry more about the student population, who are actively scouring the campus for signs of us. There's a whole underground railroad situation happening. We'll be fine. Let's get out of here. I have a lot more to say to you, and I don't want to improvise escape plans in the middle of it."

He laced our fingers together and led us on a winding route out of the building. In unspoken agreement, we stayed quiet until we passed out a nondescript side door that clanged shut behind us.

The sun had set while we were inside. Instead of turning toward the parking lot, Soren led me into the trees separating the football facility from the rest of the athletic buildings. There was a faint trail through the pines, but he seemed to know where he was going. I could see my breath in the chilly air, and the cold immediately seeped through my thin leggings.

"Is this where you murder me because I didn't tell you about the harassment?"

He glanced back at me, but the shadows hid most of his face. "Sometimes it's faster to park at the other buildings and cut through here. Also, there was a period where we were giving Mac shit about his car, and he swore revenge. I parked back here for almost a whole semester, and I kind of liked the walk so I kept doing it if I had time."

"I didn't hear a no," I muttered.

He flashed me a smile, which I *did* see, so I pushed

forward. "We should probably talk about what happened this morning... and this afternoon. All day, really."

Soren squeezed my hand. "We should probably talk about several things. You and I sort of suck at communication."

The trees thinned and the athletic facility parking lot came into view. I pulled him to a stop in the shadows of a thicker growth of pines where we still had some protection from the open space. "The second we pop out of here, we'll probably be mobbed by anyone who watched your live."

"Okay, let's do this here." He released my hand to wrap an arm around my waist and pull me close. "First, though..."

His hand threaded into my hair, and he tipped my chin up with his thumb to kiss me. I melted into him, so relieved that I hadn't permanently broken anything between us. He eased back, brushing my nose with his.

"Now that I can think again... What were you doing here? I asked you to stay at home."

"You *ordered* me to stay home, and seeing as how I'm not a pet, I didn't feel the need to obey." I tucked my cold hands under his shirt, making him hiss. "And I came looking for you because I wanted to apologize."

He nodded, not looking at all sorry for the order. "Fair enough."

"I was here because I realized how badly I'd messed up, and I wanted make it up to you."

"You didn't trust me." His quiet words were laced with hurt, and they set off an answering ache in my chest.

My fingers curled into him, as if that would be enough to keep him from leaving again. "I trust you, Soren—completely. It was *me* I didn't trust." I sighed, remembering Jackson's words. "I told myself I was protecting you, but I was using it as a buffer. Handling Colt myself let me pretend like I was in control, something I desperately clung to when I couldn't stop the freefall of my feelings for you."

"And those are?"

"I love you. Every fantastically talented, frustrating, sexy inch. I want to kick your ass at Rock Paper Scissors and wear your jersey to every game. I want to spend every night with you wrapped around me. We'll fight and maybe things will get hard because I'm still putting together my broken pieces, but nothing will pull me away from you. If you still want me."

His thumb stroked my jaw. "You are *everything*, Vi. I love you and all your broken pieces. I'm sorry I left, but I never intended to stay gone. I was always going to come back to you. I *will* always come back to you."

I let out the breath that I'd been holding, and his thumb moved across my bottom lip, causing another shiver to race over my skin. "I know."

The last bit of tension left him, and he replaced his thumb with his mouth. A demanding, claiming kiss that I gave right back to him. No more pretending or hiding. A rustle from the dark brush near us broke us apart. I met his eyes, and we both burst out laughing.

Soren nodded at the parking lot. "Ready to dodge the roaming bands of Voren fans and go home?"

I winced. "I sort of left two of my brothers at the apartment."

He laughed, backing me slowly against the closest tree, barely hidden from the parking lot where we could hear people milling around. "Guess we'll stay here a little longer then."

A shiver coursed over me at the dark promise in his voice. "What will we do while we're waiting?"

His head lowered, and he ran his tongue along the thundering pulse in my neck. "I think we need to come up with some new rules."

"Sure, you do." Wet heat pooled between my thighs, and the cold faded away. I whimpered quietly when he skimmed under my shirt to cup my breasts, teasing my nipples.

"Rule one: no more guests when I want to spread you naked across the kitchen counter." He sucked on the spot below my ear.

My breath caught at the image, but I shook my head. "That would mean no visitors ever."

He chuckled and curled his fingers in the waistband of my leggings and undies, inching them downward. "Rule two: Soren is always right."

I steadied myself against his shoulder and toed off my sneakers, giving him the chance to peel the material off my legs. "Still not a rule, and you already used that one."

"How about this one..." On the way back up, he lifted me, wrapping my legs around his hips. "I'll love you every day of my life, I'll support you in whatever you choose to do, and I'll fuck you against any tree you want."

"Rule approved," I whispered as his fingers delved inside me.

The breeze picked up, biting into my bare ass, but his body surrounded me, warm and solid. Soren freed himself from his jeans, and I bit my lip, quieting my moan as he replaced his hand with his cock.

His mouth covered mine as we rode out the fury of the day, pushing each other to take more, just a little more, until he swallowed his name on my lips and emptied himself inside me.

Soren buried his face against my neck and held tight as we both caught our breath. I threaded my hands through his hair—we'd lost the elastic somewhere again—and let the hot rush of emotion fill me to bursting.

"I love you. Every day," I murmured.

He lifted his head and gave me a wicked grin. "We'll work on rule two."

I swatted his chest, but he caught my hand and kissed my palm.

"Every day, Vi."

I didn't care that I was half-naked a stone's throw from a busy parking lot, or that we would potentially be homeless in a few weeks, or that the administration was just as likely to come after us as they were to go after Coach Lancaster—I wouldn't trade a single moment of this time for the cold, lonely life I'd been living before.

EPILOGUE

Soren

I held Vi's hand as our whole crew along with Derrick's family sat spread out in a fancy hotel suite they'd booked in Dallas. The draft would begin any minute, and I couldn't focus on shit. Despite Derrick being invited to New York as a probable first-round pick, he chose to stay here with the rest of us.

It was a miracle we were here at all after the drama with Coach. The live went viral overnight, and by morning, Teagan University had officially caved. They put him on leave while they investigated, handing off their championship football team to an assistant coach who'd never called a single play on his own.

Turned out Coach Lancaster was a bit of a control freak. He also took copious notes.

Before our next game, Colt and four other guys on the team were suspended, and there was talk our school would be disqualified from the playoffs. Luckily, the CFP board let us play. Without letting us hire an interim coach from outside the program.

Despite his many, many other flaws, Coach Lancaster

had been good at his job. Without him, we struggled in the playoffs. His assistants had really only been good at following orders.

Ultimately, we edged our way into the championship, but lost in the end. It was a hell of a season, and not a single one of us that played that championship game had a regret.

Vi snuggled closer, shoving a throw pillow out of the way, and I pulled her against my side. We'd decided not to take our chances with housing again. Thanks to Harper, I was able to pay for a 6-month lease on an apartment that would get us through the end of the school year. A one-bedroom, but we didn't need more than one.

The gym equipment was a death trap, the parking was more of a strong suggestion than an actual lot, and we had a grand total of eighteen minutes of hot water at a time, but the last four months were the best of my life.

Vi concentrated on finishing her degree, and to my surprise, Harper made regular visits out to TU. So did Vi's brothers, who liked to show up in the middle of the night with no warning.

They'd declined our invitation for today's party, but said they'd be watching from home, rooting for me. I was still getting used to the unwavering support from Vi's family. And from Derrick's.

His sister, Chloe, scooted past and plopped down on the opposite side of me from Vi. She straightened her glasses and gave me the same intense stare that Derrick got when he was about to perform a miracle on the field.

"Stop freaking out." At barely twenty, she was technically a couple of years younger than us, but her attitude came from someone much older. I'd met her a couple of times before, and we'd hit it off right away. This time was no different.

"I'm not freaking out."

She scoffed, and her dark curls fell over her shoulder from the force of it. "D's about to puke in his own shoes, and he *knows* he's going first round. There's an actual camera guy in the corner, pretending not to be filming all of us, and you ended your season by making national news for getting your coach fired. But you're not freaking out."

I winced. "Thanks, Chloe, but I'm really fine." To my surprise, I wasn't lying. My stats were good, and at this point, there was nothing else I could do. I'd get drafted or I wouldn't.

Vi laughed at something Eva said, and Chloe's gaze shifted to her then softened. "I'm glad you found someone to love you the way you deserve."

I shook my head. "It scares me when you say nice things."

She grinned, her green eyes glittering with devious amusement. "Who said that was nice? I get the feeling Vi doesn't put up with one iota of your bullshit. And you can't get enough of her." She rubbed her hands together. "Sweet, sweet revenge."

"I guess I should hope the same for you then."

One dark eyebrow rose. "Please. Love is for suckers. You and Derrick can have it all, thank you very much. I'd rather just take advantage of all the single guys looking to get laid..." Her words trailed off as her eyes flicked past me.

I glanced over my shoulder to see Noah, a closed down expression on his face, turn and head down the hallway toward the bedrooms. If I didn't know better, I'd think he was pissed, but Noah didn't get pissed—even on the field.

Something weird was going on there.

Vi nudged my side and nodded at the screen, where the

commissioner had started his speech about this year's draft class. The room quieted as the picks began.

Like we all knew was coming, Derrick was chosen early by New York. He swept Nadia off her feet and spun her around. Chloe hopped up for her own hug, but even then, Derrick didn't let Nadia get far from his side. I knew the feeling.

I watched our celebration play out across the screen, courtesy of the silent cameraman, until it was time for the next team to make their pick. Again and again, names were called that weren't mine, through the end of the first round.

Vi tucked her hand into mine and squeezed. I looked down, and she was staring up at me instead of at the screen. She'd worn the same dress as that first Halloween party at my parents' house, a joyous burst of color against the slate gray of my suit. Her short hair was styled in soft waves, and I wanted to sink my hand into it, sink into her, until the rest of the room disappeared.

A tiny smile flitted across her face as if she could read my thoughts, and maybe she could. It wouldn't be the first time she'd seen something in me no one else had.

I kissed her hand, and my tense shoulders relaxed. No matter what happened over the next few days, I'd have her by my side.

A hush came over the room as the second round began. Two of the first three names I recognized, then came one that I nearly missed.

"With the thirty-sixth pick of the NFL draft, the Houston Stallions select Soren Brehm, tight end from Teagan University."

Everything around me ground to a halt for a beat, and I was certain my mouth hung open in shock. Second round. I went second round.

The room erupted in applause, even Chloe, and Vi threw her arms around my neck.

"I'm so proud of you," she whispered under all the noise. "I love you."

I pulled her into my lap, fancy dress be damned. None of this would have happened without her.

"Every day, Vi," I breathed into her hair.

————

Want more Rule Breaker?

Yeah, me too. Get a glimpse of Soren and Vi's happy ever after when Harper visits them in Houston.

Click here for your free bonus epilogue!

If you're having trouble clicking, go to www. nikkihallbooks.com/rule-breaker

————

What about the other TU Wildcats?

Turn the page to meet Parker and Riley in Front Runner, the next book in the Wild Card series.

FRONT RUNNER

Riley

Women can't play football. The refrain played on repeat in my head, matching my steps beat for beat as they echoed off the long, empty hallway.

I've heard variations of it my whole life, but the thing is... I *can*.

The heavy door of the weight room slammed shut behind me, and I took a second to just breathe. My shoulders relaxed at the smell. The football training center had the same musky undertone that reeked of home—sweat and passion and hard work—though it was almost buried under the scent of cleaning solution.

The university logo reflected back at me a thousand times in the pristine mirrors, a scarlet TU over a snarling cat. Not a surprise since they'd slapped it on every reasonably flat surface. *Go, wildcats!* I wanted to roll my eyes, maintain my stoic distance, but a fissure of excitement traveled through me. Teagan University was a dream. One I hadn't completely accepted yet.

Wide eyes stared back at me from the mirror, and I

forced myself to take deep breaths until my pulse slowed. This place may seem like lightyears ahead of where I'd been, but I'd earned my spot here. All I had to do was show them.

I shook my head. The semester hadn't even started yet, and I was already gearing up for battle. My time would be better used prepping for the grueling practices sure to come. A division one college football program didn't succeed by going easy on the athletes.

And Teagan University was succeeding. Or they had been until the playoffs last season.

Two of their players had orchestrated a take-down of their skeezy coach, which left the team limping into the championship that they ultimately lost. My gain though, since the new coach was the one who'd recruited me.

I began my warm-up as the picture from SportsCenter flashed across my mind. Face impassive, Parker Shaw had stood on the sidelines as the clock ticked down with sports-casters questioning his actions. I respected someone who'd put doing what's right ahead of winning, but it must have been hard on him.

That same week Coach Gordon had approached me about transferring to TU. I'd watched every clip I could find on the internet, and then I spent the next seven months obsessively checking my email to make sure it wasn't a mistake. If I hadn't already committed to a football camp back home over the summer, I'd have moved as soon as my spring classes ended. Hell, I'd have moved in January if they'd let me.

My dad would have been so proud.

With my heartrate raised and my muscles warm, I eyed the rows of dumbbells and headed for the squat rack instead. All the plates were neatly organized, and I grinned at the distinct lack of dust. Did they have cleaning elves who swept through after every session? Probably some poor intern not getting paid enough.

I was no stranger to late night conditioning, but the stillness and quiet skittered across my nerves, raising the hairs on my arms. Not even the fluorescent lights buzzed above me. I purposely made more noise than normal as I set the bar to the right height and started loading my plates. Next time, I'd remember to unpack my earbuds.

Coach Gordon had warned me the weight room was dead at this time of night, but I wasn't expecting full-on zombie vibes. A loud clang echoed from the big metal doors, and I nearly dropped the weight on my foot. Quiet shuffling from around the corner made me second guess every decision in the last year that had led me here. No amount of playtime was worth getting eaten on my first night.

Instead of the shambling undead my brain insisted on picturing, a tall guy in shorts and a shirt stamped with the TU logo came around the corner. He stopped briefly when he noticed me, but then his mouth widened into a grin.

I recognized him from the months of stalking TU's team. Adam Mackenzie, up-and-coming wide receiver. A junior, like me, he'd earned a spot in the starting lineup last season. Watching him play was a whole different experience from meeting him face-to-face.

Even without all the gear, he was tall and built, but no more than any other guys I'd played with. Football tended to be full of people who were tall and built, even me. I'd dealt with my fair share of attractive teammates, and I hoped he fell on the fun side rather than the douchey, arrogant side.

He eyed me up and down, but it felt like curiosity more

than a come-on. No flicker of recognition, so I guessed the news hadn't hit yet.

"I didn't expect anyone to be in here." He punctuated the statement by dropping a small duffel bag at his feet.

"That makes two of us."

He chuckled. "Yeah, but only one of us is *supposed* to be in here. You must be a rebel, Diana."

My head tilted. "Diana?"

"Prince? Wonder Woman? C'mon, girl."

I smothered a laugh at the utter horror on his face. "I know who Wonder Woman is. What does that have to do with my presence here?"

"You look like her a little bit, and you're not afraid to enter the world of man. This weight room is for football players only, but I won't tell if you won't." He winked, and against all odds, I felt a smile pull at my lips. "Adam Mackenzie. Everyone calls me Mac."

I took his outstretched hand and felt nothing. Thank goodness. He really *was* a good-looking guy. "Nice to meet you, Mac. Riley Jones."

"Need a spotter, RJ?"

RJ. I liked that. No one had ever given me a nickname besides my dad. A quick pang of sadness disrupted the happy thought—there and gone almost before I could register it. I didn't think I'd shown any outward sign, but Mac's eyes narrowed slightly. Observant. I'd have to remember that.

I shrugged. "As long as you don't plan to offer me helpful advice on how to use the equipment."

He raised a brow at my biceps. "Please. You're cut, and those muscles didn't appear all on their own. I'm too pretty to have you coming out swinging." Mac rubbed his jaw and shuddered.

That earned a full laugh as I finished loading up the weight and took my starting position. "I'm going light today."

He whistled and moved behind me. "Sure you are."

I worked in silence for the first two sets. To my surprise, Mac's eyes stayed on the bar instead of my ass. By the third set, I was feeling the pull in my muscles, and curiosity got the better of me.

"Do you always come here late at night?"

His eyebrows rose. "I could ask you the same question, but no. I usually come during the day with the team. My nights are reserved for the cheerleaders."

"The cheerleaders?"

"Yeah, I let them use my body for practice."

I pressed my lips together to keep the laugh in and focused on my form—a slow squat down, then back up. "At least you're upfront about it."

He tsked at me with a gleam in his dark eyes. "Cheer practice, RJ. Get your mind out of the gutter."

His answer made me pause. "Like you throw them in the air and stuff?"

"Yeah, they bring the skill, I bring the muscle."

I could imagine that. Mac had an air of coiled energy, like he just needed an excuse to let it out. "I suppose it can't be any worse than football practice."

"You like football?"

I focused on finishing my reps before responding, but Mac didn't want to wait. He nodded at my butchered shirt in the mirror.

"SWU football. Plus, you're here in the football weight room."

I re-racked and wiped sweat from my forehead, deciding to go with the simple truth. "I like football."

He grinned with all the enthusiasm of a golden retriever. "Hell yeah, RJ—"

An annoyed voice interrupted him before he could say more. "Dammit, Mac. You can't bring girls in here."

We both turned, and my new quarterback scowled at me. "You can't be in here."

I'd been so focused on what to tell Mac, that I hadn't heard him approach. Parker Shaw stood a few inches taller than my six-foot frame with messy black hair, sharp features, and piercing blue eyes. All my research hadn't prepared me for the intensity I saw there, nor the way my heart suddenly took off.

If Mac was a cute golden retriever, this guy was a wicked guilty pleasure—like a fallen angel that clearly thought very little of my dazed gawking. What the fuck was wrong with me?

His eyes narrowed, and he broke our staring contest to grunt at Mac. "You know better, man. Ball bunnies aren't allowed in the training facilities."

The insult finally knocked my brain free from whatever sleep-deprived lust bubble I'd been trapped in. "Excuse me?"

Parker sighed. "No offense, but there are a million other places you guys could hook up. Try one of those."

I wasn't sure if I should laugh or kick him in the shin. Probably not the second one, since I wanted him uninjured for football reasons. Before I could correct him, Mac slung an arm around my shoulders.

"No hookups this time. I was just doing a little late-night training with my girl, RJ."

Parker's jaw ticked as he stared at Mac's arm. "Then train somewhere else."

His voice oozed with disapproval, but he dismissed us to

search around beneath one of the nearby machines. I shrugged the heavy weight of Mac's arm off and started taking plates off the bar to prep for the next exercise. Parker could issue all the orders he wanted, but I wasn't done with my session yet.

Mac scooted closer to sit on the bench next to Parker's crouched form. "You going to the frat party tonight?"

"Which one?" His muffled voice didn't sound excited.

Mac shrugged. "Any of them."

Parker stood and tucked a woven bracelet into his pocket. "You know the deal. If you go, I go."

Mac grinned. "My man."

I moved around the station to put away the last of the plates, and Parker brushed by me on his way out. A shot of sensation traveled up my arm like I'd touched a live wire. His steps faltered for a second, and I wondered if he'd felt the same thing.

He glanced back, his cold eyes skimming over me to land on Mac, who'd moved closer on silent feet. "Text me when you're done, and I'll come get you."

"No need. I'll come with you now, as long as my girl is welcome too."

Parker shook his head and strode out of the weight room without answering.

The second the door closed behind him, I realized I'd only uttered two words in the few minutes he'd been there —and I'd let Mac convince him we were fuck buddies. So much for making a good first impression.

I groaned and put back the last weight with more force than necessary.

Mac grabbed his bag, then turned and walked back-wards toward the door to waggle his eyebrows at me. "You coming, RJ? Don't worry, I'll keep you away from Captain

Grumpyass all night. If you're good, I'll even let you get a feel of these babies." He lifted his shirt to show off a six-pack that probably sent the ladies swooning. Not this lady, though. Still nothing for the gorgeous goofball. The asshole with the attitude problem, on the other hand...

Heat still lingered where he'd brushed my arm.

I shook my head and offered Mac a smile. Captain Grumpyass was a problem for another day. "No thanks. I'm going to finish up here and get some rest."

Mac dropped his shirt and shoved the door open with his shoulder. "Catch."

Out of nowhere, he tossed a phone at me. *My* phone, I realized, as it sailed through the air in a gentle arc. Years of training helped me catch it with ease.

I held it up as Mac's name echoed in the hallway. A tingle went down my spine at Parker's voice, and a sense of foreboding made my tone sharper than I meant. "What the hell, Mac?"

He sent me an unrepentant grin. "I borrowed it during your first set. Call me if you change your mind... or the next time you need a spotter." Mac winked again, then he was gone.

I woke up the phone to see he'd added himself to my contacts under Hottie Mac. Stupid of me not to set up a lock screen, but I didn't like the extra steps involved. It occurred to me that he must not have been doing a fabulous job spotting if he was breaking into my phone. The audacity pulled out another smile.

For a second, I was tempted to use the number and take him up on his offer for the party. He made it hard not to like him, but I still felt out of sorts. The last thing I needed was an early introduction to half the football team, especially after that disastrous meeting with Parker Shaw. *Hi, I'm your new wide receiver, and I may or may not be here as a publicity stunt...*

My lips pressed together as waves of nervous energy flooded my system. Even if Coach Gordon and the entire TU administration only saw me as a PR strategy, I'd prove to them I deserved to be here.

New state, new college, new team, same routine. I didn't need wild parties on a Saturday night. I needed to get to work.

————

Did you enjoy your first chapter? Snag your copy of Front Runner today!

A NOTE FROM NIKKI

Thank you so much for reading Rule Breaker! After Soren made himself known in Game Changer, I *had* to write his story next. Vi was the perfect person to get under his slick, sarcastic exterior, and her brothers... *swoon*. Maybe we'll see them again in future books. Derrick and Soren are moving on, but there are still plenty of athletes at TU waiting for their stories to be told. I can't wait for you to read about Parker and Riley next.

If you have a second, please consider leaving a review. Even better, tag me with the review so we can be besties. You can find me on Facebook or TikTok. Finally, if you want updates on future books and other fun stuff, join my newsletter. I promise not to bite.

ACKNOWLEDGMENTS

I'd like to thank (in no particular order):

- Nicole Schneider, Liz Gallegos, and Jolene Perry, my word wizards
- Angela Haddon, for another beautiful cover
- Gelato, if you know, you know
- The Hubs and kids, for letting me have several weekends all to myself
- The Denver Broncos, for finally getting a real quarterback so I can watch local games
- Google incognito mode... look, sometimes even a romance author has to look things up
- The real Stephen, who dared me to put him in a book. You're welcome.

ALSO BY NIKKI HALL

Wild Card series

Game Changer

Rule Breaker

Front Runner

Hard Hitter

Play Maker

ABOUT THE AUTHOR

Nikki Hall is a smart-ass with a Ph.D. and a potty mouth. She writes stories that have spice and sass because she doesn't know any other way. Coffee makes her happy, messes make her stabby, and she'd sell one of her children for a second season of Firefly. She also writes paranormal romance under the name Nicole Hall.

Want to find out when the newest Nikki Hall book hits the shelves? Sign up for her newsletter at www.nikkihall books.com/signup.

RULE BREAKER

Cover designed by Angela Haddon

Edited by Jolene Perry, Waypoint Author Academy

Printed in Great Britain
by Amazon

38580566R00162